JG FAHERTY

HELLRIDER

This is a **FLAME TREE PRESS** book

Text copyright © 2019 JG Faherty

FLAME TREE PRESS
6 Melbray Mews, London, SW6 3NS, UK
flametreepress.com

Distribution and warehouse:
Baker & Taylor Publisher Services (BTPS)
30 Amberwood Parkway, Ashland, OH 44805
btpubservices.com

Thanks to the Flame Tree Press team, including:
Taylor Bentley, Frances Bodiam, Federica Ciaravella, Don D'Auria,
Chris Herbert, Matteo Middlemiss, Josie Mitchell, Mike Spender,
Cat Taylor, Maria Tissot, Nick Wells, Gillian Whitaker.

The cover is created by Flame Tree Studio with
thanks to Nik Keevil and Shutterstock.com.
The font families used are Avenir and Bembo.

Flame Tree Press is an imprint of Flame Tree Publishing Ltd
flametreepublishing.com

A copy of the CIP data for this book is available from the British Library
and the Library of Congress.

HB ISBN: 978-1-78758-264-4
PB ISBN: 978-1-78758-262-0
ebook ISBN: 978-1-78758-265-1
Also available in FLAME TREE AUDIO

Printed in the US at Bookmasters, Ashland, Ohio

JG FAHERTY

HELLRIDER

FLAME TREE PRESS
London & New York

PART ONE
BEGINNINGS

Hell Rider
Roarin' through the night like a demon
Speedin' through a life without reason
Burnin' with a fire, unholiest desires
Hell Rider
Comin' for you

'Hellrider,' by Demon Dogs

★   ★   ★

Feeding from blood cursed through sins of mankind
Devouring innocents who waste their lives
Burning ships sail through the safety of night
Immortal cursed now hiding from the daylight

Sinking teeth through skin, in the sky so grim
Falling to the death, yet living again
Waking self torment, in the light that you've sent

'Lead The Way,' by Charred Walls of the Damned

BEGINNINGS....

The town of Hell Creek knew all about death. In that respect, it was no different than any other backwoods Florida town. Like so many of its neighbors, Hell Creek had been built on the bodies of Native Americans (who the locals still called Indians, differentiating between them and their Asian counterparts by tapping their foreheads and saying 'dot' or 'no dot'), settlers, and the unlucky men who'd laid the first highways through the alligator- and snake-infested swamplands.

There is a vaguely incestuous similarity to many small towns. The unconscious — and sometimes conscious — insularity hidden beneath a façade of cheerful hellos and friendly smiles. The gossip that runs daily life, operating like a cruel wizard behind a curtain of friendship.

And the verbal histories and legends of the people, often going back to before the community even had a name.

True to form, Hell Creek's residents had a variety of tales and superstitions, everything from haunts and spookems to swamp monsters and zombies. Of course, only a few old-timers still believed the old yarns; for most folk, talk of ghosts and vengeful spirits was usually nothing more than a form of entertainment, a tool to scare children or trick tourists into buying 'hand-crafted' artifacts and trinkets.

All in all, on the surface there was nothing special about Hell Creek other than its name, which it had earned because of the supposedly bottomless springs at the edge of town, from which fresh water flowed into the Everglades. To everyone who lived in the area, Hell Creek was nothing more than your average small town, a place where people still hung their washing out to dry, bacon fat was a staple in nearly every kitchen, and the Confederate flag continued to hold a place of respect on every porch and pickup truck. A place where crime most often meant drunk and disorderly or hunting out of season.

Certainly no one who lived there would ever have expected a murder in their sleepy town.

Or the horrible events that followed it.

Of course, things might have been different if they'd believed in ghosts.

CHAPTER ONE

Only a few hours before his life ended in agonizing fashion, Eddie Ryder's night was already going so badly he figured it couldn't possibly get any worse.

After another day of almost no business at the garage, of just sitting around twiddling his dick and sweating from the heat, he'd stopped at the Piggly Wiggly on the way home to grab a pack of smokes and a six-pack for dinner. As he set his purchases on the counter, the clerk's face turned sickly pale. Despite a bad reputation in town, Eddie knew his mere presence wasn't enough to warrant that kind of immediate reaction, which meant the clerk's sudden anxiety had to be the result of something – or *someone* – else.

His fear was confirmed when a loud, raspy voice spoke from the entrance.

"Lookee here, fellas. If it ain't our good friend, Little Eddie. I knew I smelled pussy."

Instead of turning around, Eddie placed twenty dollars on the counter, pocketed his smokes, and picked up his beer.

"Don't worry," he whispered to the wide-eyed clerk. "I'll make sure they don't cause you any trouble tonight."

The clerk nodded, too frightened to speak.

Eddie took a deep breath and then turned to confront the three Hell Riders who'd entered the Piggly Wiggly. All of them wore denim vests with their names over their hearts and the words 'Hell Riders' emblazoned on the back in bloody script, curved around a skull wearing a Nazi helmet, all against a backdrop of the Confederate flag.

"Not in here, Hank." Eddie nodded at the doors. "Out in the parking lot."

Henry Bowman – Hank to everyone in Hell Creek – shook his head. Long, unkempt brown hair slapped back and forth in time to his movements. "No way, fuck face. Your ass is mine."

Pointing a finger toward the ceiling, Eddie said, "Cameras, remember? You start trouble in here, you'll end up in jail just like your brother."

Leroy 'Mouse' Bates, the smallest of the Hell Riders, frowned. "He's right. That's how Ned got caught the last time. Camera got 'em."

"Shit." Bowman jabbed a finger into Eddie's chest. "You're lucky we got a party to go to, otherwise I'd smear you across the parking lot. Guess you'll have to wait for that ass beating. Don't worry, though. We know where to find you. C'mon, boys, let's get us some beer."

Eddie stood aside as the three of them walked past, all sneers and laughter, then nodded to the clerk and left the store's meager air conditioning for the wretched tropical heat and humidity of a typical summer night in South Florida.

Ignoring the mosquitoes and biting flies that dive-bombed him before he stepped two feet from the doors, he climbed onto Diablo. As the engine roared to life, he considered doing some damage to the three Harleys parked out front − kick them over, run his knife along the gas tanks − but in the end he just drove past. Even though he no longer belonged to the gang, he still adhered to the prime tenet of biker rules, the same rule that had kept Hank and his friends from touching Eddie's bike: you could do whatever you wanted to the person, but you didn't fuck with their wheels. Or their mother.

The ten-mile ride back to the house gave Eddie too much time to think about gangs, mothers, and bikes, all of them constant problems entwined together and festering in his head.

It'd been almost a year since he'd taken his lawyer's advice, pled guilty to the robbery charge, and accepted one year's probation in return for ratting out fellow Hell Rider Ned Bowman, Hank's older brother. Ned, the founder of the gang − *group*, according to the club's lawyer − and the only member currently over the age of thirty, had molded an assortment of teenage and twenty-something-year-old acolytes into a troop of beer-swilling, hog-riding petty criminals who were nothing more than Hell's Angels wannabes, although none of them knew it back then. Eddie had been right there with them, thinking he was all big and bad, believing that the police were just like the rest of the town, quivering in their boots whenever the Hell Riders tore through town on their obnoxiously loud Harleys. For three years, he'd believed he was the absolute shit, that nothing could stop him. He'd had no idea the local cops, who they'd all considered dumber than dirt, had merely been giving them enough rope to hang themselves.

Sure enough, less than an hour after he and Ned had robbed the Piggly Wiggly by pretending they had guns in their pockets, Chief Jones and the boys in brown had rolled up on his house. It was then, with his mother and brother crying in the living room, that he'd learned about the cameras in the ceiling.

And realized he wasn't nearly as smart or tough as he'd thought he was.

After three weeks in the county jail, the growing certainty of doing time in prison had changed his life. Scared the hell out of him, much as he hated to admit it. Knowing he couldn't leave an ailing mother and younger brother to fend for themselves, he'd taken the deal the DA offered, even though it meant making instant enemies out of the derelicts he'd once considered not just friends, but brothers.

Thanks to Eddie's testimony – and the bags of coke the cops found in Ned's apartment – Ned Bowman ended up getting a five-to-ten stretch in the state prison, while Eddie was back to work two days later, with credit for time served.

Since then, his life had gone from shit to worse.

The dual demon headlights of his bike spotlighted the battered, rusty mailbox at the edge of the road and he slowed to take the turn into the long driveway. By the time he reached the two double-wide trailers his old man had welded together to create a decent-sized house, the bike was coasting in neutral, its customary growl muted to a dinosaurian purr.

Eddie killed the motor, plunging the lawn back into darkness, but it didn't happen soon enough for him to avoid getting a good look at the place he'd called home his entire nineteen years of life.

Compared to some of the neighboring trailers, the Ryder place was a castle. No cars with cement blocks instead of wheels decorating the front yard. No lawn chairs with broken arms and sagging ass straps. The tiny lawn was kept mowed and free of broken toys, empty beer bottles, and other junk. Twice a year he power washed the bird shit and leaves off the roof. None of the windows were cracked or covered over with cardboard, and none of the screens were patched with that second-most common building material of all trailer parks, duct tape. He even made sure to bring in the holiday lights every January, right after New Year's, instead of just turning them off and letting them hang dark the other eleven months of the year. In short, it was the antithesis of all the surrounding trailers, a redneck anomaly.

Or, as Eddie usually thought of it, a piece of fruit in a punchbowl full of turds.

And yet he still hated the sight of it.

God, I wish I could just get the hell out of here.

The temptation was so strong, so fucking crazy *powerful*, just as it always was when he contemplated the life he'd been saddled with. He refused to act on it though, despite the never-ending pull. During those long nights in his jail cell, he'd made a vow to never be like his old man, and it was a promise he intended to keep. Even if it meant sacrificing his own happiness forever.

His family deserved that much. And more.

Before he opened the door, he took a deep breath and focused on projecting a happy attitude. Entering the kitchen, he found Carson at the table, a textbook and notebook open in front of him. The younger boy's brow was furrowed in deep concentration.

"Hey, little bro. How's it hangin'?"

"Cool. School started today."

"So I see." Eddie went to the fridge, stowed his beer, and pulled out the meatloaf he'd baked the night before. He did a lot of cooking on Sundays, since most weeknights he didn't get home from the garage until seven. As he prepared plates for microwaving, he watched Carson eagerly writing notes and flipping pages and thought how different he and his brother were.

He's probably done more homework tonight than I did in all my years of high school. And he actually enjoys it, enjoys going to school. Hell, when I was sixteen, I spent most of my time cutting classes so I could party and get laid.

Which is why you're running your father's garage, barely keeping the family above water, instead of taking classes at the community college, he added to himself.

Eddie imagined his mother shaking her head at his words. Between her being sick and Carson being too young – and too damn smart – to quit school, supporting the family had landed on Eddie's shoulders like a ton of bricks the day his father, Big Eddie, had up and left. His mother did her best at first, but her illness had quickly robbed her of the ability to work, or even clean the house. Because of that, Eddie had pretty much been working full time from the age of sixteen. At seventeen he'd officially left school for good.

And done the one thing he'd always said he wouldn't do: fallen into the spiderweb trap of holding a dead-end job in a pissant town.

After making a plate for Carson, Eddie fixed one for his mother. As always, walking down the hall to her room was the worst – and the best – part of his day.

"Hey, Ma," he said, after knocking at the open door.

"Hey, yourself," Sally Ryder answered, her pale face breaking into a smile. She was sitting up in bed, watching a game show on the little color TV he'd gotten her for Christmas, a replacement for the old black-and-white set she'd had since before he was born.

Every time he saw her, he was amazed she'd kept so much of her beauty despite the thieving emphysema that stole little pieces of her life away each day and replaced them with dead lung cells and weak muscles. Her long black hair, equally dark eyes, and bronze skin identified her as a Martinez in ways no married name could hide. Eddie was proud to have inherited her looks, including her tall, thin frame, rather than Big Eddie's freckles and red hair. Those had gone to Carson instead. Fate had evened things out, though, by passing Sally's brains to Carson and Big Eddie's temper to his namesake.

"Brought you some food." Eddie set the plate on the nightstand. He knew she'd pick at it through the evening, between bouts of sleeping and coughing. Losing her strength hadn't robbed her of her desire to fight, even though she knew it was a battle she'd never win. As different as night and day when it came to honesty and temper, one thing Sally and Big Eddie had always had in common was a spit-in-your face, never-give-up attitude, a trait both children had inherited in spades.

"How was work?"

Eddie suppressed the urge to chew his lower lip. Her voice sounded weaker than it had when he'd checked on her before leaving for work in the morning. He told himself it didn't necessarily mean anything, she could just be having a bad day, or she might have been a little more active than usual and worn herself out. These days, that could happen just from taking a shower or getting herself a drink of water.

Except deep down, he knew it wasn't true.

"Fine." After a pause, during which he regretted his terse response, he kept talking, reminding himself how much she enjoyed hearing about anything that went on outside the four walls of her prison. "A couple of jobs came in, nothing major, but it might mean things are gonna pick up again."

Another lie in a long list of them, but at least this one had a purpose. The last thing he wanted was her worrying about money. Even if the economy remained stuck in the shitter and business kept getting slower than ever.

"That's good." Sally closed her eyes and leaned back on the pillow, careful not to crimp the line to the oxygen cannula resting under her nose. "I think I'll nap a bit before I eat. You go help Carson with his homework."

"Sure, Ma. See you later." Like he could answer one question out of fifty from Carson's books.

Eddie was about to ask her how she felt, and then realized she hadn't coughed once since he got home. He glanced at the nightstand. Sure enough, the inhaler sitting there had a different label than the old one, meaning Doc Holmes had been by during the day and prescribed something stronger. Again.

She's dying. And not slowly, either.

Shut up! Eddie wished he could take care of the voice in his head the way he took care of most other problems, with threats of violence. Or his fists, if threats didn't work.

Not that he could go down *that* road anymore, either. With his track record, one more time in trouble with the police and it would mean jail, no matter how many strings his mother or Doc Holmes pulled with Chief Jones. Which was why he'd resorted to talking his way out of trouble with Hank Bowman when every bone in his body had urged him to break the asshole's nose. Back in the day, it wouldn't have mattered he was outnumbered three to one. Although skinny as a broomstick, he was quick and strong, and had no doubt he could've taken down Hank and one of the other two before the third did any serious damage to him.

Instead, he was still seething inside, his pent-up fury a living thing, adding to the storm that always boiled below the surface, just waiting for moments like tonight to erupt.

He'd learned the hard way he had to let it out before it grew too strong and he exploded at the wrong time. So he'd made sure he had an outlet. Once Carson was asleep, he would sneak back to the garage and take out his frustrations on the heavy punching bag he kept in the office, a relic from Big Eddie's amateur boxing days. Twenty minutes attacking the bag followed by a couple of hours tinkering with Diablo's engine was usually enough to bank the angry fires inside him so he could go home and grab a few hours sleep before starting the whole rotten cycle over again.

"Good night, Ma," he whispered. She didn't answer, and he tiptoed his way out of the room and back down the hall to the kitchen, where Carson was washing his plate.

"What's on the agenda for tonight, little man?" Eddie asked, putting together two meatloaf sandwiches for himself.

"I finished my homework, so I'm probably going to play some computer games for a while and then go to bed."

Eddie paused in slathering mayonnaise on white bread, pointed the knife at Carson. "Dude, you need to get some real friends, not a bunch of faceless dorks online."

Carson rolled his eyes. "They are real. They're from school. But it's better this way."

"Better? How?"

"'Cause they don't have to come over here." Carson kept his gaze down as he said it.

Eddie's first instinct was to yell. Chew the kid out for acting like a spoiled ass, remind him that at least they had food on the table and a mother who loved them. But three years of filling in as the head of the family after his father took off had taught him some tough lessons, one of which was things usually turned out better if he did the opposite of whatever their father would have done.

He's embarrassed. Just like I was at his age, Eddie realized. *Living in a trailer on the shit side of a shit town. A good-for-nothing brother. A dying mother. Geez, what a fun house for a kid. No wonder he doesn't bring friends over. Who can blame him?*

So he took a deep breath, using the time to gather his thoughts. When he knew he could talk without shouting, he nodded to Carson and went back to making his dinner. "You know, you're sixteen now. When I was your age, I didn't have a curfew. No reason you should anymore, either."

"What's that mean?"

Eddie tossed his knife in the sink. "It means you don't have to park your butt in your room every night. As long as you keep your grades up, you can go to your friends' houses and play your dorky games after dinner."

Carson's eyes went wide. "You mean it?" Suspicion tainted his voice.

"Yeah. I'll let Mom know. She'll be cool with it." He gave a beaming Carson a friendly punch on the arm and headed for his room, balancing his plate on top of the six-pack. A rare smile touched his lips as he walked.

I might not be father-of-the-year material, but tonight I think I managed to do the right thing.

★   ★   ★

At one in the morning, the humid night was as close to silent as it ever got when you lived next to the swamps and hammocks of the Everglades. Eddie pushed Diablo up the driveway, the crunch of dirt and gravel under the tires more than loud enough to drown out the chirps and whirrs of night insects, the occasional croaking frog or bellowing gator, and the distant hum of cars on the highway.

Only when he'd reached the road did he start the bike, which roared to life like the metal beast he'd designed it to look like. As always, when he climbed on Diablo and felt it vibrating beneath him, he let himself imagine it was a living creature, eager to be released from its cage and roam the night.

"Sorry, old boy," he said. "No joyriding tonight. Gas is too damn expensive." He gave the gas tank a friendly pat. Like the rest of the bike, it was painted to resemble the blood-red, scaly hide of a demon. He'd even customized a special metal plate for the front, shaped like the demon's face, with the twin headlights as the eyes. In the daylight, each scale sparkled in crimson, violet, or fiery orange, depending on what angle you viewed the bike from.

At night, the blacks and silvers took precedence, lending the monster bike an even more ominous look.

Resisting the urge to give the throttle a vicious twist, Eddie shifted gently into first and eased down the road, Diablo's engine rumbling in grudging response instead of rattling the windows of the trailers they passed.

★　★　★

From his bedroom window, Carson watched his brother's taillights disappear into the dark. Every night it was the same thing; Eddie pretending to sleep and then heading back to the garage or out for a ride. It used to be that Carson would go back to sleep, but lately things had changed. He found himself staring at the ceiling, worrying about stuff a sixteen-year-old boy shouldn't have to think about. What would they do if something happened to Eddie? Riding a seven-hundred-pound motorcycle after drinking several beers wasn't exactly being safety-conscious, even if Eddie insisted it took a lot more than a six-pack to get him drunk.

Once the first seedling of worry sprouted, the rest shot up like weeds in a garden, spreading until they took over all his thoughts.

Eddie wasn't in the gang anymore, but he still wasn't exactly a model citizen, either. Not that he ever had been. He'd inherited their father's temper, which meant anything could happen while he was out cruising on his bike. He could get into a fight and go to jail. Or worse, he might get sick of playing dad to his little brother and take off, the way their father had, just get on that stupid bike of his one night and never come back.

Then what? Where would that leave Carson? What would he do?

Quit school? Get a job? Carson knew he couldn't run the garage. He had no talent for mechanical things. All he had going for him were his book smarts. And without a high school degree he wouldn't ever get a job making more than minimum wage, not in a dinky town like Hell Creek, whose only claim to fame was being the last place to get gas or food before you entered the vast, swampy national park lands of the Everglades.

Get a job? Yeah, sure. Flipping burgers at McDonald's? Stocking the shelves at the Piggly Wiggly? If he worked hard, and got his GED, why, he might even make night manager someday.

Just the thought of it made his stomach churn.

Please, God, don't let anything happen to him. It seemed like a selfish prayer, but even at sixteen Carson was well aware that sometimes the line between selfish and self-preservation was very thin.

With a sigh, he got out of bed and turned on the computer.

It was going to be another long night of waiting.

CHAPTER TWO

Eddie's private office was a small room in the back of the garage, separated from the bays and customer service areas out front. It had originally been the women's bathroom, but when Big Eddie purchased the garage, he tore out the plumbing, sealed the outside door, and made it into a little getaway for himself, a place where he could be alone to smoke his cigars, drink cheap whiskey, and watch wrestling on a tiny black-and-white TV. After taking over the business, Eddie had changed a lot of things, but he'd left his father's mini man-cave alone, understanding that he might need the private space as well.

And he had.

Filled with a need to release the pent-up frustrations churning in his guts, Eddie put on his ear buds and donned his boxing gloves, one of the few things of his father's he'd kept after the old man disappeared.

With his phone blasting heavy metal in his ears – Demon Dogs, Charred Walls of the Damned, and Iron Maiden were his favorites – and no windows to provide distractions, he quickly lost himself in the rhythm of his fists, pummeling the bag with a fury that matched the driving beat of the music. Imagining it was Hank Bowman's face he was battering.

Twenty minutes later, soaked in sweat but calmer, Eddie opened the door that led down a short hallway into the main bay.

And found the entire left side of the garage on fire.

An angry red and orange blaze stretched from front to back, devouring shelves of tires, tools, and old, grease-covered manuals. Clouds of black, oily smoke obscured large portions of the bay and filled the space with the acrid stench of burning rubber and chemicals.

"Shit!" He thought about getting the fire extinguisher, but the flames had already reached halfway up the wall. Nothing short of a fire truck was going to put it out. Instead, he turned and ran for the customer service desk, intending to call 911 before opening the bay doors and getting the hell out.

He was halfway there when several of the front windows shattered inward. A moment later there was a new wall of fire growing before him, the flames already climbing the legs of his desk and setting stacks of paper on fire. Outside, someone shouted, "Fuck you, Ryder!"

Hank Bowman. I'd know that voice anywhere. Son of a bitch, I'll—

Something exploded behind him, the force of it throwing him against one of the big lifts. Bones snapped in his chest and his head connected hard against metal. The room faded away to nothing but black and red, leaving just a small circle, like he was looking down a tunnel. Behind the ringing in his head and the sounds of the fire, he thought he heard distant laughter. Jumbled pieces of the last song he'd been listening to, 'Fear in the Sky' by Charred Walls of the Damned, echoed in his head as he fought to breathe.

Rational thoughts overcome by fear
Overcome by fear
Overcome by fear
My destiny I can't control
The only way I can face it is to
Make myself numb
Make myself numb

He was ready to close his eyes and accept his fate when an image of Carson appeared in his head. Carson, who'd be all alone without him.

No! I won't do that to him. I won't die like this! He staggered to his feet, crying out as broken ribs grated against each other and pierced vital organs. A horrific visage appeared out of the thick, black smoke, its red, satanic face leering evilly from the fiery depths of hell, and he screamed. Then he realized it was only his motorcycle and he lunged at the bike.

Diablo! Start it. Bash down the doors. Safety.

He collapsed across the custom leather seat, no longer feeling his internal injuries, unaware his skull was so badly shattered his brain was visible through the hole.

In true Ryder fashion, his body was as good as dead but he never stopped fighting, forcing his hands to grip the throttle and clutch, paying no mind to the ceiling as it crashed down around him, ignorant of the fact that his lungs were already broiling from the super-heated air.

The idea that he might not survive never even crossed Eddie's mind. Instead, his last thought wasn't of his family, or even of his own life.

It was of revenge.

Bowman, I swear I'll find you and kill you. You and all the Hell Riders.

★   ★   ★

Outside the garage, the members of the Hell Riders watched the building go up in flames. Hank Bowman chugged the rest of his beer and threw the can at the blazing structure.

"Shit yeah! Burn, motherfucker!"

The other gang members – Duck, Gary, Jethro, Butch, and Harley – whooped and hollered along with him. Only one, Mouse Bates, was sober enough to think about consequences.

"Hey, Hank, we better get the hell outta here before the cops come."

Hank opened another beer and took a gulp. "Yeah, all right." He turned back to the building and raised both middle fingers. "Fuck you, Eddie Ryder. That's what you get for fuckin' with the Hell Riders."

As they headed for their motorcycles, Duck Miller stopped. "Hey, did you guys hear that? Sounded like someone screaming."

Hank threw his empty Bud can at him. "Stop being such a pussy. It's three in the fucking morning. Ain't nobody in there. Fuckin' Ryder is gonna have a surprise in the morning, though."

★   ★   ★

By the time the first emergency response vehicles arrived, Hank and the others were long gone.

CHAPTER THREE

Police Chief Johnny Ray Jones stood in the center of the smoldering ruins of Ryder's Garage and fought down the bile threatening to push up from his stomach. Even twenty-odd years of scraping drunks off the highway and looking at bodies in the morgue couldn't prepare a person for what his men had found after the fire had been put out.

"Sure is a helluva way to go," Doc Holmes said. One of only two doctors in Hell Creek, he was also the closest thing the town had to a medical examiner, with the nearest ME's office being way up in Miami. Although pushing seventy, he looked and moved as if he were fifteen years younger. As far as Jones could tell, the old man's only concession to age was that he'd started using a golf cart instead of walking the course each Monday and Thursday.

"No shit." Jones couldn't imagine anything worse than burning to death. Your flesh liquefying, your blood and brains boiling inside you....

Jesus, please make sure that's not how I go.

"Look at that. Fused to the damn thing," Doc Holmes said, pointing to the charred and melted body of Little Eddie Ryder atop his equally charred and melted motorcycle. "Must've really loved that bike."

"He did." Jones pressed a handkerchief over his nose and mouth in a vain attempt to block the sickly-sweet smell of barbequed meat and engine fluids. *I may never eat roast pork again.*

"Chief, we got something."

Jones turned and found Ted Moselby, his second in command, holding what looked like the neck of a liquor bottle at the end of a pencil. The green glass was deformed, reminding Jones of what happened to beer bottles when you tossed them into a campfire. "What is it?"

"Looks like a homemade Molotov cocktail." Moselby dropped

the glass into a large evidence bag. "I saw the same thing a couple of times in LA, during one of the riots."

Jones nodded. Moselby had come to Hell Creek from the LAPD, where he'd been a patrol officer for five years and a sergeant for five more. He'd left the city to get away from the violence and danger, he and his wife both sick of never knowing if his next night on duty would be his last.

Wonder how he feels right now?

"You thinking the Hell Riders had somethin' to do with this?" Moselby asked.

"I was thinkin' that even before you found the damn bomb. Nobody else has the motive. Eddie wasn't popular, not by a long shot, but if one of his customers had a beef with him they'd have either used their fists or come to me."

"Retribution for Ned Bowman." Moselby made it a statement, not a question.

"Yep. You knew it had to happen sooner or later, but I didn't expect," he waved his arm at the destruction, "anything like this. I figured a beating, or maybe running him off the road one night."

"If they were drunk, or stoned, or both, shit coulda just gotten out of hand."

"I guess." Jones stepped away from the corpse and motioned for two men to start packing it up. The fact that he'd never expected Hank and his boys to commit arson – and murder – didn't assuage the guilt he felt for not keeping Eddie safe.

"You want me to round them up for questioning?"

"Yeah. And feel free to start without me." Had it been anyone else turned into human charcoal, Jones would have insisted on being there to interrogate the suspects himself. But Sally Ryder was a dear friend.

Which meant delivering the bad news in person.

"I've got to tell Sally her boy is dead."

★   ★   ★

Carson Ryder was waiting for the school bus when Chief Jones pulled up. Although it wasn't uncommon for the Chief to stop by and chat with their mother, Carson had never seen him come over so early in the morning. Or look so serious. Not even when they'd arrested Eddie for robbing that store.

Remembering all the sirens he'd heard earlier in the morning, his stomach did a slow flip and his legs threatened to buckle as he watched Jones approach him.

Oh, no. Oh, God, no.

"Mornin', Carson. You'd best come inside with me. I've got to talk with you and your mom."

Carson didn't even ask why, just nodded. Although he'd never heard it in person, he'd watched enough police shows on TV to recognize the voice cops used when they had to tell people a family member had died. His whole body felt numb, and when he spoke his voice seemed to come from somewhere outside his body.

"I'll go get my mom."

Even after they were all seated in the living room, his mother looking frail and worn in a bathrobe that had once fit her but now was two sizes too big, Carson felt detached from the whole scene. Chief Jones fiddled nervously with his hat while he broke the news, his usually confident air replaced by a series of starts and stops as he spoke. Through the binoculars of shock, Carson watched his mother break down in hysterical tears, watched Jones get up and sit next to her, put his arm around her. Thoughts popped into Carson's head in random, surreal fashion as he sat in his chair, frozen in place by the twin weights of fear and disbelief.

Eddie's dead. In a fire.
We're alone now.
Eddie's gone forever.
The garage was burned down.
Chief Jones is in love with my mother.
What are we going to do?

"Carson? Carson? Are you all right?"

The low ringing in his ears, which he hadn't even noticed until then, faded a bit as he looked up and saw Jones staring at him with a worried look.

"Yeah. Yeah, I'm okay. I...I have to...I'll be right back."

With no idea of where he was going, Carson ran down the hall and locked himself in the first room he came to, which happened to be the bathroom. Wedging himself between the tub and toilet, he sank to the floor. Only then, with his face buried in his hands, did his mind go blissfully blank and his own tears burst free.

By the time he returned to the living room, Jones was gone and his mother was already on the phone, making funeral arrangements.

Because Eddie's dead.

He waited until she hung up the phone and then sat down next to her on the couch. Neither of them said anything. They didn't need to.

Instead, they just held each other and cried.

CHAPTER FOUR

"I'm fucking dead."

Eddie Ryder knew it, as sure as he knew his own name. How else to explain regaining consciousness surrounded by pure darkness? No light, no sound, no sense of touch. It was like floating in space, nothing but his mind and the vast emptiness of a starless galaxy.

He had to be dead because no one could have survived the inferno he'd been trapped in. He wasn't in a coma, or coming out of anesthesia, or plain old sleeping. He remembered everything, and because he remembered, he knew the truth.

He'd failed.

He'd died, which meant he'd left his family behind, left them worse off than when he'd been alive.

Thoughts he hadn't had time for during his struggle to escape the fire came rushing in. His mother. Carson. In the end, he'd done just what his father had done, even if it wasn't a purposeful act like Big Eddie's had been. He'd abandoned them.

What will they do now? How will they survive?

His mother was too sick to work. Carson was too young, and besides, he didn't know a thing about running a garage.

Asshole, there is no garage.

That brought back the memory of the fiery objects crashing through the windows. The laughter he'd heard.

It wasn't an accident. Someone set that fire on purpose. They killed me. And he knew who *they* were.

The Hell Riders.

They stole me from my family. Forever.

Sudden rage rose up, more powerful than anything he'd felt when alive, driving out the remorse, the guilt, the sorrow. A tidal wave of black fury, overwhelming all other thoughts.

As if burned away by the heat of his vengeful wrath, a circle of white light appeared.

Heaven? It didn't seem likely, not with his track record. But something about it drew him. He found himself heading toward it without any sense of physical movement. Or maybe it was just growing larger. He had no way of telling, and he didn't really care. He just wanted to see where it would lead.

And it wasn't like he had anything else to do with his time.

Curiosity gave way to fury again when the circle expanded and an image appeared inside it. Like a window had opened, he found himself looking down at his own body.

Charred to something resembling a centuries-old mummy, it shouldn't have been identifiable, but Eddie was somehow able to see past the flaking, charcoal skin and exposed muscle and tendons, past the empty eye sockets and the stump of cartilage that had once been his nose. See through all the destruction and recognize himself.

And as he did, a horrible thought came to him.

That's what my mother is going to see when she has to identify me at the morgue.

That vision, even more than his dead corpse, stoked his anger to new heights. He tried to get closer to the body, filled with a seething desire to force his consciousness back into it, to become a living monster capable of exacting vengeance on the ones who'd killed him.

He couldn't do it.

No matter how hard he tried, how much he focused all his will on re-entering his dead self, he couldn't get any closer than hovering about six feet above it. He was still trying when two orderlies in blue scrubs entered the room and approached the table.

"This one?" one of them asked, paying more attention to his phone than the corpse.

The other one checked a chart. "Yeah. Eddie Ryder, DOA. Gee, no shit. Fuckin' guy's beef jerky. Stick him in locker ten."

Fuck you, scumbags! Have a little respect for the dead.

Static crackled from the orderly's phone and he jumped.

Serves you right, asshole.

Ignorant of the disembodied sentience floating over them, the two men wheeled the cart to a wall of storage lockers and slid the body none too gently into one. Then they left the room, the closing door cutting off their jokes about having barbeque for lunch.

Bastards. Go ahead, laugh. I'll put you on my list, right after those fuckers who did this to me.

That reminded him. The Hell Riders. He had to find them, figure out some way to get them back for what they'd done.

But how?

He willed his consciousness to rise up.

Nothing.

He tried again. No change. He was still sitting just below the ceiling, right above the door to his temporary crypt.

Don't tell me I'm stuck with my body forever. What's the point of my spirit hanging around if I can't fucking move?

Once more, he tried pushing himself back up to the blackness he'd awoken to.

Failure. Again.

Goddammit!

At his mental shout, the lights in the autopsy room flickered on and off before resuming their steady, greenish glow.

Well, that's something, at least.

Let's see what else I can do.

* * *

Johnny Ray Jones leaned back in his chair and stared at the paperwork on his desk. For the first time in his twenty-odd years with the Hell Creek police force, including the past ten as Chief, he felt helpless.

And he didn't like it.

Contrary to what most people thought, Chief of Police in Hell Creek wasn't an easy job. The town might look like Mayberry's long-lost twin to the casual eye, but he knew it for what it really was: a place where the real trouble hid below the surface, like a gator floating beneath the scum and algae of a pond, just waiting for the right moment to leap out and grab an unsuspecting victim. As one of the last outposts of actual civilization before entering the wilds of the Everglades, the unincorporated lands around Hell Creek were perfect places for drug dealers and smugglers to use as stepping stones for their trades. Over the years, he'd taken part in more than his fair share of busts, assisting various government and State Police task forces.

Assisted? Ha. Sat around with my thumb up my ass is more like it, he thought, taking a sip of cold coffee and then tossing the cup of vile sludge into the trash. The Staties had no more use for local cops than the Feds did; both saw him and his men as uneducated gophers. Still, being part of the task forces looked good in the papers and sure as shit helped out at election time.

He'd seen people shot, helped pull half-eaten corpses from the swamps, and cleaned up after drunken highway wrecks. He'd broken up more bar fights than he could count, and he'd had to identify more bodies of friends and family than any small-town lawman should have to.

But through it all, he'd felt he was making a difference.

Today was different.

Even if Moselby, who at that very moment was grilling Mouse Bates in the tiny storage area that doubled as the station's interrogation room, got one or more of the Hell Riders to confess – which was highly unlikely – it still wouldn't be good enough.

Shit, even if we send all their dumb asses to jail, it won't be good enough.

Because it wouldn't bring back Sally Ryder's boy.

Had it happened a couple of years earlier, he might have felt differently about the whole situation. Back then, Little Eddie was nothing more than a punk, hanging out with other punks, going nowhere fast. Sally was still healthy, and Jones had harbored hopes – slim hopes, but hopes nonetheless – that he might win her heart after she got over Big Eddie disappearing. Something he'd been waiting for ever since he chickened out on asking her for a date back in high school.

Things had changed, though, when Sally took ill. She went downhill fast and there was no longer room in her life for anything except spending time with her boys and trying not to die. At the height of it all, Little Eddie'd gone and gotten himself in real trouble with that robbery. But just when Jones thought the kid would turn into a full-time criminal, Eddie'd turned his life around and actually got things on track. Went to work each day. Kept food on the table for the family. Became the man of the house. Most of all, got free of that damn gang and stayed out of trouble.

And now this.

Goddamn Hell Riders.

No matter how hard he'd tried, he never felt as if he'd done enough to put an end to their troublemaking, never come down on them as hard as he'd wanted to, all the way back to when his own son had gotten involved with them. Did that make Eddie's death his fault? Maybe a small part of it was. But he'd never imagined they'd amount to more than petty criminals, getting busted here and there for DWIs or dealing, possibly the occasional drunken robbery, like Eddie and Ned Bowman.

Not arson. Or murder.

Mostly they kept to themselves at the clubhouse they'd built way out in the swamps. Out of sight and out of mind, that was how he usually looked at it. Just like everyone else. Folks in Hell Creek preferred not to make a fuss unless it was absolutely necessary.

Besides, a couple of the Hell Riders came from old town families, families who still had a lot of pull. The kind of pull that could cost an elected cop his job. Even if that cop happened to have a son who'd died as a result of their stupid antics.

Was that my fault too?

Another question he'd asked himself for years. Jeff had been fifteen when he'd lost control of his bike, wacked out of his mind on coke and booze.

Could I have stopped it?

Logic said no. The kid had lived with his mother, out on the edge of town. She and Johnny Ray had never married, and although he'd tried his best to do right by Jeff and stay involved in his life, there'd never been any love lost between them. Their relationship had grown even worse after Johnny Ray married Angelina, although after Kellie was born Jeff had been pretty decent to her. Made sure to show up on birthdays and holidays to give her presents. She'd taken it hard when he died, and that had been a lot of the impetus for Johnny Ray increasing how much attention he paid to the Hell Riders.

Increased, but never to the point where I ruffled feathers among the people who got me elected.

Could I have done more?

The answer was yes, of course. But would it have been enough to break up the Hell Riders?

If I'd tried, I might have gotten the axe, and maybe not been around to help Eddie when he got in trouble. Of course, then he'd be alive now. In jail, but alive.

"Shit." Jones stood up, the taste of guilt and self-loathing even more bitter than the break room coffee. "I might as well make myself useful now."

So far, Moselby had only brought in three of the Hell Riders.

Why should he have all the fun?

CHAPTER FIVE

Carson Ryder stared at his brother's grave and reflected on how wrong it was to be burying someone on such a warm, sunny day.

It should be cold and rainy, like you see in movies. People standing around in long, black coats with umbrellas, not baking in the sun and sweating through their shirts as they toss their roses on the coffin and walk away.

Then, as it had so many times during the wake, the burial mass, and even the funeral itself, his mind circled back to the same thought.

Why, Eddie? Why'd you have to be such a jerk? It isn't fair! What are we going to do now?

Carson knew it was selfish and wrong to think that way, that it wasn't Eddie's fault. Chief Jones had told them what happened. Eddie'd been the victim of a crime. But in Carson's mind, it *was* Eddie's fault. *He* was the one who'd gotten involved with that stupid gang in the first place. *He* was the one who snuck over to the garage every night, instead of staying home with his family. *He* was the one—

The one who abandoned us. Who left us alone.

Alone and broke. Can't forget that last part. With the official verdict of arson on the records, the insurance company had already told them no claim would be paid out until the investigation was complete. Which could be weeks. In the meantime, they barely had enough money left in the bank to cover this month's mortgage plus household expenses. After that they'd need public assistance to supplement his mother's meager government check.

The urge to kick over the assorted potted plants and sympathy wreaths ran through Carson so unexpectedly that his foot actually came several inches off the ground before he got control of himself. Even then, his legs and arms trembled as he fought to keep from running amok through the flowers, destroying everything he could get his hands on, a giant-sized temper tantrum that would leave him exhausted and crying but maybe, *just maybe*, satisfied.

What stopped him was the realization that it was exactly what his brother would have done. Or his father. Flown into a mindless rage.

I'm not like them. I'm not—

"Carson, it's time to go."

Carson took a deep breath before turning around. His mother, seated in her wheelchair, her face frighteningly skull-like behind the black veil she wore, waited a few yards down the path. Chief Jones, standing straight and tall behind her, looked super-official in his dress uniform with all the medals and ribbons. Carson knew the honor was more for his mother than for Eddie. Hell, the only other people who'd come to the funeral were his mother's friends from town and a few patrons of St. Maria's, the church she still attended whenever she could find the strength.

Not a single person under the age of thirty-five.

That alone showed how unpopular Eddie'd been.

And me, too. None of my friends came.

Not that he'd expected them to. It was a school day, after all, and how many parents were going to let their kids miss school to attend the funeral of a local delinquent? Carson was well aware that's how the town still thought of Eddie. That much had been evident when only a couple of them showed up for the wake, staying just long enough to be polite before their parents ushered them out. The same parents who'd gossiped about what a loser Eddie was, while still bringing their cars to him for repairs.

Of course, they didn't have much choice. Unless you wanted to drive twenty miles to Homestead, it was either bring your car to Eddie or use Spencer's Gas Station at the other end of town. And while Eddie might have a bad reputation, Carl Spencer hadn't seen a sober day in thirty years. His gas was cheap, but he wasn't the kind of person you wanted fixing your brakes.

"Carson, we have to go. We have guests coming to the house."

Guests. A handful of people bearing casserole dishes and platitudes. Semi-false sympathies would be on everyone's lips. They'd feel sorry for Sally Ryder's grief, but no real sense of loss over the death of someone they secretly felt she was better off without.

Carson they'd ignore completely.

"Carson!" Not a shout, but enough emphasis on the word to let him know she was getting impatient.

"Coming." He dropped a final rose on the ground in front of Eddie's casket and ground it into the sun-baked ground with one dress shoe.

"Thanks a lot, bro. You really screwed us this time."

★　　★　　★

Eddie wanted to smash his non-existent head with his equally non-existent fists as he watched his brother walk away from the casket. The past three days had been hell for him. Whatever he was – soul, essence, ghost – he'd remained a prisoner to his dead body, dragged along as it was sliced, diced, sewn together again, driven to the funeral home, and locked away in the cheapest coffin available. No open-casket viewing, not when you looked like something dredged up from the bottom of a deep fryer. Then there'd been the wake, with his family weeping and his mother's friends alternately offering condolences and gossiping. That had been a real joy to watch. Even worse was after they'd left, when he'd had to spend the night bored out of his skull staring at a dark room.

He'd tried to repeat what had happened in the morgue, when he'd somehow managed to affect the electrical system. But no matter what he did, he couldn't make anything happen. All his efforts got him was a headache, which totally didn't make sense since he didn't even have a fucking head to hurt.

On the morning of the funeral, his anger had grown exponentially at the thought of spending the rest of eternity staring down at his grave while his killers went on enjoying life. Did this happen to all ghosts, or was it just more of the Ryder family bad luck? Watching his mother cry again and then listening to Carson curse him out hadn't improved his mood.

Eddie paused his ongoing rant as he saw a young girl approach Carson. They looked about the same age, although he couldn't get a clear look at her face. *Good. Maybe a girlfriend will help him get his head out of those video games.*

Then it struck him that he'd never see Carson grow up, never see him graduate high school or college or become a success. Never get the chance to high-five him the first time he scored with a girl or stand next to him when he got married.

It was too much.

All his anger, all his regrets, came rushing up and out in one huge, bellowing scream, a scream only he could hear.

A scream echoed by sudden thunder in the cloudless sky.

★   ★   ★

"Carson?"

Carson, momentarily distracted by a rumble of thunder, turned as Kellie Jones, the Chief's daughter, approached him. He'd seen her standing by her father during the funeral, a familiar face not only from the classes they'd had together over the years but from the times she'd stopped by the house with her father to drop off food. Not that they were friends. Except for those few visits, they'd never really said more than hello, and when he'd noticed her during the ceremony he'd assumed her father had made her come. It wasn't like anyone as hot as Kellie would ever give a second thought about a bookworm like him.

Still, he had to be polite, especially with his mother and the Chief right there.

"Hi, Kellie. Thanks for coming."

She glanced back at her father, who crouched next to Sally, deeply engaged in conversation. Then she turned to Carson and lowered her voice.

"I made my father take me. Told him if he didn't, I'd just cut school and come anyway."

"What?" Carson felt as if the world had slipped sideways a few inches. It was a feeling he'd been having a lot since Eddie's death. "Why would you do that?"

She tilted her head and he missed her next words, his attention focused on the red highlights in her brown hair and the way the sun sparked in her green eyes.

Something hit his arm, and he realized she'd punched him.

"Hey!"

"Hey, nothing. Did you hear what I said?"

Slow fire crept up his neck and into his face. "Umm, I...."

Kellie laughed, a good-natured sound, not at all like the mocking, derisive laughter he usually heard from his classmates. "That's what I figured. I'll give it another shot. I came because it was the right thing to do, and 'cause I thought you might, you know, need someone to talk to. If you want."

She kept smiling at him, and he wondered what she was waiting for.

Then it hit him. *She's flirting with you.*

On the heels of that came another thought: *Yeah, right.*

Not a girl like Kellie. No, she probably just felt bad for him. Or her father had told her to do it. Of course, it would be nice to spend some time with her. And being seen in public with one of the cutest girls in school wouldn't exactly tarnish his reputation, either. One thing he knew about Kellie, she wasn't the type to be mean or cruel. Not like a lot of the other girls his age.

So go for it.

The voice in his head seemed more like Eddie's than his own, but he followed the advice just the same.

"Um, that would be, um, kinda cool, actually. Maybe we can grab a soda or a coffee or something?" As the words left his mouth, he felt like biting his tongue off. *Coffee? Soda?* He sounded like a bad fifties movie.

"That sounds great. I've got to get back to school, but I'll call you tomorrow." She surprised him a second time by taking his hand in hers. "I really am sorry about Eddie. I know he was trouble, but he was your brother. I'm sure you loved him a lot."

Then she walked away, the memory of her soft skin still tingling his palm. She stopped and said something to Carson's mother, gave her father a quick kiss, and headed down the path toward the entrance to Eternal Rest Cemetery. From there it was only a three-block walk to the high school.

That was when Carson remembered she'd lost her own brother, a half brother actually, back in middle school. Jeff Sanchez had been a Hell Rider, too, around the same age as Carson was now when it happened. He'd died when he lost control of his bike on a rainy night and slid across the road right into a utility pole. From what Eddie used to say, Jeff had been too wasted to drive. He'd also complained that it was around then when Chief Jones started going out of his way to make life difficult for the Hell Riders.

He should have tried harder. Maybe they'd both be alive.

Carson's thoughts returned to Kellie. She probably did know how he felt, even if she hadn't grown up in the same house as her brother.

"I'll call you tomorrow."

Her words echoed in his head as he helped his mother into Chief Jones's car while the Chief put the wheelchair in the trunk. Kellie Jones was going to call him. He climbed into the backseat and felt a sudden nervousness as Chief Jones slid behind the wheel.

What if he doesn't let her call me? He's the Chief of Police. What if he's pissed she was talking to me? He never liked Eddie, and he's probably only nice to me 'cause of my mom.

For the entire ride home, Carson stared out the window, afraid to face the man whose daughter he'd just touched hands with. When they got back to their trailer, he quickly made himself busy in the kitchen, helping his mother's friends with the food and dishes.

He didn't relax until Jones went home. But even then, he kept thinking about Kellie and her father, scared and thrilled and worried all at the same time. Had she really meant what she said, or was she just being polite? Would she call, or just blow him off? Would Chief Jones even let him within a hundred yards of his daughter? By the time he went to bed, he was so wound up again that he found himself staring at the ceiling, just like all those nights when he'd waited for Eddie to come home.

Except it wasn't the sound of his brother's motorcycle that reached Carson in the dark silence of the house.

Instead, it was his mother's crying that kept him awake all night.

CHAPTER SIX

With all the mourners gone, Eternal Rest Cemetery grew as beautifully tranquil as a secluded glen or rarely visited park. Birds sang and insects buzzed, but their soft, mellow noises created subliminal harmonies that increased the feeling of serenity instead of disturbing it. Eddie's funeral had been the only one scheduled for the day, and since it was a weekday afternoon, there were no visitors at the other graves. They would come later, after work or dinner, in ones and twos, bearing flowers and tears for the departed. No more than ten on an average evening; it was a sad but true fact that once the initial shock and heartbreak wore off, most people only visited the graves of their loved ones on weekends or special occasions.

After a few years, sometimes not even then.

Floating helplessly over the gaping hole of his grave, Eddie Ryder listened to the chirping and whirring below him and felt resignation push away a tiny bit of his anger. If he had to be stuck somewhere forever, the cemetery wasn't such a bad place to be. There was a nice view, and hopefully his family would come by once in a while to visit. Maybe they'd even talk to his grave, the way some people did, and in so doing fill him in on the details of their lives.

It was at that moment the cemetery's two groundskeepers came down the path, shovels over their shoulders. Eddie didn't need to see their faces to recognize them. Lenny Bates – Mouse Bates's father – and Elmer Dinkley, Hell Creek's resident town idiot. Their job was to operate the crane that lowered the casket into the grave, and then use the backhoe and shovels to fill in the hole. It took them over an hour to maneuver the casket into place, while Eddie fumed above them.

Goodbye, me, Eddie thought. *Hello, a thousand years of staring at the ground.*

Except something quite different happened.

The moment the first load of gray, sandy dirt landed on the casket with a metallic thump, something snapped painfully inside him, a digging, twisting agony that would have had him rolling on the ground if he'd still been alive.

Then it vanished.

And he was floating up, up, and away from the grave, his former ties to his body severed in one toe-curling snip.

What the…?

I'm free!

With that realization, all his fury erupted and he screamed with joy. Thunder shook the sky and he rocketed skyward.

Guess what, Hank? Eddie fucking Ryder is back!

And I'm coming for you!

★   ★   ★

Blissfully unaware that his son was being interrogated by the police for the hundredth time in his relatively short life, Lenny Bates threw the backhoe in neutral and looked up at the sky in surprise as sudden thunder, louder than the 'dozer's engine, shattered the cemetery's quiet.

"What the fuck?"

"Mebbe a storm comin'," said Elmer, leaning against the backhoe's cab to spit a stream of tobacco juice on the grass. "Guess we better finish this fast."

"Ain't a cloud up there." Lenny knew that didn't mean a damn thing, not in South Florida in the fall, when a thunderstorm could show up out of nowhere, much like his mother-in-law, just as loud and unwelcome.

"Whatever. Just hurry up. I don't feel like gettin' soaked."

Elmer scooped up some loose soil while Lenny aimed the backhoe for another run. He couldn't shake the feeling that something was wrong, though, and every few minutes he found himself looking over his shoulder, thinking someone was watching them.

"Shouldn't work in no damn cemet'ry, dey's full of haunts." Lenny remembered his father's words, back when the old man was still alive, on the day Lenny quit high school to take the assistant

groundskeeper's job. In the thirty years since, he'd never once felt like he'd rather be working somewhere else.

Until now.

Fuckin' haunts. Now I'm gonna be creeped out all goddamned day.

★   ★   ★

The interrogation room at the Hell Creek police station stunk of cigarettes and body odor. The former was a permanent fixture, from years of drunks, punks, and assorted lowlifes cadging smokes from police officers. The second, and by far stronger, *eau de funk* emanated from the pores of Mouse Bates, who, much like his grave-digging father, considered bathing something best left for holidays, weddings, and semi-annual trips to the whorehouses in Homestead or Miami.

Doing his best to breathe through his mouth, Johnny Ray Jones fought to keep from slamming a fist into Mouse's greasy, zit-infested face. Instead, he pushed a pack of Camels toward the so-far uninformative gang member, hoping that if he couldn't get the asshole to talk, he could at least knock a few weeks off the shit-bird's life.

And in the process maybe burn away some of the foul stench the kid wore like a pole-cat jacket.

Johnny Ray waited until Mouse lit up and exhaled before starting in on him again. It was the second time that week they'd brought him in, on the slim hope he might slip up and contradict his previous statement. "So let me get this straight. You're telling me you don't know anything about what happened at Eddie's place? You gotta do better than that, Mouse. We know somebody torched the garage. And there's a kid in a grave because of it."

The skinny teenager flipped his long, greasy hair back and gave Johnny Ray a shit-eating grin that was equal parts yellow teeth, leftover food, and chewing tobacco.

"It's the truth, Chief. We wasn't anywhere near the place that night. We spent the night partyin' at the clubhouse."

"Really? I got a videotape shows you, Hank, and Duck jawin' with Eddie the night he was murdered."

Mouse's smile fell off a bit, just enough for Johnny Ray to

know he'd hit a nerve, but the boy did a good job of regaining his composure.

"Yeah, well, we was just lettin' him know who's boss, ya know? Keep him on his toes a little. We'd have prob'ly busted him up a little, too, if it wasn't for the cameras. But teachin' someone a lesson's a lot different than killin' him. Alls we did after that was buy our beer and go to the party."

Johnny Ray gritted his teeth. Mouse wasn't smart — not book smart, anyhow — but like his namesake he had a kind of animal intelligence, a knack for scurrying into a hole whenever there were signs of trouble. The kind of slimy little asswipe who always managed to escape by the skin of his balls while his friends got caught red-handed.

The worst part was, the little fuck knew it. His toothpaste-challenged grin was back in full force, showing enough accumulated sludge that nine out of ten dentists would have lost their lunches just looking at it.

When Johnny Ray didn't immediately say anything, Mouse figured correctly the questioning was over. He stood up and dropped his cigarette to the floor, crushed it with one road-worn work boot. "Hey, if that's all you got, Chief, I guess I'll be goin'. Have a nice day."

Johnny Ray put his arm across the door, halting Mouse's exit. "You can go, Leroy," he said, and was rewarded with a dirty look. Mouse hated his given name more than anything. "But before you do, know this. I sometimes look in the other direction on a lot of the shit that goes on in this town. Easier that way. Less paperwork. But when it comes to murder and arson, I tend to get very serious. And when it happens to involve the family of a person I'm very close to, someone who's one of my dearest friends in the whole *goddamn world*, I guarantee I will find who did it and *put their fucking ass in jail for life!*" By the time he finished, Johnny Ray had his face nose to greasy nose with his suspect and he'd let his voice rise until he was shouting.

Mouse's eyes went wide and for the first time Johnny Ray saw something in them other than arrogance.

Fear.

He stared for a minute longer, and then moved his arm away. As Mouse opened the door, Johnny Ray whistled softly.

"Hey, Leroy."

No longer smiling, Mouse looked back.

This time it was Johnny Ray's turn to smile.

"Have a nice day."

★　　★　　★

The poorly muffled roar of Mouse's Harley was still vibrating the windows of the police station when Ted Moselby joined Johnny Ray by the brew pot in the break room.

"So, what do you think? When do we make our move?"

Johnny Ray filled two plastic cups, set them down on a counter stained from years of spilled coffee, and considered the question. Moselby knew better than anyone that the Hell Riders were guilty. But once again his big-city experience worked against him. Things moved differently in small towns. Slower. In a close-knit community like Hell Creek, you couldn't lock someone up unless you had real, hard evidence. The kind that even a councilman or bank president couldn't pay to make disappear.

"I think," Johnny Ray said, sipping the tepid, bitter brew, "they're as guilty as fuckin' sin. But we ain't got a lick of proof. And as long as Duck Miller's uncle is mayor around here, we can't do squat until we have that proof. Lots of it."

Moselby shook his head. "And here one of the reasons I left LA was to get away from the political bullshit."

With a shrug, Johnny Ray said, "You never get away from it. It just comes out of different assholes. Here's what we're gonna do. We keep a close watch on them. Bust their balls for every little thing. I mean everything. One of them changes lanes without a signal or goes a mile over the speed limit, we ticket their ass. Maybe we'll make 'em nervous enough that one of them slips up. Christ, they're all dumb as friggin' roadkill. One of 'em is bound to get wasted and open their mouth to the wrong person."

Johnny Ray took another sip of his coffee and groaned as it hit his stomach like a shot of acid. It didn't matter what coffee they bought, or who made it. Somehow the machine turned it into pure factory runoff. *Damn thing's possessed*, he thought, and then wondered where that idea had come from. If there was one thing Johnny Ray Jones didn't believe in, it was haunts and ghosts.

That would come later.

CHAPTER SEVEN

From two hundred feet in the air, Hell Creek revealed itself as truly insignificant.

If you type 'pissant town' into Google Maps, I'll bet this is the picture that comes up, Eddie thought, looking down with a mental sneer. His irritation was due in part to his growing frustration with the invisible leash, longer than before but no less unbreakable, keeping him tied to his corpse, but also because rage was as much a part of his genetic makeup as his black hair or wiry frame. He'd had the bad luck to inherit Big Eddie's temper rather than his mother's calm, rational demeanor, a temper that at times during life had been uncontrollable, a demon inside him that constantly wanted to be set free.

And death only seemed to have made it worse.

He'd spent the past two days trying to get a handle on his new condition, with little success. While being released from his short lead seemed like a blessing at first, in actuality it had left him more aggravated than ever, because he'd had a taste of real freedom only to find he was still stuck in a cage; a larger cage than before, but still a cage. And he had no idea how to get out.

Rising higher from the ground had been easy; all he had to do was stop thinking about doing anything else and away he went. Coming back down had been harder. After some practice, he'd found that it helped to visualize an anchor sinking into the deep blue depths of a lake.

So far, though, he'd had little luck moving in other directions. No matter how much he concentrated, all he'd managed was a few yards left, right, back, and forward, with a little bit of rotation thrown in for good measure. Instead of staring right at his grave, now he could look down at the whole cemetery, while the town stretched off to the left and right before fading back into the swamps it'd been dug from.

This will not do. I'm like a dog on a chain, except the view is a little better.

Not much better, though. Not when you were stuck over Hell Creek. By spinning himself around, he could see the entire town. From the cemetery, Main Street extended south for all of three miles before becoming the interstate again and eventually curving down toward Everglades Park proper. Dividing Main Street perfectly in half was River Road, which Eddie'd always thought was the stupidest name they could have come up with, since there wasn't even a stream near it, let alone a river. The intersection of River and Main marked the center of the town and its pitiful business district. From his vantage point, Eddie was able to follow River Road as it stretched out to the west, right into the wilds of the swamps. Just outside of Hell Creek, in a no-man's land of swamp and overgrown fields ignored by county and state governments alike, was where the Hell Riders had their clubhouse, an abandoned airboat repair shop Ned Bowman had somehow scraped up the money to buy. They'd cleared it out and filled it with secondhand furniture, a half-assed bar, and a couple of TVs.

Eddie'd often wondered where Ned had gotten the money for the place. He suspected the gang leader was into shit the others didn't know about. Like moving drugs for the Colombians or Mexicans. Not all the time, just here and there. Enough to put some real cash in his hands, not like the small-time dealing he did around town. Which did come in handy. Not only did it keep him and the gang supplied with plenty of weed and coke, it made him popular with the kind of people who were always looking for a party and didn't care what they had to do to get in on the good times.

Assholes like me, Eddie thought. *I always looked down on the wannabes and the coke whores, but I wasn't much different.*

Regardless of how it had been paid for, the makeshift clubhouse was a perfect place to party because it was just past the Hell Creek town line, meaning Chief Jones couldn't bust their balls, and it was so remote the Staties never bothered with it.

A new kind of frustration rose up in Eddie as he remembered all the times he'd banged Sandy Powell there. She'd been his steady girlfriend for over a year, right up until he ratted on Ned. Then the bitch had dumped him cold. Bad enough, but the very next day she'd taken up with Hank Bowman and Eddie'd leaned the hard way she'd been nothing but a cycle slut, that she'd been into him more for his status as an original Hell Rider than because she loved him.

Another thing I owe that asshole Bowman for. Impotent rage coursed through him and he knew that if he'd had a real body he'd have been red-faced and shaking, ready to lash out with his fists at something. Or someone.

Spinning on his metaphysical axis, Eddie turned away from what he'd once considered a second home and stared in the other direction, looking past the shops and town buildings, past roads with names like Cypress, Big Pine, and Mangrove, to the far edge of town. A charred square marked the spot where his garage had been. His memories of that night were spotty, but something he definitely remembered was climbing onto Diablo and trying to escape.

How'd that work out for ya, Eddie?

One of the many things that sucked about being dead was he had only himself to talk to. He hadn't expected to miss conversations with his brother, his mother – even his customers – so much. Now there was only his own brain, and it was starting to be a real pain in the ass.

Staring at the remnants of the garage, he found that he missed his bike almost as much as he missed his family. He'd built Diablo with his own hands, crafting all his customizations around the frame and engine of a 1975 Harley Electra Glide. Pure power and comfort. No riding around with his hands and arms over his head like a baboon. He'd even done the paint himself. It'd taken him more than a year, and every extra cent he could muster. The bike had been his pride and joy.

Motherfuckers took that away, too.

If only I could've brought the bike with me. Think what I could've done. In his thoughts, he pictured himself like Ghost Rider from the comics, his skull flaming and Diablo a fire-breathing demon, racing through the streets of Hell Creek while people cowered behind store windows.

I'd ride that beast to my house, so I could—

Without warning, the ground flashed by beneath him, his consciousness moving so fast it raced past the cars on Main Street.

What the—?

A familiar feel came over him; his arms extended, his knees bent. His fingers clenching and unclenching as he shifted gears.

The rumble of a seventy-horse-power engine vibrating beneath him.

Diablo! But how?

It didn't make sense. But then, neither did his presence as a spirit or the fact that he couldn't see himself, or the bike, yet he could feel everything as if he had a body. As if he were real.

Eddie no longer cared. All that mattered was not being tied to one spot anymore. With a whooping war cry, he opened the throttle and let the bike take him where he wanted to go.

Home.

CHAPTER EIGHT

Seated on a small bench outside the Dairy King, Carson Ryder and Kellie Jones looked up as unexpected thunder rumbled overhead.

"That's weird," Kellie said, returning her attention to her pistachio cone. "It's not supposed to rain today."

"Yeah." Carson continued staring at the sky. Something about that thunder hadn't sounded right. Almost as if it wasn't thunder at all, but....

He couldn't place it.

"How's your ice cream?"

"What?" Carson glanced at his cone, where streams of chocolate and strawberry threatened to run down the sides. He quickly licked the drippings away. "It's, um, good."

Carson kept his gaze on the ice cream. His tongue felt numb, and not because of the cold dessert. True to her word, Kellie had called him the day after the funeral. He'd been so stunned by the call that he'd found himself unable to put a coherent sentence together. It'd taken him several agonizing minutes to get up the nerve to ask her if she wanted to do something after school later in the week, all the while fearful that she'd hang up before he got the words out. When she'd said yes, he'd felt excited and relieved and happy and all sorts of things he couldn't put into words.

Until they'd actually gotten off the school bus at the Main Street stop and walked over to the Dairy King. Then outright terror had hit him as he realized he'd be expected to make conversation without sounding like a total dork.

He kept desperately trying to think of something to say, something that would show her he was more than just the smart kid in class, more than someone from the Trailers, as his neighborhood was known.

So far, the best he'd managed was, "Boy, it's really hot today," and "What kind of ice cream would you like?"

She's only putting up with this because her dad and your mom are friends. As soon as she finishes her ice cream, she's gonna say how she's got homework, or—

"How are you and your mom holding up?"

"Huh?" It took him a moment to switch mental gears. "Um, you know, it's been weird. Like he's not really gone. Not for good. My mom cries a lot, and she's been spending more time in bed than usual. I fix her meals now, and make sure she takes her medicine. All the stuff Eddie used to do. But then there's times when...." He let his voice trail off, wishing he hadn't opened up so much, and knowing Kellie wouldn't let it drop.

"When what?" Kellie finished the last of her cone, gave her fingers a wipe with her napkin, and then flicked her tongue over her lips. Carson knew it wasn't any kind of come-on, but it still set his heart beating faster.

"Well, it sounds stupid, but when I go to bed, I feel like Eddie's still out there somewhere. I lie there and I find myself listening for the sound of that stupid motorcycle. He always started it or shut it off at the road, thinking we wouldn't hear him. But it didn't matter. His bike was so loud it could wake the dead."

Stunned by how much he'd said, Carson stopped talking, even though there was more inside him, words and emotions suddenly pounding to be set free.

When Kellie didn't say anything, he figured he'd really gone and blown it. Instead of just being a dork, now he was a weird dork.

"I told you it was stupid."

Then she surprised him again. "No, it's not. When my brother died, I couldn't believe he was really gone. And I was angry all the time. Angry that he got wasted and drove off the road. Angry at the people he hung out with. Even angry at my dad, although it wasn't his fault. It took me a long time to get over it. And then when my parents got divorced, and my mom left, a lot of those feelings came back. I felt abandoned. I don't know how my dad put up with me, I was such a bitch. I just couldn't believe I'd lost her, too, you know?"

"Yeah!" Carson nodded his head. "That's it exactly. Why the hell did he have to go to the garage that night? Why couldn't he have just stayed home for once? If he had...."

"He'd be alive."

Fighting back tears – no way was he gonna cry in front of Kellie! – Carson found himself nodding again. "Yeah. He'd be alive. And we wouldn't be alone."

Something touched his arm and he almost jumped when he realized it was Kellie's hand.

"You can't think like that," she said, her voice soft but firm. "It took me a while, but eventually I started to understand that it wasn't my fault, or my parents' fault, or even Jeff's fault. It was those damn Hell Riders. They got a kid drunk and let him drive. And whatever happened to your brother, that's not your fault or your mom's. It's not even Eddie's fault. He did nothing wrong by going to the garage. You can't blame him for what someone else did to him. You can't ask yourself 'what if?' He was just in the wrong place at the wrong time. Sometimes things like that happen."

"Yeah." Carson barely heard her. He was looking at her hand, reveling in the feel of her skin against his.

Thunder rumbled again, only this time it didn't come from the sky. Kellie turned to look up the street, and her hand fell away. Anger, the same anger he'd just confessed to, churned in Carson's stomach as he watched four motorcycles take the corner at River Road. Polished chrome turned the afternoon sun into a thousand burning daggers of light and windows rattled as the four Hell Riders accelerated down Main Street.

"I hate them." The expression on Kellie's face told Carson how much she meant it.

"I hated Eddie's bike." The words popped out of Carson's mouth before he even knew they were there. "He called it Diablo. Who names their motorcycle? Sometimes I think he loved that bike more than he loved us."

"Is that why you hated it?"

Carson wished she'd put her hand back on his arm. Or that he had enough guts to touch her like that. The Hell Riders had ruined the mood, though. Now there was just talking. He looked at her, and she stared back at him.

"No. I hated it because I knew someday it would take him away from us forever. Except I figured it would be him getting on it and just riding away, going out for a pack of smokes and never coming back, the way my dad did. Or ending up dead on the highway 'cause he had too much to drink. But you know what?"

Kellie shook her head, never breaking their intense eye contact.

"I'd give anything to hear the stupid motorcycle again."

★　　★　　★

"I didn't leave!" Eddie shouted, hoping that from two stories up some part of his essence would make it down to Carson. "I'd have never left you and Mom."

After the thrill of experiencing Diablo again, even if only in an imaginary sense, and finding out he could move to different places in town, the afternoon had quickly soured for Eddie. He'd looked into the windows of his house and seen his mother, paler and more drawn than ever, sleeping in her bed. He'd planned on sticking around until she woke up or Carson came home, but his guilt – *it's my fault she looks like that* – lay too heavy on his invisible shoulders, so he'd headed back into town. There, he'd found Carson and Chief Jones's daughter coming out of the Dairy King.

"Way to go, little brother," he said, watching the two kids sit down on a bench. So they'd gotten together after all. He floated down until he could hear them talking. At first, he felt a little weird for eavesdropping. Sort of a voyeuristic excitement accompanied by embarrassment. Like when you were a kid and you caught your parents fooling around when they thought you were asleep.

Then he heard what they were talking about.

Him.

It was like dying all over again, listening to his brother's words.

"Goddammit!" As if the curse was an ignition key, Diablo rumbled to life beneath him once more, and just like *that!* he went roaring down the road after the four Hell Riders.

★　　★　　★

"Did you hear that?" Carson looked around.

"What?" Kellie asked.

"That weird thunder again. Like before. Except it didn't sound like thunder."

"More motorcycles, probably." Kellie stood up and tossed her napkin in the trash. "I've got homework to do."

"Sure. Homework." There it was, the blow off, just as he'd expected. "Me too."

Kellie's hand, cool and a little sticky from the ice cream, slid into his and pulled him up from the bench. "Well, we're in some of the same classes. Why don't you come to my house? We can study together."

It took Carson almost a full block to find his voice.

CHAPTER NINE

Eddie stayed with the Hell Riders as they cruised past the town limits and took a short, unpaved road that led into the Everglades. He'd known where they were going as soon as they got onto the highway; the road to the clubhouse was as familiar to him as his own driveway.

The four bikers went inside and Eddie took a moment to rest. Unlike his other trips across town, this one had left him feeling punky, like back in the days when he'd stay out all night partying and then go straight to work. Even sinking down to window level was an effort.

He forgot all about being tired when he looked inside and saw Hank Bowman, Duck Miller, and Harley Atkins laughing as they clapped Mouse Bates on the back and high-fived him.

"Nice going, Mouse!" Hank handed the smaller rider a beer. "Fuckin' Police Chief Dickhead thinks he can try to scare us? Shit. He might as well put his arson case in a box and file it unsolved, 'cause he ain't never gonna get nothin' on us."

Staring through the window, Eddie ground invisible teeth. *Bastards! I'll kill all of you! I'll see you in fuckin' hell!*

"Yeah, I could tell he was pissin' in the wind," Mouse said. "But I think we oughtta be careful for a while, lay low."

"Lay low? No way!" Duck opened a beer, spraying foam all over the place before he got the can to his mouth.

"Shut up, Duck," Hank said. He glared at Mouse. "What'd you hear?"

Mouse shrugged. "Somethin' Jones said before he cut me loose. He's takin' this real personal, he said. And he had a look.... Man, I never seen him like that. Like he was just itchin' for a reason to take a swing at me."

"He knows he's fucked." Harley lowered his barrel-shaped body into a dusty, worn reclining chair. The wood creaked under his weight and when he leaned back, his massive belly formed a medicine ball-sized dome beneath his dirty Rage Against the Machine t-shirt. "He's...what's the word? Flusterated."

Hank snorted. "That's frustrated, you idiot. And we knew it was personal. Ain't no secret Jones is all cozy with Eddie's mother. So what's the big deal?"

Mouse swigged beer and belched before replying. "I'm tellin' ya, I don't remember ever seein' him so pissed. Not even when your brother decked him that night down at Lanie's."

As mad as he was, Eddie couldn't help but smile at the memory of the night Ned Bowman had punched Chief Jones. Lanie's was a biker bar on the highway between Hell Creek and Homestead. Well outside of Jones's jurisdiction and Ned had known it. Jones had been nosing around about a sudden influx of pot in Hell Creek, and Ned was six tequilas over his normal limit, which meant he was being a bigger douchebag than usual. They'd gotten to jawing and Ned had clocked Chief Jones right in the mouth. Knocked him out cold. The whole gang had boogied out of there, of course, laughing their asses off all the way back to Hell Creek. Afterward, Jones had made their lives hell – and their wallets a lot thinner – for about a month, hitting them with everything from speeding tickets to citations for disturbing the peace.

But they'd all agreed it'd been worth it.

"Fuck him," Hank said, and threw his beer can at the wall.

Eddie flinched as the can hit right next to the window, momentarily forgetting no one could see him.

"He's gonna keep comin' down on us."

"So what?" Hank held out his hand and Duck tossed him another beer. "If he does, you just keep your mouth shut. How fucking hard is that? If Jones had any real brains, he'd be a cop in a real town, 'stead of a shit burg like Hell Creek."

"He was smart enough to break Eddie and put your brother in jail." Mouse stepped back as he spoke, putting himself out of range of Hank's fists. But instead of getting angrier, Hank gave a nasty laugh.

"Yeah, and we paid Ryder back for that, didn't we? He got what he deserved, and the same thing'll happen to anyone else who opens his mouth. Any problems with that?"

Eddie seethed as the other three gang members shook their heads. "Good." Hank slammed his beer against the stolen picnic table they used for poker and meals. Foam sprayed out, adding to the innumerable stains in the rough wood. "Let the rest of the boys know. I don't want to hear nothin' else about it."

Watching his ex-friends laugh and joke as they finished their beers and prepared to get the evening's party started fueled Eddie's rage even further. They'd just admitted to killing him, while he stood there helpless to do anything about it. Every part of him burned, blazing with a mad energy worse than anything he'd ever felt while alive.

When the four Hell Riders walked outside to dump some empty beer kegs in the back, he couldn't control himself any longer. All his wrath came out in a furious scream.

"I'll kill you all, you motherfuckers!"

At that exact moment, just as Hank shut the door, every window in the clubhouse exploded inward, filling the place with deadly glass shrapnel.

"Holy fuck!" Hank dove to the ground, Mouse and Duck close behind him.

Harley simply stood there, staring at the clubhouse, his eyes wide and his mouth hanging open.

"Get down!" Duck shouted at him, pulling out a pistol. He was the only one in the gang who had a permit to carry, thanks to his uncle the mayor. "Someone's shootin' at us."

Harley remained standing, a perfect target if someone had been firing at them. "They are? I didn't hear no guns. And how'd they do that?" He pointed to their motorcycles.

All the rearview mirrors were shattered.

"Son of a bitch." Hank got to his feet and looked around. The others joined him, although Duck didn't put his pistol away. "What the hell...?"

★   ★   ★

What the hell? Eddie's thoughts mirrored Hank's. *Did I do that?*

After the explosion of glass, he'd shot up into the air, an instinctive reaction that caught him by surprise. By the time he got control of himself, he'd been almost a hundred feet over the clubhouse. Below him, Hank and the others were cursing at the damage to their bikes and wondering what had happened.

Eddie's anger remained, but at the same time he felt exhausted, drained of all strength. When the Hell Riders climbed on their cycles and roared off, he didn't bother following them. Instead, he let himself slowly float back toward town like an empty boat drifting to shore on an invisible current.

His thoughts, however, raced at top speed.

What the hell am I? Am I a ghost? An angel?

Why am I still here instead of heaven or hell or wherever fuck it is dead people go?

Are there others like me, and I just can't see them, or am I alone?

His questions kept circling around to two main questions.

I can control energy. I can move from place to place. What else can I do? And....

Why? Why am I here?

Looking deep inside himself, he found he didn't care about the second question. He was still around, for whatever reason. For how long, he didn't know. But he'd been given a chance.

A chance to get revenge.

And he planned on making the most of it.

CHAPTER TEN

Over the next two days, Eddie worked harder than he ever had while alive. Without the need to eat or sleep, he found it easy to devote his total attention to learning as much about himself as he could. He quickly discovered that even though he had no actual body, he still had certain physical limitations, some of which he managed to overcome, at least to a degree.

The first thing he realized was that his ghost form remained tied to his body somehow. The farther from his grave he traveled, the weaker he got. Riding to the clubhouse – Diablo was as much a part of him now as his own thoughts – tired him out. Any more than a mile farther and he grew so exhausted he had to stop. The same thing happened no matter which direction he took, leaving him trapped in a circle roughly twelve miles in diameter, which encompassed all of Hell Creek plus a little bit more. Better than being stuck hovering over his own grave, but having no real freedom added more fuel to the inferno smoldering inside him.

That same passionate rage seemed to be the basis of all his powers. By channeling it, forcing it into a focused thought or action, he could affect the physical world. Trickle some energy out and he could make streetlights flicker or car alarms go off. Gather up all the hate and fury festering inside him and let it loose in one huge eruption, a mental projectile vomiting of pure hatred, and the effects were far greater. A row of motorcycles knocked over in front of Hickey Tavern. A dozen shattered windows at the elementary school.

The only problem was, channeling all that energy into one blast left him totally drained, so weak that sometimes he couldn't even conjure Diablo to life. On those occasions it took hours for his strength to return.

In between his experiments, Eddie inevitably ended up returning to his house to see his mother or Carson. Although it gave him a slightly creepy feeling to spy on them, he couldn't stop himself from doing it. He'd peer through a window or sit across the room while his family went on living without him. Watching them was an oddly wonderful and terrible experience. Wonderful because even though he couldn't interact with them, he took some joy from knowing they weren't gone forever, that he'd at least get to see how their lives turned out.

Terrible because he remained invisible to them, helpless to provide comfort or aid or support when they needed it. And from what he'd seen, they did need it. His mother looked sicker than ever, as if his death had drained the last of her will and strength and she was just marking the days until she joined her son in the afterlife. Carson put on a brave front for her, and in public, but it hadn't escaped Eddie that his little brother had cried himself to sleep every night since the funeral.

Even now, while the two of them sat in her room finishing a late dinner, a desolate silence filled the air, a sense of gloom reached Eddie from the other side of the window. Watching them, the words to a song came to him, a song by Charred Walls of the Damned that he used to listen to whenever he felt depressed, usually about bills or his mother's declining health.

Struggling in a world so cruel
Trying hard not to fail
Sometimes making it through the day
Is like walking on nails

Walking on nails. That's exactly what it was like. Nails that pierced all the way to his heart. Only now, instead of wishing he could rid himself of the anguish, he embraced it, because the horrible sadness of their lives re-stoked the hatred inside him, re-charged his batteries and filled him back up with rage toward his murderers. He welcomed it, let his wrath expand within him until he felt he couldn't contain it, and then he forced himself to slowly rise up until he was well above the house.

Usually, at that point he'd conjure Diablo and race toward town, just like when he'd been alive, shaking the heavens with his thunder.

There he'd practice using his destructive energies, pointing his finger at clouds and firing energy bolts like the super-villain he imagined himself to be at those times.

Tonight, however, he had something else in mind.

★ ★ ★

Wednesday night had always been the unofficial start of the weekend for the Hell Riders. They'd gather at Hickey Tavern for a dinner of chicken wings, beer, and tequila shots. Around ten o'clock they'd either stumble out and bring some girls back to the clubhouse or they'd be rousted out by Chief Jones or some other cop and *then* stumble back to the clubhouse.

Eddie doubted anything had changed since he'd died. After all, it wasn't like the gang had lost one of their own. Sure enough, when he arrived at the Hickey there were seven gleaming Harleys parked out front. He didn't even have to look at the bikes to know who they belonged to; only full club members and their girlfriends were allowed to attend the Wednesday night pre-party. Pledges, wannabes, and assorted sluts would be at the clubhouse, getting things ready for the main event. With him dead and Ned in prison, that left only seven full members.

Passing easily through the wide front window, Eddie went inside, experiencing a moment of nostalgia as he took in the familiar booths, dark walls, and assorted neon signs of the bar. He hadn't been back since ratting on Ned Bowman and getting kicked out of the gang, preferring to keep a safe distance from any Hell Rider hangout after that.

The Hell Riders had their usual corner table, the top crowded with baskets of wings and fries, pitchers of cheap beer, and empty shot glasses. When Eddie arrived, Hank was just finishing a joke or story that had the others laughing so hard they were spraying beer and food all over.

His intention had been to come up behind one of them and see if he could give somebody a good shock, place a hand on them and funnel a little bit of his energy right into their flesh. Hell, if he was lucky, he'd give one of the bastards a heart attack.

Instead, something far stranger happened.

The closest rider was Jethro Cole, a scrawny kid who'd dropped out of high school after two failed attempts to pass tenth grade. He had buckteeth and more freckles than brain cells, and Eddie'd often thought the Bowman brothers only kept him around to be their gofer boy.

Eddie reached out to touch Jethro's shoulder, but rather than stopping, his hand kept going – right into Jethro's body.

There was a burst of white, followed by a moment of pure blackness, and then without warning he found himself staring directly into Hank Bowman's face.

And he was *alive*.

I can feel! The sensations were so overwhelming he thought he might faint. His heart pounded strong and hard inside his chest. Air moved in and out of his lungs. A wave of coolness from the air-conditioning washed over the skin on his arms, raising goosebumps and tickling each individual hair. The sweet-bitter tang of beer and the spicy, greasy kick of chicken wing sauce filled his nose and made his mouth water.

"What's wrong with you?" Hank's voice boomed like a cannon in Eddie's ears, deafening him.

He looked around to see who Hank was talking to and noticed all the other Hell Riders were staring at him.

No, not me. They're looking at Jethro. Holy fuck, I'm inside him!

As soon as he thought it, he knew it was true. Somehow he'd taken over Jethro Cole's body, was now in control of it. Whatever he told it to do, it responded, just like his own body.

Which opened up all sorts of possibilities.

"Dude, what's your fuckin' problem?"

Eddie realized Jethro's body was still in the same position as when he'd entered it, beer half-raised, a wing in his other hand.

Goddamn, this is going to be fun.

Eddie looked straight at Hank.

"You're my problem, dickhead." Then he threw the wing across the table. It hit Hank dead center in the forehead and bounced to the side, leaving a greasy, red inkblot of hot sauce right above Hank's nose.

Hank's mouth dropped open but no words came out. Before

anyone could say anything, Eddie leaned over and poured his beer in Hank's lap. For a moment, time seemed to stand still, with everyone at the table frozen in their seats.

Then all hell broke loose.

Duck Miller and Gary Rock dragged Eddie/Jethro out of his chair and tossed him onto the floor. Eddie laughed out loud at the pain. It was a distant sensation, as if Jethro's brain had taken the brunt of it, and the remaining dull ache was so much better than feeling nothing at all that he reveled in it, embraced it. He continued laughing as Duck and Gary lifted him back up and held him while Hank waded in, hammering Jethro's stomach and face with both fists. That hurt a lot worse but Eddie forced himself to keep laughing. He saw a couple of teeth fly past and spatters of blood covered Hank's hands and shirt.

A grayish cloud descended over Eddie's vision and he couldn't tell if Jethro was losing consciousness or if the supernatural connection had started to weaken. Eddie didn't know what would happen to him if Jethro passed out – or died – while he inhabited the biker's body, but he didn't want to find out.

Better make this fast.

It took a lot of effort to raise Jethro's head and smile at Hank. It was even harder to form words with half his teeth gone and both lips split and swollen.

"Hey, fuck nuts. Watch out. Eddie's coming for ya." Eddie raised his hand and gave a middle-finger salute.

"Yeah? Here's a fuck you for ya." Hank pulled back his fist for another blow, and for the first time, Eddie felt a twinge of fear.

He had no idea how to get out of Jethro's body.

Then he pictured himself riding away on Diablo, and just like *that!* he was moving, the imaginary bike's engine straining as if climbing a steep hill, tires spinning and smoking. There was a *snap* like a giant rubber band breaking and then he rose up, up, and away, heading toward the ceiling while Hank's fist connected loudly with Jethro's already broken nose.

Below him, people jumped up and looked around at the sound of thunder booming. Windows rattled and glasses shook. A waitress screamed.

Eddie, incorporeal again and weaker than a sick puppy, found enough strength to fight the encroaching darkness and let out a bellow of laughter. Although no one in the bar heard it, lights flickered and the TVs went dark.

With a silent sigh, he let the blanket of gray fall over him and take him away.

★   ★   ★

Hank Bowman stared at the unconscious form of Jethro Cole and shivered as a cold sensation spread from his belly, numbing him until he felt like he stood in the eye of a hurricane, immune to the chaos around him. People cried out as thunder crashed outside. Someone shouted to call the police. Duck and Gary dragged Jethro toward the men's room, and Mouse tugged at his sleeve, saying something about getting the hell out of there.

Hank stood apart from all of it, let it flow around and past him.

What the hell had Jethro said? Those last words, right before Hank's fist flattened his nose and knocked out two more teeth. They'd been low, almost lost beneath the sounds of people shouting and running away, and twisted nearly beyond recognition by the damage done to Jethro's mouth.

"Hay fu nuth. Washout."

That part Hank translated easily. *Hey, fuck nuts. Watch out.* He had no idea why Jethro would say something like that, practically write himself a death sentence, but the words at least made sense.

But the last part? It'd come out sounding like a drunk with a mouth full of oatmeal.

"Ethys cum."

Someone grabbed his arm and Hank swung around, fist cocked and ready. It was Mouse again.

"C'mon, man, we gotta move. Cops are coming."

"Yeah. Okay." Hank followed the others outside. Halfway to his bike a thought came to him so suddenly he almost tripped over his own feet.

"Cops are coming."

"Ethys cum."

Cum. Coming? *Something coming?*

"Ethys." Hank placed his tongue between his lips and said the word out loud.

Said it again, this time using teeth Jethro hadn't had.

"Ettys."

Eddie's? Eddie's coming?

"Hey, fuck nuts. Watch out. Eddie's coming." Were those the words Jethro had struggled to get out?

It didn't make any sense, but it sounded right. Now that he'd said it once, he couldn't imagine it being anything else.

Eddie's coming.

Despite the ninety-degree temperature and the hot sauce sitting in his stomach, the cold wind inside Hank grew stronger.

CHAPTER ELEVEN

Eddie regained consciousness as the morning sun crept over the tops of the pine trees at Eternal Rest Cemetery. The first thing he saw was a temporary grave marker with his name on it.

Oh, man. I feel like shit.

He didn't remember returning to his grave. Everything after leaving Jethro's body was a complete blank. Like the time he'd drunk a whole bottle of tequila. His head had that tequila hangover feeling, too. Like being trapped inside a steel drum while someone pounded on the outside with metal sticks.

Head? What head? You're a fuckin' ghost. You shouldn't even be able to feel pain.

But he did feel it. Pain. Exhaustion. And that wasn't all.

Sadness. Hatred. Rage. Regret. As if all the bad shit in life came with me when I died.

But it's not all bad, is it? he asked himself, remembering what he'd done the night before. In fact, some things were pretty damn cool.

I can motherfuckin' possess people! How awesome is that?

Now that he knew how to do it, his plans for the Hell Riders needed to change.

Things are gonna get a lot more personal.

With a groan, he rose to an upright position and conjured Diablo. He'd thought he'd have trouble, but even though his non-existent skull ached like hell, he felt stronger than he had since…well, since he'd returned from the dead.

The whole possession thing wasn't just fun. It felt good. Real good. Better than coke or whiskey, despite the hangover. Like booze and energy drinks mixed together, but stronger.

Fuckin' A. I think I like it!

With a thundering roar that startled birds from their roosts and sent small animals scurrying for their burrows, Eddie and Diablo exploded up into the new day.

★ ★ ★

"Did you hear about the fight last night?"

Carson Ryder looked up to find Kellie Jones standing by his lunch table. As usual, he'd been eating alone. Thanks to bad luck in scheduling, the few friends he had didn't share a lunch period with him.

For a moment, Carson struggled to find his voice. The stunned looks on the faces of the kids at the nearby tables told him everyone felt the same shock as him that Kellie had stopped to talk to him. Over at the popular table, where Kellie normally sat, several of the guys looked ready to fall off their seats.

Carson couldn't help smiling as he turned his attention to Kellie. *How cool is this?*

"You mean down at the Hickey? It's all over the school. Probably all over town. I heard Hank Bowman nearly killed Jethro Cole."

Kellie set her tray down. "Scoot over. I'm hungry."

Carson's heart jumped and he slid to one side, making room for her. She hadn't just stopped to say hello. She was actually going to eat lunch with him!

"It's true," Kellie continued while she unwrapped her sandwich – mixed veggies on whole wheat. "Jethro's in the hospital."

Dumbfounded that she was sharing a table with him, he nearly knocked his iced tea bottle over when he reached for it.

Jeez, whatever you do, don't spill on her, you idiot!

He took a deep breath before trying again. This time, his hand didn't shake.

"Is your dad gonna arrest Hank?" Carson wished the cops would arrest the whole damn gang and lock them up forever.

Kellie shook her head. "He brought him in, but they couldn't charge him with anything except disturbing the peace. Mr. Hickey said that as long as Hank pays for the mess, he won't press charges. My dad says he's probably too afraid of Hank, plus he needs the business. And Jethro's not pressing charges, either. He's practically on life support, but he insists it was just a misunderstanding. And since no one else got hurt there isn't much my dad can do. Hank will probably have to pay a fine, but that's about it."

"That sucks."

"I know. Somehow those guys always manage to weasel out of everything."

"It should be like on TV. One of your dad's men plants some dope on them, they all get busted, and they spend the next twenty years in jail."

With a roll of her eyes, Kellie said, "Please. Don't let my father hear you say that. The only person more by the book than him is Moselby."

Remembering how many strings Chief Jones had pulled to keep Eddie out of jail, and not knowing if Kellie knew about it, Carson decided to change the subject. "So, what's your dad think about all the vandalism around town?"

"It's crazy, isn't it? He's going nuts. He thinks it's Hank and the others, 'cause people have been hearing motorcycles in the same areas where the windows got broken. But there's no witnesses and no proof."

Her remark about motorcycles triggered something in the back of Carson's brain. "You know, I've been hearing motorcycle sounds at night lately. Except—" He stopped, suddenly too embarrassed to finish.

"Except what?"

"You're gonna think it's crazy." She would, too. Even he couldn't believe it.

Kellie stopped nibbling a cookie and looked right at him, her large brown eyes filled with sincerity. "I won't. And even if I do, I promise not to laugh."

What the hell. "I said I've been hearing motorcycles at night, but that's not exactly true. I only hear one. And it sounds just like Eddie's."

"Diablo?"

He nodded, and Kellie nodded back. "You told me you'd heard it before. Maybe you're hearing a different bike, but it sounds kinda the same, so you—"

"Imagine it's Eddie's. I know, I thought of that. But there's something else. Something...stranger."

"So far it's not so strange."

"Sometimes when I hear the sound of his engine, it's over the house. Like, way over. Up in the sky."

He waited for her to laugh, and when she didn't, he wasn't sure if he should be relieved or worried. Laughter would mean she thought he was goofy.

Taking him seriously might mean she thought he was really crazy.

"Maybe it was thunder." This time Kellie kept her eyes on her food.

That's it. This'll be the last conversation we ever have. By sixth period she'll be telling her friends what a nut job I am.

"It didn't sound like thunder. Not at all. It sounded just like when Eddie used to start Diablo out in the driveway, except...."

"Except it was in the sky."

"Yeah."

Kellie put down her cookie, and Carson was sure she was about to say 'sayonara, doofus'.

She didn't.

She leaned forward and lowered her voice to almost a whisper. "Carson, something very strange is going on in this town. I think we should be extra careful."

"What?" He felt like he'd missed something. "Careful about what?"

"I don't know. But things have been really weird lately. Ever since...ever since the fire."

He didn't have to ask what fire she meant.

Before he could respond, the bell sounded, announcing the end of the lunch period. Kellie stood and picked up her tray. "I have a yearbook meeting today after school, but maybe we can grab some pizza tonight?"

Carson nodded, too surprised to speak. Even after she walked away, he kept staring at the spot where she'd been, thoughts spiraling through his head.

Maybe she's crazier than me.

But she asked me out for pizza!

Why did she act so weird? Is it a set-up?

We're going on a date!

He was still sorting through his feelings when the second bell rang, reminding him he better hurry or he'd be late for class.

This time, he didn't even notice the dirty looks Kellie's friends gave him.

CHAPTER TWELVE

Eddie tailed the Hell Riders at a height of several hundred feet, hoping the distance would be enough to dim Diablo's growl until it seemed like nothing more than distant heat thunder. He'd been watching the gang for most of the day, trying to think of the best way to use his new power. Hank and his boys had spent most of the afternoon boarding up the windows of the clubhouse and getting questioned by Chief Jones, who'd ended up storming away in a frustrated huff. Eddie almost felt sorry for him; with everyone refusing to press charges against Hank, Jones had been left holding his dick.

The best part of the afternoon was when Eddie learned about Jethro being in the hospital. He'd burst into laughter, which had set the lights flickering all over the clubhouse. That, in turn, had caused Hank to practically jump out of his pants, and led to the whole gang searching inside and out, trying to figure out who was screwing with them. It was like watching a sitcom, a private show just for him. Their increasing frustration only made Eddie laugh harder and caused the electricity to malfunction even worse.

Finally, Hank had shouted for them all to get the hell out, that he'd meet them later in town.

And that's when Eddie got his idea.

It was so simple he didn't know why he hadn't thought of it before.

Scare the fucking shit out of them and then kill them.

Eye for an eye. It was what they'd done to him. Made his life miserable. Now he'd pay them back, with interest.

And he'd save Hank for last.

But that didn't mean he couldn't have fun with his old friend first.

At that moment, Hank was flicking light switches on and off, trying to figure out where the problem lay. While he did this, he called out to the empty room, "Anyone here? C'mon, you fuckers. Show yourselves!"

Through hours of practice on street lights and car windows, Eddie had developed more control over what he called his 'hate energy'. He'd found that by imagining his rage as a weapon, like a gun, he could vary the amount of power released, rather than having it just leap out of him. A small gun released a little zap; a shotgun more. And for big jobs he pictured himself like Rambo, wielding a ridiculously oversized rocket launcher.

Time for a real *shock, Hank.*

Pointing his finger like a kid pretending to shoot a pistol, Eddie pulled his mental trigger. Although no visible discharge occurred, the light switch suddenly popped and sparked in Hank's fingers. He stumbled backward, hair standing on end and the tips of his thumb and forefinger blackened and smoking.

"Goddammit! Motherfucking cocksucking no-good whorebag!"

Eddie pointed again. *Bang!*

The forty-five-inch color television, a three-hundred-pound relic from the times before flat-screens, exploded in a fireworks display of colored sparks. A hailstorm of glass shredded the chair where, just an hour before, Mouse had sat while being grilled by Chief Jones about the fight between Hank and Jethro.

Hank let out a terrified shriek and dove behind the bar Ned and some of the others had stolen from a junkyard in Homestead.

In his mind, Eddie tried to picture the wiring behind the walls. He let his hand pass through the cheap paneling under a light switch, imagined himself gripping the wires, and channeling his energy into them, overloading them.

Instantly, all the light bulbs blew out and several electrical cords melted right into the sockets. From his hiding place, Hank shouted for help.

That's right, you piece of shit. You fucking douche. Scream like a baby. Remember this. Eddie was here. Eddie was h—

A massive bolt of pain punched through Eddie's brain, worse than any hangover. He cried out and grabbed his head. The moment he stopped using his power, the pounding lessened to a dull ache.

Overdid it. Still not that strong. Gotta rest. The metaphysical him stumbled over to Diablo and climbed on, his hands and feet automatically starting the engine and putting the demon bike into gear.

Weak and nauseous, Eddie instructed the bike to take him to his grave.

★   ★   ★

In the near darkness of the boarded-up clubhouse, Hank Bowman pressed himself against the bar, his arms wrapped around his knees, his body trembling. The whole damn place was going crazy around him. He found himself wishing he'd left with the others instead of staying behind to see if he could draw out whoever was fucking with them. Now he regretted that decision, as obviously more than one or two people were involved.

But who? Hell Creek had no rival gangs. *It couldn't be the cops. Not their style. The Cubans from Miami? That wouldn't make sense. They had a good deal going, him transporting their shipments of pot when they came through the 'Glades in return for some cash and stash.*

A dull roar sounded outside, interrupting his thoughts.

A motorcycle? Son of a bitch! Was it his own gang pulling this shit on him? If so, they were gonna pay.

Fright gave way to an embarrassment that quickly turned into fury. Hank bolted from his hiding spot and ran for the door, expecting to see the other Hell Riders outside, laughing their asses off at his expense.

Instead, he found an empty parking lot.

Empty, and yet he could still hear the motorcycle.

The throbbing, growling, coughing noise could only be a Harley. A big one. In fact....

It sounded familiar.

Hank looked down the road toward the highway, which was a long, straight run several miles into Hell Creek. It appeared as deserted as the parking lot. Same thing in the other direction, the black top arrow-straight as it headed deeper into the swamps.

The cycle's rumble faded away, almost as if....

Hank looked straight up. *Impossible. It had to be thunder. There'd been a lot of that lately. From the weather. It made sense. Damn heat lightning probably made the lights go haywire, too. Overloaded the circuits or something.*

That has to be it. Either that, or the fuckin' heat's driving me crazy.

Cursing at his unwarranted fear and the hellish weather they'd been having, Hank entered the clubhouse, figuring to drink a couple more beers before they got warm.

Then he stopped short.

Across the room, over the big, stained couch, someone had burned letters on the wall.

Eddie was h

Hank's body shook as sudden shivers ran through it. *Eddie?* Just saying the name brought back memories of the night before.

"Eddie's coming."

The last words Jethro had spoken before getting knocked unconscious.

It also triggered another memory.

Eddie's bike. Diablo. *That* was the motorcycle he'd heard outside. Eddie Ryder had been a genius with engines, and he'd customized his bike so that nothing else sounded like it.

Eddie was h

Eddie was *here*? Was that the message?

No. It was goddamn impossible. They'd burned Eddie Ryder to a fucking crisp. His body was already buried.

Another idea came to him, one almost as frightening as someone coming back from the dead.

Somebody knows what we did. And they're trying to spook me.

And it was working. How had they gotten in and out without him seeing? Not through the front door, that was for sure. And the back door was locked.

It didn't matter. Whoever it was, they were as good as dead when he found them. 'Cause if someone knew, then it was just a matter of time before they tried to use that information against him. And he couldn't have that.

"You're dead, motherfucker. Just like Eddie Ryder."

Tough words.

But not tough enough to take away that nasty feeling in the pit of his stomach, or the acid burning the back of his throat.

Eddie's coming.

Eddie was here.

With a shiver, Hank headed for the door.

CHAPTER THIRTEEN

Hell Creek Pizza was one of the most popular gathering spots in town, right after Hickey Tavern and Hell Creek Lanes. And there was a good reason for this. Before 2007, the residents of Hell Creek had to make do with frozen pizzas from the Piggly Wiggly on River Road, or take the long trip to Homestead and visit one of the pizzerias there.

That all changed with the opening of Hell Creek Pizza, which quickly built a devoted following, especially on Friday, Saturday, and Sunday nights, when reservations were a necessity. So Carson was glad Kellie had gotten there early and grabbed one of the few available booths.

"Sorry I'm late," he said, sliding in across from her. "My mom decided she had to look at my homework before I could leave."

"You say it like it's a bad thing." Kellie handed him a menu.

"Well, yeah, it is. I've had straight A's all my life. Now all of a sudden she has to check my homework?"

Kellie shook her head. "You know, for someone who's so smart you can be kinda dumb."

"What?" Carson didn't know how to react. Was she insulting him or praising him?

"Think about it. Your brother just died. All she has left is you. Checking your homework is just an excuse to spend time with you. To talk to you."

A tingling heat crept up Carson's neck and into his face. He imagined himself turning as red as the vinyl seats in the booth. How could he have been so stupid?

"Oh, man. Now I feel like an idiot for getting mad at her."

Kellie didn't let him off the hook. "You should."

"Thanks a lot." He stared blindly at his menu, fighting back tears. He was doing a good enough job of hating himself. He didn't need her help.

Then she touched him.

Carson looked up in surprise. The last thing he'd expected at that moment was to feel her hand closing over his. Suddenly, he was looking down a tunnel, a dark tube where everything was gone except the perfect circle containing her face, which was so serious and beautiful he wanted to keep the image in his mind forever, a mental screensaver for his brain.

"Hey, it'll be okay. I acted the same way when my brother died. It's hard not to. Between being a teenager and losing your brother, you start to think about how crappy your life is and you get all depressed and angry. You forget that other people are hurt and sad, too. But you can make it up to her. Spend some time with her each day. She'll appreciate that."

"You think that will work? She was awful upset."

Kellie smiled and leaned forward. "You're too cute to stay mad at. In fact—"

Whatever she'd been about to say was ruined by a machine-gun-loud eruption of noise from the parking lot. A quick look out the window told Carson all he needed to know.

"It's them," he told Kellie, as if anyone in town couldn't recognize the sound. "The whole freakin' gang." He wasn't sure what pissed him off more, the sight of his brother's murderers or the fact that they'd interrupted what Carson was pretty sure had been about to be his first real kiss.

"We can go somewhere else."

He thought about it. He knew Kellie wouldn't hold it against him. A couple of families were already standing up to leave and several others signaling for their checks while casting nervous looks toward the door.

They killed Eddie. The more he thought about it, the angrier he got. Why should he have to leave? They were the ones who didn't belong. Besides, they weren't going to bother him, especially not in a public place. And if they did....

That wouldn't be so bad. They'd get arrested and it might make Kellie like me even more. That would be worth a few bumps and bruises.

Then he thought about Jethro, half-dead in the hospital. He'd gotten a lot worse than bumps and bruises. And he was part of their gang. What would they do to the brother of the guy they just murdered?

So my options are stay safe and look like a pussy, or stick around and maybe get my ass kicked, but impress the girl.

The choice was obvious.

"No, we'll stay. If they start trouble, you can call your dad."

Kellie's expression said she didn't think he'd made the best decision, but she didn't object. Instead, she opened her menu and pretended Hank and the other riders, along with several girls, weren't entering the building in a cloud of gasoline fumes and pot smoke.

"Wanna split a pizza?"

"Sure," Carson said, keeping an eye on the gang members stomping their way between the tables toward the private room in the back. Mr. Zefron, the owner, normally kept it reserved for large parties, but Carson imagined he'd be more than happy to let the bikers have it. Especially since it would keep them out of sight, if not out of sound, from the rest of the customers.

Kellie asked him another question, but he didn't hear her because he suddenly found himself staring at Duck Miller, who stared right back at him.

He recognizes me! Fear and hatred battled in Carson's guts, making him feel close to puking. Duck stopped, and for one terrifying moment Carson thought the biker might change direction and head toward their booth.

Instead, Duck gave him the finger and then followed the rest of the gang into the back room, pausing just long enough to steal a basket of garlic bread off a nearby table.

The couple at the table wisely said nothing.

"Carson, are you listening?"

"Huh?" His heart thumping madly, Carson turned back to Kellie, who gave him a strange look.

"Are you okay?"

"What? Oh, yeah. Fine. Pizza. Splitting. I'm there."

"I asked what kind you want."

"Um, anything except mushrooms or olives." He wished she'd stop staring; he imagined she could see right through him, see that he'd been frightened half to death.

With a small sigh, Kellie closed her menu. "I like pepperoni or sausage."

"We'll get half and half," Carson said, signaling for the waitress. A pizza with toppings, sodas, and maybe dessert would practically empty his wallet, but he remembered something Eddie had told him one time.

"Chicks cost money. Dating costs money. Get used to it, little bro, 'cause it only gets worse the older you get."

Looking at Kellie as she brushed a lock of hair from her face and gazed out at the setting sun, he felt pretty sure it was worth it.

★　★　★

Eddie fought down a surge of anger when he saw Duck Miller flip Carson the bird. *Who the fuck does that asshole think he is, doing that to my brother?*

The temptation to zap the hell out of Miller was so great Eddie's entire body practically vibrated with unseen energy. But he reined it in, common sense telling him that the restaurant wasn't the best place for lightning bolts and thunder.

Besides, he had a much better plan, one that didn't include exploding windows and deadly flying glass in a crowded place.

After scaring the shit out of Hank at the clubhouse, he'd taken some time at his grave to recover his strength. He still didn't feel a hundred percent, but the idea he'd come up with had him so psyched up he didn't want to wait. It was all he could do to contain himself while Hank and the others grabbed chairs and loudly ordered ten pitchers of beer. Several of the guys had girls with them, their 'cycle sluts', as they called them in private, local girls who got off on being with the baddest boys in town.

Hank had one arm around Sandy Powell, who wore one of her usual dignified outfits: ragged cut-off denim shorts so tight she had major camel toe and an equally tight t-shirt sporting the slogan 'Zero to Naked in Ten Beers'. Eddie felt a sharp pang when he saw it. He'd bought it for her at a county fair, the same night he'd banged her for the first time.

Now she was banging Hank.

Stole my life, stole my girl. I am so gonna fuck you over, Skank-man.

And the time to start was right then.

He'd already chosen his target for the night. Butch Franks, a lowlife even among lowlifes. With his outdated mullet haircut, a bushy mustache that always seemed crusted with old food, and an assortment of bad tattoos covering his arms, neck, and chest (including his favorite, a naked woman on his belly with her legs spread so that his fuzz-filled navel served as an outrageously oversized vagina), he was the ultimate definition of trailer trash. And proud of it.

Waiting until the bikers were drunk wasn't easy. All of them could hold their booze – including the girls – and Eddie knew it would take several pitchers each before they even got buzzed.

Then he remembered how he'd experienced everything through Jethro while possessing him.

Why should Butchie have all the fun?

This time Eddie was prepared for the transformation when he placed his hand on Butch's shoulder. The sudden burst of white light followed by pure darkness, like a camera flash going off in a lightless cave.

And then that amazing, wonder-fucking-ful feeling of being....

Alive!

He'd entered Butch in the middle of eating a chicken wing. Caught mid-swallow, Eddie found himself choking on fiery hot sauce. *Christ, I never realized how hot he liked his food!* Ignoring the laughter of the others, he grabbed his beer and chugged half of it down, relishing the explosion of bitter flavor across his tongue while the cold liquid diluted the lava heat of the wing sauce.

Able to breathe again, Eddie leaned back and forced Butch's face into a sheepish smile. "That one was hotter than a donkey's ass." It was something he'd heard Butch say before. Butch's one redeeming quality had always been his seemingly endless storehouse of good-old-boy quotes, most of them obscene. This one made the whole table howl with laughter.

The waitress came over, a cute girl Eddie remembered from high school. Rhonda something. It came to him that as Butch, he could get away with all sorts of shit he'd have never tried while alive. Things the other guys never worried about, because their families were either just as rude and obnoxious as they were, or because they simply didn't care what people thought.

So when Rhonda approached him to take his order, he took the opportunity to give her nice, tight ass a squeeze.

With a surprised squeal, Rhonda raised her hand to slap him.

"I wouldn't do that," he said, showing her his fist. His response surprised him as much as her. He'd never hit a girl in his life, but his hostage body had responded almost instantly, like an instinctive reaction coded into his genes. "Jes' get our food and be quick about it." Eddie forced the fist down to the table, two thoughts foremost in his head.

Gotta keep better control. Can't have pieces of Butch sneaking out like that.

And....

What the hell kind of home life did Butch have?

He wasn't sure he wanted to know.

Eddie was half-afraid Rhonda would bring the manager back, but when she returned it was just to place more beer on the table.

"I'm sorry." The words were whispered in his ear as she passed by him. At the same time, she dragged one hand slowly across his shoulder.

Jesus. She wasn't just apologizing to him, she was coming on to him. He didn't know what made him feel sicker, that everyone was so scared of the Hell Riders, or that so many supposedly nice girls got turned on by being frightened. He'd never thought about those kinds of things when he'd been part of the gang.

Fear does some fucked-up shit to people, but that doesn't make it right.

Hank Bowman stood up. "Time to water the garden," he said, giving Sandy's shoulder a squeeze. "Don't miss me too much, baby."

Sandy laughed and smacked him on the ass. Eddie found his attention focusing on her to the exclusion of everything else. He hadn't realized how much he'd missed touching her, being touched by her. Since leaving the Hell Riders, he hadn't been with anyone else. He'd thrown himself into his work and family to forget the pain of her publicly cursing him out and dumping him right on the courthouse steps following Ned's trial.

The next day she'd taken up with Hank.

Lousy bitch. I oughtta take care of both of them right now, like they did to me.

He pictured Hank and Sandy lying in the morgue, their bodies charred and unrecognizable. The image made him pause.

What the hell is wrong with me? Getting pissed off was nothing new, not with his temper, which had always been as much a part of him as his eye color or his love of heavy metal and southern rock. But he'd always managed to keep in mostly under control. Now it seemed like the rage inside him had grown from a simmering pool of lava to a full-blown volcano, ready to erupt at the slightest provocation – and sometimes without any warning at all.

Even weirder, despite his anger, he still wanted her. Was, in fact, growing hard at the thought of it.

Why not? It would sure piss Hank off, and be more fun than just killing them.

He commanded Butch's body to stand up and walk around the table. No one paid any attention to him, not even when he sat down in Hank's empty seat.

But they all took notice when he grabbed Sandy, pulled her close, and planted a huge kiss on her mouth. The table went silent, except for one of the other girls, who whispered, "Oh, my God!"

Sandy resisted the kiss at first, but after a moment, her tongue snaked into his mouth and she stopped struggling. His hand crept up her shirt and cupped one braless tit, the nipple hard and pointed between his fingers. Her fingers slid down to his crotch, started squeezing his cock through his jeans. She moaned into his mouth, reminding him of all the times they'd done it at the garage or in the back of the Hell Creek Movie Theater, which her daddy happened to own. He knew just by the way her hips wiggled that she was already getting wet.

Goddamn. She's getting off on this. Right in front of Hank's buddies. She'd probably fuck me right here.

How many times did she cheat on me?

That brought his resentment back in full force, a thunderhead of fury that rolled in like a hurricane. By then he had both hands up her shirt, kneading her breasts like fresh dough.

Fuck you, you little whore.

He grabbed both nipples and twisted as hard as he could.

Her hand clamped down on his cock and he came as she screamed.

"What the fuck?"

Eddie turned at the sound of Hank's voice. His rival stood in the doorway, eyes wide and mouth hanging open. Something hit Eddie's face with a stinging blow; it took him a moment to realize Sandy had slapped him. She jumped away, tugging down her shirt, tears of pain flowing down her face. Tears she immediately put to good use.

"Hank! He fuckin' attacked me!"

Eddie nodded. "Couldn't help it," he said, savoring the look on Hank's face. "I been wantin' to get my hands on them titties for a long time. Little bitch liked it, too."

Hank's face turned bright red. "You motherfucker. I'll fuckin' kill you." He grabbed a steak knife off the table and advanced on Butch/Eddie.

Eddie stood up and spread his arms, laughing. "You already killed me once, dick wad. See if you can do better this time."

Hank stopped at Eddie's words and all the color drained from his face. "What did you say?"

Drawn by the noise, other diners gathered by the doorway to watch the fight. Someone yelled for the manager, and another voice called out to get the police. Eddie glanced over at the crowd and realized he needed to finish things in a hurry. He wanted someone hurt before the cops came.

Someone like…*Sandy. She deserves more than a twisted nipple. Plus, it'll piss Hank off even further.*

Two quick steps brought him within grabbing distance. He took hold of Sandy's arm and yanked her forward, then quickly put her in a headlock. She struggled and kicked at his legs, leaving painful bruises that just fueled him further. The pain was good! Feeling anything was better than being a ghost.

With his free hand, he unzipped his pants, pulled out a cock way larger than a dumb shit like Butch deserved, and wagged it at Hank. "See this? Your little bitch had her hands on it right under the table. Made me cum like a bastard. I almost forgot how good she was."

Duck Miller made a move toward them and Eddie yanked harder

on Sandy's neck, making her gasp. "I'll snap her fuckin' neck like a chicken," he said. "Stay right there."

"Who the fuck are you?" Hank asked.

"Your worst fuckin' nightmare." Eddie was about to add, 'I'm the guy you fuckin' burned to death,' but a commotion behind Hank stopped him.

"Let her go." It was Dave Martin, the manager. In his hands was a gleaming double-barreled shotgun.

Eddie laughed. *This keeps getting better!*

Dave raised the gun. "I said, let her go, Butch."

That's when things went very wrong for Eddie.

For the second time in less than an hour, Butch's body betrayed him. His muscles clenched and his arm tightened more than he'd planned.

The *crack!* of Sandy's neck was no louder than someone snapping their fingers, yet somehow it drowned out all the other sounds in the room.

What did I do? I didn't mean to— His grip loosened and she hit the floor like a sack of laundry, her head flopping side to side. Before Eddie could raise his eyes from her, a tremendous explosion filled the air and what felt like a speeding car hit him in the chest and slammed him into the wall. His legs collapsed under him and he tumbled over.

Jesus Christ! He motherfucking shot me!

Eddie stared at the gaping hole where his stomach had been. The pain was so intense he couldn't move, couldn't even think.

Visions of lying across Diablo came back to him and he was dying in the fire all over again. The room slid sideways and he found himself surrounded by distorted faces that seemed too high up in the air, a forest of people-trees towering over him. Some of the trees parted and he caught a glimpse of a face he recognized.

Carson! Jesus, not again. He reached out to his brother, who seemed a mile away and fading fast. *Goodbye. This time it's for—*

The world swiveled around him again and he stumbled, disoriented by the return of physical sensation. A warm hand grabbed his arm and steadied him.

What the—?

He was standing in a crowd of people. Across the room lay Butch

Franks, his blood and intestines all over the floor. The wall above Butch resembled a piece of modern art, a melting tulip painted in crimson. Next to him lay Sandy Powell, her head resting completely parallel to her shoulders. The stink of gunpowder mixed sickeningly with the odors of greasy baked cheese, hot sauce, beer, and fresh shit.

Eddie's stomach did a slow flip and he fought the urge to puke.

Where...who did I—

"Carson, c'mon, let's get out of here. I don't want to see this." The hand on his arm tugged at him.

Carson? Eddie turned and saw Kellie Jones staring at him.

Holy shit, I never realized how beautiful she was.

On the heels of that thought came another.

Jesus, I've possessed my own brother.

Eddie took a step and almost fell again. The differences between Carson's sixteen-year-old body and the adult bodies he'd used since his death – which had been much like his own in how they worked – were astounding. Energy simmered in every muscle, aching for release. He felt anxious and excited and horny and confused all at once. When Kellie pulled his arm, her touch sent shivers through him that ended in his groin, which started to sprout an erection.

"Are you okay?" Her voice was a wonderful song that only he could hear.

Christ on a cross. He's head over fuckin' heels for her. And somehow I'm feeling it.

"No." It wasn't a lie. Between struggling with Carson's body and dealing with the after-effects of dying again, Eddie knew he needed someplace to just sit down and get some goddamn air or he'd pass out. He'd thought that when he possessed people, he had total command. But now he wasn't so sure. Did a part of them remain, a part that could take back some control if he wasn't careful? Maybe Butch's body had just done what came naturally to it.

An even darker thought rose up.

What if it's not them? What if it's me?

The voices of the people in the room blended into one giant roar, like an audience at a concert, and the bodies became colored blurs whose faces he couldn't distinguish.

"Let's go outside. The fresh air will help." Kellie steered him away from the crowd.

They were halfway to the door when everything went black.

CHAPTER FOURTEEN

"Jesus fucking Christ." Police Chief Johnny Ray Jones stared at Butch's corpse while Doc Holmes signaled to the EMTs that it was okay to put the remains into a body bag. The ambulance with Sandra Powell's body had already departed.

"No problem determining cause of death for this one," Holmes said.

"The question isn't how he died, but why." Jones looked at the notes he'd jotted down in his pad, hoping there'd be something new there to explain the massacre.

Holmes stripped off his bloody latex gloves and tucked them into a biohazard bag while one of the EMTs, Roscoe Jackson, who also served as Holmes's assistant when needed, began the unenviable task of scooping pieces of organs and flesh into evidence bags.

"I figured that was pretty straightforward, too. Butchie finally lost his last marble, attacked the Powell girl, and got himself a stomach full of buckshot for his trouble."

"See, that's what doesn't make sense." Jones pointed his pencil toward the outer room, where Officers Moselby and Dennis were questioning Hank Bowman and his cronies. "Franks was a lowlife. Everyone knows that. And probably borderline crazy."

"Borderline?" Holmes snorted. "That boy was nuttier than elephant shit at a circus."

"Whatever. Why now? What triggered it? What did he have against her? Or Hank, for that matter? Even attacking her is goddamned strange. Witnesses say she was all over him before he...."

"Killed her."

"Yeah." It was still hard to believe. Despite Sandy's habit of dating bikers and other creeps, the Powells were a respected family in Hell Creek, not the kind of people who got murdered in the middle of the dinner hour at the Pizza House. And there'd be a shit-storm coming down from on high because of that, too.

Of course, I never expected anyone to get murdered in this town. And now I've got three in two weeks.

Not for the first time since Eddie Ryder's death, he found himself wondering what the hell had happened to his normally quiet town. It was like they'd been cursed or something.

"I know what you're thinking, Johnny Ray." The Chief turned and found Holmes staring at him, his left eye squeezed almost closed, a sign the doctor was dead serious about something. "Weird shit going on in town these days. And you're wondering if it's all related somehow."

"And you're going to tell me to stop being so foolish, right?" Just saying it made Jones feel a little better. After all, what could murdered teenagers, random power surges, and vandalism possibly have to do with each other?

Holmes shook his head. "Just the opposite. Like I said, weird shit is going on these days. Odds are it's all related. You just need to figure out how. But I'll tell you one thing."

A cold feeling snaked its way up Jones's back. "What?"

"You better find out fast. I got a hunch things are gonna go from bad to worse real soon."

★   ★   ★

From the corner of his eye, Hank Bowman watched the EMTs wheel Butch's body out the back door. He felt cold and empty, like a refrigerator with no food inside. The fact that Butch and Sandy were dead wasn't affecting him nearly as much as the circumstances of their deaths. Hell, he'd only let them hang around 'cause they entertained him. One with his jokes and the other with her mouth and pussy. Neither of them meant much to him.

But before they'd died....

That was the fucked-up part. The part that had him shaking so bad Doc Holmes had asked him if he wanted something to calm him down. Ordinarily he'd have jumped at the chance for a free high, but this time he'd said no.

Something told him he should stay straight.

He'd answered all the cops' questions honestly – another thing he normally wouldn't have done, although for once he didn't have to worry about getting in trouble for telling the truth – but the whole time they talked to him he'd really been thinking about what had happened, replaying it in his mind.

Walking into the room and seeing Sandy makin' out with Butch and rubbing his crotch like a fuckin' two-bit whore. Yeah, she'd said Butch attacked her, but Hank knew better. He'd seen what was going on before Butch gave her that titty squeeze.

That was fucked up enough, but what'd you expect from a slut? And then....

"You already killed me once, dick wad. See if you can do better this time."

You already killed me once. It didn't make sense.

Unless....

Eddie's coming.

Eddie was here.

It was impossible. But who else had they killed, had *he* killed?

How, though? People don't come back from the dead. There's no such things as ghosts, no matter what they say in the movies.

"That's all for now." Ted Moselby – who was big and tough enough that no matter how they felt, neither Hank nor the other Hell Riders had ever dared utter the word nigger in his presence, let alone to his face – closed his notebook. "Get yourself home, Hank. You look like you've seen a ghost."

Hank jerked in surprise at the words, but retained enough composure to scowl. "Ain't no such things as ghosts."

If only I believed it.

PART TWO
THE ROAD TO MADNESS

Empty roads leading to empty souls
The Dark underground swallowing whole
Lives once so fertile now all but lost
No hope for life
No hope for today
This ghost town stands
Overwhelmed by decay

'Ghost Town,' by Charred Walls of the Damned

★   ★   ★

Highway burns beneath chromed heat
Devil riding in the seat
Charred asphalt lies for miles behind
Evidence of Satan's ride
Hell is coming down the road
Bring death for eons foretold
Hell Rider!
Coming for you.

'Hellrider,' by Demon Dogs

CHAPTER FIFTEEN

Eddie opened his eyes to a world of pure white. For one brief instant he thought maybe he'd finally left all the sorrow and pain behind, gone on to someplace better. Then his other senses kicked in as well.

Sound. The droning of a distant airplane engine. A barking dog. The squeak of bed springs.

Touch. The cool softness of cotton sheets on bare skin. The comforting – yet somehow wrong – squoosh of a pillow beneath his head.

Smell. A mélange of good and bad. Faint hints of bacon and meatloaf and grease and fresh corn on the cob, odors that told him immediately he was in his own house. But there were other scents as well, identifiable but not familiar. Sweat. A man-odor, but not his own. Dirty socks, but not his feet.

He sat up and his body almost tumbled off the bed when it moved faster than he expected.

Across the room, a woman in a bright yellow bikini stared at him from a movie poster advertising *American Pie 10: Back to the Beach.*

Recognition finally kicked in. *I'm in Carson's room.* He looked down, saw a skinny, hairless, summer-tanned chest. *And I'm still inside him.*

Memories of the previous night crawled out of the darkness and into the light of consciousness. Getting dizzy and passing out at the Pizza House. Waking up on the floor, with Kellie Jones and someone else looking down at him. Telling her he was all right, he just wanted to go home and lie down, he'd call her tomorrow. Sneaking in through the window so he wouldn't have to talk to his mother.

He'd never expected to remain in his brother's body.

Sandy.

Her face appeared in his thoughts, eyes bulging, neck lolling to the side.

I killed her. Oh, goddamn, I killed her. Guilt stabbed at his chest. *I didn't intend...I just wanted to hurt her a little, piss Hank off in the process. Payback for what they did to me.*

Now she's dead, and it's my fault.

Or was it?

There'd been that sense of losing control in Butch's body. First with the waitress and then when he'd been holding Sandy. It just happened. Like it was something Jethro had wanted to do. Or would do in that situation.

Butch's arm tightening on Sandy's neck. The snap of the bones.

He'd known just how to do it, how much pressure to use. Did that mean Butch had killed someone before? The more he thought about it, the more Eddie believed it possible. Butch's family lived outside of town, generations of swampers who still jacked deer for food and made their own moonshine, wicked strong shit that could melt the paint off a car. Even the youngest among them knew how to hunt and trap. Who knew what kind of trouble they got into out there?

That has to be it. I'm no murderer. The Hell Riders don't count. They have it coming.

Sandy, I'm sorry. And he meant it. At the same time, it worried him that he didn't feel worse. Guilty, yes, but no real sense of loss. No sorrow that Sandy Powell was gone forever.

She deserved it.

Which wasn't true. She'd done him wrong, but she hadn't been part of his murder.

How do you know? Maybe she was there.

Eddie frowned. Even if she hadn't been at the garage when it happened, she'd still played a part in his death just by letting Hank do it. After all, she had to have known what Hank was up to. She was sleeping with him, for fuck's sake. She could've told someone. Gone to the police.

Instead of him getting roasted like a Thanksgiving turkey.

She's just as responsible as Hank and the other assholes.

So fuck her. She did deserve it.

Feeling better, his remorse already a distant memory, Eddie sat up. Then groaned as a violent ache ran through his stomach, accompanied by a loud gurgling sound. *God, I'm starving!* He'd forgotten what it was like to feel hungry, how crazy good the craving for food could be. His mouth and tongue grew wet at the thought of eating and he bounded out of bed, still dressed in his pants from the night before.

Carson won't mind me using his body a little more, just long enough to enjoy a real meal again.

Or would he? How did he know what Carson was feeling, what any of them felt when he hijacked their bodies? Was it painful? Did they just go to sleep? Could they see and hear everything, like an unwilling captive in front of a TV screen? Carson might be cursing him right now for what he'd done, was still doing.

How much of a person remains while I'm inside them?

Eddie paused before opening the bedroom door. The last thing he wanted to do was hurt his brother, or put him in danger of any kind. And, until he vacated the body and then waited to see what happened after, something he hadn't done with Jethro or Butch, he really had no idea of what the effects of his forced entry were.

I should get out right now.

"Carson? Are you up?"

Mom. He glanced at the bedside clock. Almost nine. Time for her breakfast and medicine. A different kind of pain blossomed in his chest, a desire to see his mother again. Talk to her. Another thing the Hell Riders had stolen from him.

Sorry, little bro. I know it's selfish, but I need to do this. Don't hate me.

"Be right there, Mom."

★ ★ ★

Eddie put the last dish back in the cabinet, biting his lip to keep from crying. Sound carried too well in the trailer and he didn't want his mother to hear.

Being in his mother's presence again had been harder than he expected. He'd almost broken down when he entered her room. Everything had hit him at once, overwhelming him. The sour smells of dirty sheets, unwashed hair, and stale food, combined with the faint, lingering whispers of her perfume and body wash. And on top of that something worse, something indefinable, an odor that was kind of like the sick breath people got when they had a cold or flu, but darker, as if he could smell the very illness that was slowly robbing her of her life.

Her voice had been different, too. A little weaker, a little raspier. But clearer at the same time. He'd understood then that in his ghost or spirit state, the sounds of the real world were slightly muffled. Hearing his mother through Carson's young ears – free from the damage years of exposure to motorcycle engines and heavy metal music had done to his own – made him want to just sit by her side and listen to her talk for hours.

But he couldn't. It would be too out of character. It was one thing to sit and chat or watch TV on those rare occasions when she joined them in the living room, and they could all pretend everything was fine. The bedroom was different. Neither of Sally Ryder's boys had ever been able to spend too much time in their mother's impending death room. They did their duties, made some small talk, and after ten or fifteen minutes took advantage of any opening – her being tired, school work, chores – to make a graceful exit.

This time, though, Eddie'd made sure to stay longer, savoring each word, each touch of her hand, the feel of her soft sheets under his palms. He looked around the room, burning every detail into his memory. It might be the last time he ever got to be with her, alive and in person. Hijacking Carson's body wasn't something he wanted to do again. It was one thing to take over his enemies. But not someone he cared about.

So he'd stayed in the room even after she finished her breakfast and he polished off the peanut butter sandwich he'd made for himself, holding her hand and telling her how nice a time he'd had with Kellie Jones. When she'd asked him about the murder – it was all over the news by that time – he'd brushed it off, saying he and Kellie had already left the restaurant by the time the trouble happened. A white lie, one he hoped Carson would never have to explain. Only when her eyes started to close and she'd said she needed a nap did he finally leave.

"Goodbye, Ma," he'd whispered, kissing her gently on the forehead. "Love you." Something he'd never had the chance to say the night he'd been killed.

And that was the moment when things got to be too much. All his feelings — guilt, anger, sorrow, loneliness — came storming in, riding a wave of teenage hormones like a champion surfer hitting the barrel of a lifetime. He'd hurried down the hall to the kitchen, eager to get as far away as possible before he lost control.

Then he'd sat down at the table and cried like a damn girl.

Now, with the dishes done and nothing holding him back, Eddie went to Carson's room and lay on the bed. Closing his eyes, he concentrated on Diablo.

This time the separation came gentle and easy. He slipped out of Carson's body as smoothly as taking off a jacket. In less than a second he stood next to Diablo again, a Diablo he could see and feel as strongly as if it were real. Only this Diablo had eyes that turned and looked at him, eager to be up and away. He imagined himself pushing the bike up the driveway, like the old days, so he wouldn't wake his mother. Except now the bike weighed next to nothing, and he felt more energized than ever before.

When he finally climbed on and kicked Diablo to life, the bike roared like a true beast from hell, flames spouting from nose and tail pipes, reddish-yellow eyes fixed on the open road ahead.

Snug in his seat, he took off toward the bright morning sun, Diablo's stereo blasting heavy metal that suited his dark mood perfectly.

Suffering on poisoned ground
Suffering in this ghost town
Dark clouds from above, bring darkness and doom
Effortlessly shattering, what lies in its course
A deafening roar, it feels no remorse

★　　★　　★

Up and down Cypress Flats Road, the sudden boom of thunder rattled windows and sent knick-knacks and potted plants tumbling to floors.

In her bed, Sally Ryder woke with a start and sat up so quickly she pulled the oxygen cannula from her nose. She'd been dreaming that both of her boys were back with her, each of them holding one of her hands.

And then the sound of Eddie's motorcycle had shattered her dreams, like it had on so many other occasions when he'd thought he'd been far away enough that they wouldn't hear it.

It took several moments for her heartbeat to calm down, desperate moments during which she struggled and wheezed for air until she had her oxygen line in place again.

When she finally lay back on her pillows, tears dampened both her cheeks and she continued crying long after she fell asleep again.

CHAPTER SIXTEEN

Carson Ryder woke to the sound of thunder. He'd been dreaming of Eddie. They'd eaten breakfast together and then Eddie'd taken off on Diablo, heavy metal music blasting in counterpart to the bike's roaring engine. As sleep gave way to awareness, the sound of the motorcycle blended perfectly into the heat thunder rumbling overhead.

A brief moment of disorientation greeted him when he opened his yes. Nothing in his room looked right, even though he recognized all of it. As if he was the one out of place rather than the objects surrounding him. He sat up and the world took a sickening spin. With a groan, he gripped the bed so he wouldn't topple over.

What the hell happened?

The last thing he remembered was being at Hell Creek Pizza. There'd been a commotion in the back room and people had screamed. Kellie'd tried to pull him away, and then there'd been a gunshot. After that....

Nothing.

Did I hit my head? He ran his fingers through his hair and across his face. Nothing hurt. His stomach churned and gurgled, and he fought the urge to throw up as another bout of bed spins hit him. His stomach felt stuffed and the vile aftertaste of peanut butter coated his mouth. That alone was enough to make him queasy. He hated peanut butter. It looked and smelled like something you'd find in a baby's diaper. It used to drive him crazy when Eddie would eat it for breakfast.

Like in my dream.

Along with his nausea, his head ached as well. *A hangover?* He'd never done more than taste a beer, certainly never been drunk, but he'd heard Eddie describe the after-effects often enough. But where – and why – would he and Kellie have been drinking?

Had he come down with a bad case of the flu? Possible, except since when did the flu make you lose your memory?

None of it made sense, just like waking up in the same clothes he'd worn the day before didn't make sense.

Kellie. I'll call her. Maybe she knows what happened.

Hoping he hadn't actually drunk alcohol and done something stupid, Carson fumbled through his pockets until he located his cell phone.

★   ★   ★

"God. I can't believe I don't remember any of that." Carson slumped on the couch, a glass of Mr. Pibb cradled between his hands. Kellie sat across from him in Eddie's old armchair. She'd sounded frantic when he'd called, said she'd been worried about him all night. When he'd told her he felt too sick to leave the house, she'd shown up ten minutes later, sweating and out of breath from riding her bicycle in the sweltering heat.

"Maybe you bumped your head when you fainted," she said, helping herself to one of the cookies he'd put out. Oreos and soda. Not fancy, but there'd been nothing else in the kitchen.

"My head does hurt, but now it's just a regular headache, like when you watch too much TV." He rubbed the back of his head. "No bumps or anything."

"You should see a doctor," Kellie insisted, as she'd been doing since she arrived.

"See a doctor for what?"

Carson looked up at the sound of his mother's voice. "Ma, you shouldn't be out of bed."

"Nonsense." His mother shuffled into the room, pulling her oxygen tank along on its rolling frame, and lowered herself onto the loveseat. Just the effort of walking down the hall had her wheezing, and it took several seconds before she could speak again.

"Why do you need to see a doctor?"

"I don't," Carson said, before Kellie could state the real reason. "I woke up feeling kind of crappy today and Kellie thinks it might be the flu or something. Probably just a bug."

"You don't feel well?" His mother gave him a funny look. "It must have hit fast. You were fine when you brought me breakfast this morning."

"I was? I did?" For the third time in a day that was barely past noon, Carson felt like he'd fallen through the looking glass into Wonderland.

"Yes. In fact, you were very talkative. You even watched some TV with me while we ate. You should have told me you were sick."

A phantom taste of peanut butter, oily and salty-sweet, passed through Carson's mouth. "Uh, Ma? What did I eat? Do you remember?"

Sally Ryder took a few breaths before answering. "Let me think. I believe it was toast. Toast and peanut butter."

A hole opened in Carson's stomach, dark and cold and filled with things he didn't want to think about. "Oh, yeah. Now I remember. Maybe the peanut butter was too heavy so early in the morning. That might be why my stomach hurts."

His mother gave a laugh that turned into a series of hacking, wheezing coughs. Carson bit his lip and waited, accustomed to her attacks but hating them nonetheless. Kellie feigned interest in her cookie.

When she recovered, Sally shook her head and pushed herself to her feet. "The way you eat, I can't imagine anything bothering your stomach. Do you want me to get you something for it?"

Carson shook his head. The last thing he wanted was his mother wasting what little energy she had on him. "No, I'm fine with the soda. You should get back in bed. I'll bring you your lunch in a few minutes. How does ham and cheese sound?"

"Okay." She gave him a kiss on the cheek and then smiled at Kellie. "Nice to see you again, Kellie. Tell Johnny Ray I said hello."

"I will, Mrs. Ryder. Feel, um, better."

After Sally Ryder left the room, Kellie stood up. "I better get going."

"No." Carson motioned for her to sit. "There's something I have to talk to you about. Just hang out while I fix her lunch, okay? I'll be back in a minute."

"Sure. It sounds like it's something important."

He nodded. Outside, thunder rumbled, raising goosebumps along his arms.

"Yeah. Like maybe life or death."

★   ★   ★

It had taken three sound barrier-breaking trips around town, urging Diablo faster each time, for Eddie to take the edge off the tremendous energy boiling inside him after exiting Carson's body. Each turn, each rev of Diablo's engine, sent wicked thunder rolling across the flat swamplands of the Everglades and rattled the windows of Hell Creek's houses and buildings. Eddie soared too high, high in the sky, *high as a fucking plane, man,* to see the expressions of the people down below, but he laughed at the commotion he imagined his actions were causing. Children cowering in their rooms. Pedestrians turning their faces upward. Dogs howling in fright. Never in his life had he felt such power, and he was motherfucking *loving* it. And it seemed like it happened each time he possessed someone. After Jethro and Butch, he'd definitely felt stronger.

After Carson, he felt like a fucking god!

You can't keep it up. What about Carson?

That calmed him a bit, dampened the crazy forces racing through his being. He'd been having so much fun he'd forgotten his promise to himself.

Gotta make sure the kid's okay.

He shot across town to the trailer park, and then, with Diablo's engine rumbling as softly as possible, lowered himself until he had a clear view into Carson's room. He caught the last few sentences of his brother's call to Kellie, enough to ease his conscience. No problems except some memory loss and feeling tired? He could live with that. Carson would be fine in a little while. Hell, Eddie'd had hangovers that were worse, both before and after his death.

It also got Eddie to wondering. Was that the same effect he'd had on Jethro and Butch? Only one way to find out. He told Diablo to take him to the hospital. Maybe he could learn something from looking in on his old club brother.

As luck would have it, Jethro was awake and talking to another

Hell Rider, Harley Atkins, when Eddie arrived. After passing through the glass, Eddie took a seat on the window ledge to listen to their conversation.

"—probably never remember, least that's what the doctors is sayin'." Jethro's face was still a swollen mess, and the bandages wrapping his head made him look like someone had abandoned a mummy before finishing the job. When he spoke, several gaps showed where teeth had been knocked out. Together with his split, puffy lips, his new dental situation made his words sound like someone trying to talk through a mouthful of food.

"That sucks, dude," Harley said. With his long beard and mustache, he looked like one of the characters from *Duck Dynasty* or *Moonshiners*. "'Cause everybody wants to know what the fuck you were thinkin', goin' after Hank like that."

"I don't fuckin' know!" It came out 'Uh doan fthuckin' go,' but Harley understood it all the same.

"He's still mighty pissed. We ain't even supposed to be visitin' you until Hank decides if you can stay in the club. I'm only here 'cause Hank sent me to ask you some questions."

Jethro moaned and shook his head. "He's gotta believe me. I don't know why I freaked out. Maybe there was somethin' in the weed."

"Somethin' that didn't bother none of us?" Half-hidden by the curls of straw-blond hair falling over his forehead, Harley's raised eyebrows indicated his disbelief.

"Yeah? What about las' night?"

Harley scowled. "How'd you hear about that?"

"Bad news travel fasht, man. Heard a couple nurses talking 'bout it. Was Butch smokin'?"

"Not with me." The uncertainty in Harley's voice made Eddie want to laugh out loud. He held it in, afraid he might set the lights flickering. *Stupid bastards, thinking somebody messed with their weed. Wait 'til they found out the truth.*

"Don't mean he wasn't." Jethro lay back and closed his eyes. Harley just sat there, a look of confused concentration on his bearded face.

Reminds me of when the teachers used to call on the kid in the back of the class, the one who was always eating paste or staring at the big ol' booger he'd just dug out of his nose. If he says 'Duh' right now I won't be able to control myself.

Harley stayed silent, though. After a couple of minutes of intense but ultimately fruitless thinking, he stood up. "Guess I'll be headin' out. Don't know when I'll be back. Depends on what Hanks says."

"Wait." Jethro's eyes remained closed, and his final words were so faint Eddie barely heard them. "You listen good. Bad shit goin' on around here. Somethin' not right."

Harley chewed his lower lip before replying. "Yeah. Things are fucked up for sure." He waited for Jethro to say more, until the sound of heavy breathing told him there was no point in sticking around.

After Harley left, Eddie got bored watching Jethro sleep and floated outside the window while he considered his next moves. More than ever, he wanted every last Hell Rider dead. It had to be soon, too, because he had no way of telling how long he'd be around to do the job. It wasn't like being a ghost came with an owner's manual.

"But I think I got enough time to scare the shit out of a few of them first," he said to Diablo, who growled in response.

"Besides, if it's true I take a little energy each time I'm inside someone, then I should keep getting stronger, right?"

I'm like a vampire, he thought, and the idea of it made him feel damn good. Better than he had in a long time, even before he died. Vampires were powerful motherfuckers. You didn't mess with vampires.

Not if you wanted to live.

CHAPTER SEVENTEEN

Carson returned to the living room to find it empty. For a heart-dropping, gut-wrenching moment he thought Kellie'd decided not to wait for him after all. Then he heard noises coming from his bedroom. Looking in, he found Kellie sitting at his desk, watching a YouTube video on the computer.

The intensity of his relief surprised him, and scared him a little, too. He'd had a crush on Kellie for a long time, a crush he'd had no problem admitting to himself, although no one else knew. Not that anyone would have been surprised; half the boys in their junior class had a crush on her. But now...now it seemed like his feelings had grown stronger, that spending time with her had been the equivalent of a springtime rain, allowing the seed of something to grow. Something more than just a crush.

Something like love.

But is it? Or is it just a reaction to her attention, something no girl had ever given him before, combined with the stress of everything going on?

Carson's heart wanted it to be the former, but his head knew it could be the latter. Love, lust, infatuation, gratitude, loneliness, acceptance, rejection – the emotional soup of adolescence was a dangerous and confusing mix, and usually he was glad that he tended more toward calm logic than wearing his emotions on his sleeve the way Eddie always had.

But he didn't want to live life like a robot, either.

"Just trust your instincts and go with the flow, dude. Don't overthink things." The words came to him as he sat down on the bed. It was something Eddie'd told him the previous year, when he'd been worried about a big test. Although his older brother had never been one for dispensing – or following – good advice, that particular bit of wisdom had made sense.

And it still does. You trust Kellie. She's stuck with you through all the craziness of the past couple of days. Either she'll stick with you through this, too, or she won't. But no matter what, you'll know where you stand with her.

"Thanks for waiting," he said, as she turned off the video.

"Sure. So what's so important? You looked really freaked out before."

"Yeah." Carson took a moment to gather his thoughts. How did you tell someone something so crazy you didn't even believe it yourself? Especially someone you'd only known a few days. It was hard to trust a close friend with your deepest secrets, let alone a stranger.

Kellie stared at him, waiting. Neither bored or impatient. Just... there for him.

Just tell her, already!

"Okay, but hear me out before you say anything. And don't laugh. It's gonna sound kinda wacked out. I mean, really out there."

"Go ahead. I won't laugh, I promise."

Carson looked down at his hands, which were twisting the material of his t-shirt. "Remember when my mom said I ate peanut butter and toast for breakfast?"

"Yeah?"

"Well, the thing is, I hate peanut butter. I mean, I really freakin' hate it. Always have. My mom probably forgot, 'cause she isn't... she...."

"Has other things to worry about," Kellie said, rescuing him from both bad thoughts and getting off topic.

"Yeah. And, like, I don't remember anything from this morning that she was talking about, but I must have done those things, must have made breakfast and then cleaned up. Except...when I went into the kitchen to make lunch, I noticed that the juice carton was open in the fridge, not folded closed. And there was a knife in the dishwasher that still had peanut butter on it."

Kellie shrugged her shoulders. "So? I don't get what's the big deal."

Carson took a deep breath. *Here it goes.* "Eddie is the one who used to love peanut butter and toast for breakfast. It always grossed me out when he ate it. And he'd always lick the knife and then put it in the dishwasher, but there'd be some leftover peanut butter on it that would get all hard, and me or Mom would always be telling him to clean it in the sink first. And he'd always stick the juice or the milk in the fridge and leave the top open, so he could just grab it and drink if he wanted to."

"I still don't...." Kellie stopped, frowned. "Wait a minute. Are you trying to say your brother...?"

"Is haunting me. Yeah. I know it sounds stupid. Crazy, right? But think about it. I've been hearing his motorcycle at night, and sometimes even in the day. And now I had this blackout where I did things only he would do."

"Carson, there's a perfectly good explanation for what's happened to you."

"Wait, I'm not finished. There's more. What about all the strange things happening in town lately? They've all involved people in Eddie's old gang, the same gang that...." He paused, couldn't say the words.

"Killed him. And that's probably why you're acting like this." Kellie scooted her chair over to him, took his hands in hers. "Don't you see? Those assholes killed your brother. You'd have to be made of stone not to be upset over it. And on top of that, now you're the only one looking after your mom. You're trying to be strong for her, but subconsciously you're all messed up. And then you saw someone get murdered. That's why you fainted or blacked out or whatever. It's the stress. It could happen to anyone. I'm surprised *I* didn't pass out when that gun went off."

"What about doing those things my brother used to do?" Now instead of staring at his own hands, Carson was staring at their hands joined together. A much safer thing to do than looking into her eyes. If he did that, he might cry.

"Your subconscious again. You're trying to fill Eddie's shoes so you're acting like he used to. You want to become him, 'cause he took care of you both and you need him around still."

He shook his head. "But—"

"No buts." Kellie squeezed his hands harder. "I know what you're going through. I went through it, too, when my mom died. I told you before. I used to hear her voice down the hall, smell her perfume. Sometimes I'd wake up at night and swear I'd seen her standing by the bed, and then she'd be gone."

"So you don't think I'm crazy?"

"Carson, look at me." She tugged at his hands, forcing him to acknowledge her words. He looked up, saw she was staring back at him, her eyes earnest and free of judgment.

"What?"

"I'd think you were crazy if you *didn't* feel this way."

Her eyes stayed locked on his, and he felt her gaze grow stronger. Her head moved closer, just a fraction of an inch, but he noticed it. And although he'd never kissed a girl in his life, he knew he was about to.

He moved his head forward.

Their lips met.

And all his worries melted away in the sweet, gentle softness of her mouth.

CHAPTER EIGHTEEN

After leaving the hospital, Eddie spent the better part of an hour randomly possessing people, strictly for practice. He didn't want a repeat of his unplanned occupation of Carson to happen, not with family or any of the Hell Riders.

Of course, he made sure to enjoy every minute of it.

In Publix, he used a skinny old man to knock over a pyramid of grapefruits into an aisle. While an assistant manager chewed out the confused man, Eddie swooped to the other side of the store and made the meat clerk tell a series of filthy jokes to three old ladies waiting to purchase cold cuts. Then he left the clerk and went across the street to Sal's Barber Shop, where he forced Sal to shave a giant bald spot on the back of Principal Robinson's head.

"That's for all the detentions you gave me," Eddie said with a laugh, as Robinson exited the shop, unaware of his new look.

Each time he entered a new body, his ability to control it improved, so that by the time he made Wilbur Dennis, one of Hell Creek's finest, back his car into a mailbox, he felt sure there'd be no more surprises like the one Butch gave him with Sandy.

Even better, he discovered that possessing people definitely recharged his supernatural batteries. Even a few minutes was enough to power him up, wash away any trace of fatigue.

With energy literally crackling around him, he rocketed up from the town's center in a burst of thunder and headed south, where he found Hank Bowman pulling out of the Hell Riders' clubhouse parking lot.

Perfect.

Entering Hank took no more effort than thinking about it. There was a second or two of disorientation while he got used to the body, shorter and heavier than his own had been, and the feel of Hank's Harley between his legs. The bike tilted dangerously to one side and then Eddie righted it. Much like Hank himself, the bike was heavy and squat, not streamlined like Diablo. But Eddie'd ridden plenty of different bikes in his pre-ghost days and it only took a few labored beats of Hank's heart to get comfortable.

Jesus, I never realized how out of shape he is. Even if I wasn't gonna kill him, the drugs and booze will do the job in a couple of years. That's if he doesn't crash his fat ass on the highway before then.

The bike wobbled and Eddie nearly crossed into the other lane trying to correct it, his reflexes – or rather, Hank's – a hair slow. Hank had definitely been partying hard. The tingling buzz of primo coke counter-balanced the mellow fog of a good joint. The bittersweet-smoky taste of Jack Daniels still coated his tongue and warmed his stomach.

I could just drive this bike into a tree, or off a bridge, and the police would chalk it up to a drunken accident.

It would be so simple.

Eddie frowned and shook his head.

Screw simple. When Hank's time comes, he's gonna make fucking headlines. Right now, I want him to suffer, like he made me suffer. And I know just where to start.

Humming Molly Hatchet's 'Flirtin' With Disaster' and cursing the lack of a radio on Hank's bike, Eddie headed toward Hell Creek.

Time to throw some real misery in Hank's life.

And have some fun at the same time.

★   ★   ★

As he'd expected, Eddie found Kristy Flood behind the bar at Sheehan's, an aging pub on the south end of town. When he entered, the afternoon crowd – three old men and a girl with too many tattoos who he vaguely remembered from some of the club's parties – turned and looked at him, and then at Kristy, whose eyes immediately narrowed when she saw Hank's face.

A part-time stripper and full-time bartender with a fondness for nose-candy, she'd been Hank's main girl before he'd hooked up with Sandy, and word around town was she'd been royally pissed when he dumped her.

Which made her the perfect weapon to use against him.

He'd always thought she was hot, as in, a hot mess. Not the kind of girl you'd bring home to meet the family, but definitely too good for Hank. Waist-length black hair, perfect rack, and ice-blue eyes that could freeze you from across a room. And a take-no-shit attitude. Back when he was alive, he'd have never considered going with her. Not only was she several years older than him, but she was Hank's, and therefore off limits to everyone else.

Things are different now, though. I could have her if I wanted.

Only he had something else in mind.

"You got some nerve showing up here" she said, the smell of cheap weed wafting around her. Her friend with the jailhouse tats snorted laughter. The old men wisely said nothing.

Eddie went to the end of the bar and motioned for her to join him. Despite his intentions, the sight of her in her tight black Lynyrd Skynyrd t-shirt was getting him horny and angry at the same time. The booze and drugs didn't help, dulling his senses and getting his thoughts and memories all mixed up in his head. Images of Hank and Sandy kept pushing their way in. Had she ever cheated on him? Back when he was alive, he'd have said no. But after seeing how fast she got into it with Butch, now he wasn't so sure. Knowing her, it would have been fast and dirty. She liked it like that. A BJ in the bathroom, a quick fuck behind a bar or at the clubhouse.

How many times did I end up with sloppy seconds without even knowing it?

The mere thought of it fueled his anger to new heights and he forced it back, afraid he might accidentally zap Kristy or burn down the bar. The rage fought him like a wild animal, stronger than ever before. Darker. *Is it me getting more powerful, or is it something inside Hank making me feel this way?* There'd always been a fury inside him, a twisting, living snake waiting to strike. But never like this. Now the cage was open, the beast free. And Eddie wasn't sure if he could control it.

Or if he even wanted to.

I could send the whole damn town to hell. And maybe I should. What'd anyone in this shit hole ever do for me?

No. Stick to the plan. This is about Hank.

Taking a deep breath, he forced a smile to Hank's face.

"I came to apologize. I was a fool, baby. I didn't know how good I had it with you."

"Fuck you. Take your sorries and shove 'em up your ass."

"Yeah!" shouted tattoo girl, and pumped her fist. Eddie shot her a look and she backed away, glaring at him, but didn't leave.

"I mean it. And to prove how much I love you, I got you something. Something special." He reached into his pocket and pulled out the black box containing the diamond ring he'd purchased earlier, maxing out Hank's credit card in the process. Flipping it open to expose the ring, he went down onto one knee.

"Kristy Flood, will you marry me?"

"What?" Kristy's eyes grew wide. "Are you serious?"

"Hell, yeah," Eddie said, fighting back his laughter. His voice shook from the effort, and he hoped it added conviction to his words. "I've always loved you. I want you to be my old lady forever. Nobody rides the back of my bike except you."

Kristy's mouth hung open but no words came out. Tattoo girl's eyes had gone wide and she'd pulled her phone out, was videoing everything.

Even better! By the time he left, the Hell Riders and all their followers — shit, the whole town! — would know Hank Bowman had gone—

"Yes!"

"Really?" Eddie had half-expected she'd either laugh at his proposal or tell him to get lost. Who would take back a loser like Hank? *She must be desperate.*

She grabbed the box and slipped the ring on her finger. The diamond was huge, gaudy, and poor quality, which Eddie figured matched Hank's tastes perfectly.

"Ohmygod! I love it! It's perfect!"

"You make me complete." Eddie stood and gave a loopy grin right into the other girl's phone. "My heart belongs to you."

She squealed again and wrapped her arms around him. Kissed him, her mouth tasting of pot, vodka, and unbrushed teeth, a perfect match to Hank's. Her tongue attacked his, twining and pushing like an animal trying to force its way into a cave. Eddie found himself responding, dimly aware of the old men clapping and tattoo girl narrating something into her phone. When Kristy finally broke the kiss and leaned back, her ample chest heaving as she caught her breath, Eddie wished she hadn't stopped. In fact, there was no reason they couldn't go into the back room and—

"Damn, I missed that." Kristy stepped out of his arms. "But I ain't surprised. I figured you'd get tired of that skinny-ass bitch sooner or later and come crawling back. But I didn't expect this." She held up her hand, the ring shining dully in the overhead lights. "I'd have kicked your ass out the door if you hadn't had it. See this, Sandy Powell? Karma's a bitch. I got a ring and you're dead!"

Eddie's rage ignited at her words. Who the fuck was she to talk about Sandy? His arm lashed out and he grabbed her by the wrist, slammed her hand down on the bar.

"Watch your fuckin' mouth."

"Ow! What the fuck? Don't tell me you're still hung up on that skank?"

Eddie's other hand came around and slapped her across the face, hard enough to leave a red, hand-shaped mark but not hard enough to bruise. What Ned Bowman used to call a warning rather than a lesson.

"Oh, shit." Tattoo girl leaned closer with the phone.

Eddie paused, his hand raised for another blow. *Control. Gotta keep—*

Pain exploded between his legs as Kristy smashed her knee into his balls.

"Fuck you, Hank Bowman!" she shouted. Humiliation painted her face and fury burned in her eyes. "Get the hell out of here!"

Doubled over and cupping his injured nuts, Eddie still managed to choke his next words out through teeth gritted against the pain.

"You're a terrible fuck. Sandy did it better."

"You sonofabitch!" She kicked him again, in the thigh. He laughed, and she attacked him like a cornered wildcat, slashing at him with her long nails and pulling chunks of hair. Instead of fighting back, Eddie covered his face. He needed Hank's eyes intact for later.

Something hard bounced off his shoulder and glass shattered on the floor. He looked up. Kristy had a beer mug in her hand. Before he could move, she thumped it against his head. Bright lights filled his vision and he stumbled to his knees. Her foot lashed out again and the pointed toe of her cowboy boot stabbed him in the ribs. Cold liquid drenched his back as the tattoo girl poured a beer on him.

"You fucking bitch!" He pulled himself up and cocked his fist, ready to send Kristy's friend into Neverland.

The three old men stood behind her, all of them gripping mugs like brass knuckles.

"Time for you to get your ass out of here, Bowman," one of them said. Despite his age, he looked in good enough shape to do some damage.

The urge to let loose his rage and bring the roof down on them was so strong his muscles trembled. A little burst of energy sneaked out, just enough to make the lights flicker and the jukebox squeal.

No. Not them. Not today. You got other business to take care of.

He turned and stared at Kristy, who'd grabbed a baseball bat from behind the bar and looked ready to use it.

Today's you're lucky day. You just don't know it.

"We'll settle this later. At home, darling." He stretched out the last word so that it dripped with sarcasm. "You know what they say. Practice makes perfect. Maybe someday you can be good as her."

"Get the fuck out of my bar, you asshole!" She swung the bat, but he was ready. He dodged out of the way and then grabbed it from her hands and threw it across the bar. Bottles shattered and booze sprayed in all directions.

"I'm gone, but you'll see me again. And when you do, make sure to tell me Eddie was here."

Kristy's eyebrows scrunched together as she tried to make sense of his words.

"Eddie? What are you talking about? He's dead. And you're—"

"I'm the guy who just can't die." Eddie laughed, "And this is just the beginning. Ask your new fiancé if he believes in ghosts yet."

Still laughing, he turned and headed for the doors. Kristy's shout followed him as he pushed them open.

"You're fuckin' crazy, Hank! Eddie's dead! You killed him!"

He started Hank's bike, letting the engine's roar cut off the sound of her voice.

One more thing to do, and then Hank could wake up to a whole new world of trouble.

★ ★ ★

The hospital dozed in that quiet period between lunch and dinner when Eddie marched Hank's body down the hall to Jethro's room. Most of the doctors had finished their rounds, and the nurses were at their stations, updating the charts. The perfect setting for the afternoon's grand finale. He'd already called Mouse and Harley, told them to meet him there.

"Shit, man," Mouse said as Eddie walked in. "You look like hell."

"Yeah, what the hell happened to you?" Harley asked.

Eddie gave them a big grin. He knew what the others were seeing. His face and arms covered in scratches from Kristy's nails. His hair and beard wet with beer. His eyes red from partying.

They think I look crazy now? Wait 'til that video from the bar hits the 'net.

"Been a fuckin' helluva day," he said, shutting the door behind him. "I've been doin' a lot of thinkin'." He went over to the bed, his smile growing wider as Jethro grew more nervous the closer he got.

"There's been some weird shit goin' on lately. We all know it. But we can't let that get between brothers, right? Hell Riders gotta stick together."

"Damn straight," Harley said.

"Hell yeah." Mouse pumped his fist.

On the bed, Jethro just nodded. His eyes flicked from Hank to Harley and back again.

"So, after reflecting some, I figure whatever made Jethro here act like a fuckin' dipshit the other day, maybe it ain't his fault."

"It wasn't me, I swear," Jethro whispered.

"I believe you. And to prove it, I'm gonna give you somethin' special, somethin' I wouldn't let no one else have. My cock."

"What?" Jethro started to move back, but Eddie grabbed him by the neck, held him in place. With his other hand, he unzipped his jeans and took out his dick.

"Yep. Just a quick blow job and I forget you ever crossed me."

Eddie leaned forward and rubbed Hank's dick across Jethro's lips and nose. The injured Hell Rider turned his head back and forth, pushing at the bed railing with his hands, but couldn't avoid the contact.

"'Course, there's some jizz mixed in. Sorry 'bout that. And with Kristy, you might never know who else's stuff is in there. She's a regular sperm bank, ain't that the truth?"

"What the fuck, Hank?" Harley grabbed his arm and pulled him away.

"Get your fuckin' hands off me or I'll cut 'em the fuck off!" Eddie shoved Harley away. The fluorescent tubes in the ceiling flickered and buzzed. The IV pump hooked to Jethro's arm dinged twice.

Mouse let out a yelp and backed away from the bed.

Eddie took a deep breath and the lights steadied. He smiled again and waved Hank's dick around while Jethro frantically wiped at his face and lips with both hands and Harley frowned like he'd been given a math problem.

"Things are gonna be different, now, boys. We got business to take care of. We're gonna make this fuckin' town our own. I'll be right back, gotta take a piss."

Eddie headed for the door, his dick still dangling, the stares of the three riders warm on his back. When he exited the room, he made sure to leave the door open so Harley, Mouse, and Jethro had a clear view. Aiming himself in the direction of the nurses' station, he let loose a long stream of piss right onto the floor.

And then took his leave of Hank's body.

CHAPTER NINETEEN

The last thing Carson wanted to do was stop kissing Kellie. But his stomach rumbled, reminding him he'd need to start thinking about making dinner soon. And he should check in on his mother.

"I'll be right back," he said, reluctantly tearing himself away. "I just hafta see if my mom needs anything."

"Okay. I'll be here when you're done." Kellie lay back on the bed, and Carson almost gave in to the temptation to join her. His lips and tongue tingled, and like him they wanted more. However, as the closest thing to the man of the house, he knew he had responsibilities to take care of.

"Mom?" He knocked on the door. When there was no answer, he knocked louder. "Mom? It's almost time for your medicine. Do you need water or anything?"

Nothing.

A feeling of dread blossomed in the pit of his stomach, the kind of dread that comes from living with someone who has a terminal illness. The idea that this might be it, that his mother might be gone forever.

He pushed open the door, while telling himself to stop being so foolish, she was just asleep.

Except she wasn't.

Sally Ryder lay sideways on the bed, one arm extended outward toward the pill bottles on her nightstand. Her eyes were closed, and a line of spittle dangled from the edge of her bottom lip.

Carson's heart kicked into overdrive.

No. Not now. NO!

"Kellie! Call 911!"

★　　★　　★

Johnny Ray Jones was contemplating dinner menus at his desk, trying to decide between the meatloaf special from Hickey Tavern or a couple of loaded hot dogs from Dairy King, when the call came in. Drunk and disorderly at the hospital. He'd been ready to send Moselby until he found out it was Hank Bowman who'd decided to take a piss in the hallway.

Got you, you stupid asshole. Let's see you talk your way out of this one.

D and D wasn't as good as murder, but it meant he'd get to keep Bowman locked in a cell for a day or two. Which would give him ample opportunity to pry some information out of the dumb bastard, especially if Hank still had a load on.

Except it turned out Bowman was apparently so stoned he didn't even know where he was or what he'd done.

"I swear, I didn't do nuthin'," the disoriented biker kept repeating, as they rode back to the station. Every time he said it, Johnny Ray just shook his head. They had him dead to rights. Not only were there a half-dozen witnesses, but the security cameras had caught the whole thing on tape. On top of that, his jeans were still wet and stinking of piss. Yet he kept insisting he'd never gone to the hospital, never spoken with his buddies, all of whom looked spooked to hell by his crazy actions.

"Let him sleep a couple of hours," Jones told Ted Moselby after they ushered Hank into the drunk tank and shut the cell door. "Then I'll try talking to him again."

"You got it, Chief."

Johnny Ray barely had time to sit down before the phone jangled.

"Chief! We got a 911 call!" Cindy Emerson, the evening receptionist, shouted. Something in her voice told Johnny Ray it wasn't an ordinary emergency.

"What is it?" he asked, already up and reaching for his hat.

"It's your daughter. She's at the Ryder place. Her and Carson just found Sally unconscious."

"I'm on my way!"

Johnny Ray was out the door before Cindy finished acknowledging his words. A terrible pain gripped his heart as he flipped on the siren in his SUV, a pain that had no physical origin.

Please don't let her die.

He raced down Main Street, cursing the gods of Fate for continually raining tribulations down on Sally. First they saddled her with Big Eddie, a textbook definition of an abusive, good-for-nothing loser. Because of his laziness she'd been forced to help support the family by taking a job at the fertilizer plant, where she inhaled enough toxins over the years to ruin her lungs and immune system. But, no, that wasn't enough. They'd sent her an evil present in the form of Little Eddie, who'd picked up right where his father left off.

Of course, the Fates hadn't shot their entire load on Sally. They'd saved a good one for Johnny Ray. The one he'd found out thirdhand not long after Sally got knocked up by Big Eddie. It'd been Cindy Emerson who'd told him, long before either of them joined the police force.

"I can't believe you two never got together. She was so sweet on you all through school."

That was his own private hell, the knowledge that if he'd only gotten up the nerve to ask her out the first time he met her – or any time before Big Eddie did – she might never have started dating Big Eddie in the first place. She'd be healthy and happy today and he wouldn't be a widower.

Please, God, if you're listening. Give me another chance. I swear I won't make the same mistake twice.

★　　★　　★

Johnny Ray arrived at Sally Ryder's trailer just as the EMTs jumped out of the ambulance and ran to the front door. By the time he got inside, Carson had already led the two techs down the hall.

"Daddy!"

Kellie practically leaped into his arms. Black trails of mascara ran down both cheeks, turning her pretty face into a Halloween fright mask.

"Are you okay, honey?" he asked, holding her tight against his chest.

"Yeah."

"You sure? Can you tell me what happened?"

She nodded, and then pulled back a little. "We were in Carson's room, just...um, watching TV, and he went to ask his mom if she wanted dinner. That's when...."

Her voice trailed off and Johnny Ray hugged her again. For a moment it was as if they'd gone back in time, back to when Angelina had died. Kellie was still young, still hurting from the loss of her brother. The years dropped away and his pain was as cold and solid as it had been that night. He could only imagine how it felt for her.

How it had been seeing Sally on that bed, wondering if she was alive.

Not for the first time, he wished Kellie'd had a good female role model in her life. Of course, the lack of one fell entirely on his shoulders. He'd never been good at choosing women. After high school, a string of one-night stands had led to Jeff, and that had been a hard life lesson to learn. But it was one he'd taken to heart. From that point on, he'd stayed away from 'bad' girls and eventually met Angelina, who turned out to be the perfect woman. Smart, from a good family, and pretty as hell. So perfect she'd actually made him forget about Sally.

Life had been great for twelve years, until the day Angelina went to the doctor with stomach pains and died two weeks later from an infection she developed during the removal of a burst appendix.

Leaving him to raise a teenage girl with major abandonment issues.

A little therapy and a lot of love, combined with Kellie's amazing inner strength, had enabled father and daughter to work things through and come out better for it. Still, he harbored a deep resentment toward Fate or God, depending on the day, and knowing those old memories were playing a part in how Kellie felt at the moment brought all his bitterness to the surface again like fetid waters rising in a swamp.

"Look out, folks!"

Johnny Ray guided Kellie out of the way as the EMTs exited the hallway and headed for the front door. One of them pushed an ambulance gurney holding a very pale Sally Ryder, while the other worked on getting a drip bag of some kind going. Above the oxygen mask that covered her nose and mouth, Sally's eyes were open but unfocused. Carson trailed behind, looking like a lost child in a department store.

"How is she?" Johnny asked one of the techs, a lanky fellow named Russell.

"Better than she looks," Russell said, steering the gurney around the couch. "Prob'ly had a dizzy spell and passed out reaching for her meds. Unless the doc finds something different, she should be good as new in a day or two."

Then they were out the door and wheeling toward the ambulance.

Carson stopped by the couch, his eyes moving between Johnny and the EMTs, clearly unsure of whether he could ride in the ambulance.

"I'll take you to the hospital," Johnny said. "And we'll stay with you until your mom's settled into a room or sent home, whatever the doctors decide."

"Thanks." Carson's relief showed in his eyes and on his face. "I just…I have to get the insurance cards. They're in her pocketbook."

"Sure." Johnny watched Carson hurry back down the hall to Sally's room.

How sad that a kid his age has to know about things like insurance paperwork and emergency rooms.

Then he felt Kellie's hand in his and realized how similar their situations were. If anything ever happened to him, it would be Kellie looking for insurance cards and wondering how she would get to the hospital.

I think when this is over, she and I are going to have a long talk. Make sure she knows what to do and who to call in case of an emergency.

On the way to the hospital, he prayed she'd never have to put the information to use.

CHAPTER TWENTY

Eddie shouted his joy at the heavens as he blasted his way through the darkening sky, an invisible comet shooting through the cosmos. Possessing Hank had filled him to overflowing with radiant energy, energy he was afraid to use too close to the ground for fear he might destroy entire buildings. Instead, he'd settled for lighting a few trees on fire out in the 'Glades before heading back to town.

Even better than the power flowing through him had been the thrill of seeing Hank Bowman arrested for his lunatic actions at the hospital. God, the look on the nurses' faces when they'd seen Hank spraying the hallway like a homeless drunk.... *Man, that was priceless!*

Flashing lights far down below caught his eye and he swooped down for a better look. He spotted Chief Jones's SUV pulling into the hospital, siren wailing and dome light splashing red and blue across the ER entrance.

What gives? Why's Jones back again?

Not that it mattered.

Hey, maybe I'll jump inside him, make him act like a fool, too. Do a chicken dance in the lobby. That oughta—

Eddie's thoughts stumbled to a halt as he saw a familiar figure get out of the Chief's truck.

Carson? What the—?

Carson, Johnny Ray, and Carson's little girlfriend took off at a run into the hospital.

A terrible chill welled up inside Eddie. There was only one reason other than personal injury for his brother to be at the hospital.

Oh, no. Ma?

Eddie aimed himself at the emergency entrance, all thoughts

of Hank and Johnny Ray gone in an instant. He passed through concrete and steel as if they were air and arrived at the front desk just in time to see Carson sprint past, following Chief Jones down the hallway to the exam rooms. It was easy enough to see which one they were heading for: the only one with doctors and nurses waiting while paramedics transferred a body onto a bed.

One of the EMTs stepped back and read from a clipboard while the doctors and nurses dove in like vultures attacking roadkill. "Thirty-eight-year-old female with chronic emphysema. Her son found her unconscious at the scene. She revived when placed on oxygen."

Ma! Eddie floated over her body as the nurses attached her to a series of machines. A green oxygen mask covered her face, but the rise and fall of her chest let him know she was still alive. Small comfort, but a lot better than the alternative.

"Looked like she sat up too fast and passed out," said the second EMT.

"Is my mom gonna be all right?" Carson asked. He dodged back and forth, trying to see past all the taller figures standing between him and his mother.

"She's going to be fine," one of the doctors said, without looking up. "We just need to get her breathing stabilized and her oxygen levels up, and she'll be able to talk to you. Give us about fifteen minutes, okay?" This last was aimed at Chief Jones, who nodded, put a hand on Carson's shoulder, and led him out of the room, with Kellie following close behind.

Like a nice little goddamn family, Eddie thought, and then wondered why the idea made him so angry.

I should be happy there's someone around to help him. And my mother.

Maybe that was the problem. Someone else was caring for his family instead of him, and doing a good job of it. Better than he had, when you thought about it.

I did my best. I busted my ass to keep food on the table and pay the bills, and now it seems like they didn't even need me.

Like a spark in a field of dry grass, Eddie's anger ignited, spread outward. Lights flickered, and one of the machines hooked up to his mother gave a stuttering beep.

"What the hell's going on?" A doctor pushed several buttons on the misbehaving machine. In the hall, Carson turned around, a nervous, almost anticipatory look on his face, as if he expected something else to happen.

Gotta calm down. It's too dangerous to let my emotions loose in here. Not when Ma's life depends on that equipment.

Eddie took a deep mental breath and forced himself to relax. Immediately, the lights steadied and the affected machine returned to its normal hum.

"Must've been a power surge." The doctor gave the machine a final tap and then left the room.

I'll give you a power surge, Eddie thought, then instantly forced the image away before anything else happened.

Now what?

There's nothing you can do for her, asshole. You're dead.

Figuring the safest thing was to tag along after Carson, Eddie caught up with his brother and the Joneses in the waiting area, where Carson and his new squeeze sat in cheap plastic seats while Johnny Ray played dad and got sodas and snacks for everyone from the vending machines.

Bastard!

Eddie's anger returned with a vengeance and a trickle of energy slipped out before he regained control. On the other side of the room, sparks flew from the soda machine and Johnny Ray stumbled away as a conga line of soda cans tumbled out of the dispenser. Eddie laughed to himself while Jones fell on his ass and scooted backward, the soda cans rolling in all directions. His laughter died when he noticed that Carson, unlike Johnny Ray and Kellie, wasn't looking at the soda machine.

He was staring around the room, as if trying to locate a hidden culprit.

Hidden, or invisible?

Shit, he couldn't know about me, could he?

It seemed impossible, but Eddie knew all too well how smart his little brother was. And with all the clues Eddie'd been leaving behind lately....

Clues, or memories. He said everything's a blank from the time I was inside him, but what if some of it's coming back to him? I need to be more careful, at least until I get rid of the Hell Riders for good. Then it won't matter anymore.

Rising slowly so neither he nor Diablo created any noise, Eddie left the hospital and found a spot on the roof where he could see the Chief's car. He already had his next move planned.

Now it was just a matter of waiting.

★   ★   ★

"That was really weird about the soda machine, huh?" Carson kept his tone neutral as he spoke to Kellie. He'd waited until Chief Jones went looking for a maintenance person before bringing the subject up.

"Freaky," Kellie agreed.

"A lot of that going around lately." He glanced over at her, hoping she'd catch his hint.

She did. "Carson, there's nothing supernatural about a soda machine having a short circuit."

"What about the lights flickering when we left my mom's room?"

"What about it? Maybe the hospital's having electrical problems. Maybe there was a power surge. It doesn't mean your brother's ghost is hanging around. Besides, what reason would Eddie have for breaking a soda machine?"

"Maybe he didn't do it on purpose." The words sounded lame even to his own ears, and Carson shook his head. "I know it sounds dumb. It's just...I have this feeling that something isn't right."

"Of course you do." Kellie glanced at the hallway and then placed her hand on his arm. "Your world's a mess right now. Your brother, your mom...it's going to take time to get over it all, get used to the new order of things."

"Easier said than done." Even the softness of her touch couldn't keep him from feeling bitter over the cards he'd been dealt lately.

"Lucky for you I'm here to help."

Before Carson had a chance to process her words, Kellie leaned over and gave him a short but passionate kiss. He was about to reach out and pull her closer when the sounds of people talking in the hallway reached them. They had just enough time to sit back in their chairs before the doors to the lounge opened and Kellie's father walked in with a heavyset man in blue coveralls.

"That's the one, over there," Johnny Ray pointed at the soda machine. "Damn thing went haywire and attacked me. I pulled the plug so it wouldn't start a fire. Scared the heck outta me and the kids."

Johnny Ray glanced at them, his eyebrows furrowed, and Carson's cheeks grew hot. He wondered if he looked as guilty as he felt. He imagined a cartoon version of himself with a neon sign on his forehead proclaiming *I made out with your daughter!* in big red letters. But the Chief just nodded at them and then returned his attention to the maintenance worker, who was examining the machine's half-melted electrical cord.

Kellie cleared her throat and Carson jumped in his seat before he realized where the sound came from. She was blushing as badly as he knew he was. He opened his mouth, but for a frightening moment no words came to mind.

Don't just sit there with your jaw hanging, like the village idiot. Say something!

"Um, you want a soda?" He held up one of the cans he'd scavenged from the floor.

"Thanks." One word, but she sounded as grateful as if he'd just rescued her from a surprise math test. He opened one and handed it to her, savoring the momentary tingly contact of their fingers, and then opened another for himself.

They spent the next ten minutes in silence, until a nurse entered the room.

"Carson Ryder? Your mom wants to see you."

"That's me!" He jumped up so fast he spilled soda on his jeans, but he didn't even bother mopping it up as he hurried after the nurse.

Carson wasn't sure what to expect – after all, only an hour ago his mother had looked ready to die – but it certainly wasn't the sight of her sitting up in bed, the oxygen mask replaced by the usual cannula under her nose and most of the color returned to her face. Only the darker-than-normal smudges under her eyes served as evidence she'd been seriously ill.

"Hey, Mom. How are you?" He went to the side of the bed and she took his hand. For the first time, he understood how different a girl's hand and a woman's hand could feel. Both brought comfort, but only one sent delicious shivers through his body.

"Sorry I gave you such a scare." Her smile was as strong as ever. "I should have called for you the moment I felt dizzy, but I thought it would go away."

"How long are you gonna be in the hospital?" Carson bit his lip as he waited for her answer. The longer the stay, the worse off she really was. Even he knew that.

"Actually, your mom's ready to go home right now," the nurse said. She checked a number on one of the machines and made a note on the patient chart. "The doctor's already signed the release. We're just waiting for her new prescription to come down from the pharmacy."

"That's great news, Mrs. Ryder."

Carson looked back and saw Kellie and her father standing in the doorway. He turned away quickly, embarrassed by the tears brimming in his eyes.

"Thank you, Kellie," Sally said. "It will be good to get home. Lord knows I hate hospitals. Oh, God." Her eyes went wide and she brushed at her hair with both hands. "I must look like a complete mess."

"Yeah, you're definitely feeling better. I'll bring the truck around," Chief Jones said with a laugh. "We'll be downstairs waiting whenever you get sprung loose, Sally. C'mon, Kellie."

"See you in a little while, Carson." Kellie flashed him a quick smile.

"Okay." Carson waved his hand, but avoided direct eye contact. His hope at seeming casual was quickly erased by his mother's next words.

"Kellie's a nice girl. Are you two getting serious?"

"Aw, geez. I don't know. We're just kind of hanging out, you know?" Carson felt his face grow warm again. Lately it seemed like he spent more time feeling foolish than not.

Sally took a couple of deep breaths before speaking again. "Good for you. You should invite her over for dinner sometime."

At that moment, the doctor returned, saving Carson from

continuing the conversation, which was fine by him. He had a strong notion that a couple more minutes and he'd be getting the dreaded lecture about being safe and using protection.

"You're all set, Mrs. Ryder. Just sign these papers and you can be on your way. Hopefully we won't see you again for a long time." He gave her a nod and a smile and then placed a folder on the tray next to the bed.

Five minutes later, Carson was pushing her wheelchair down the hall. By then he'd already managed to change the topic of discussion from Kellie and dating to ordering pizza for dinner.

CHAPTER TWENTY-ONE

Eddie was hovering outside the hospital entrance when Chief Jones and his daughter came out of the building. He'd figured Jones would go back to the jail, perhaps stopping long enough to drop his daughter off at home. Except instead of exiting the lot and heading into town, Jones drove around to the hospital's front entrance and parked there with his hazard lights flashing.

It didn't take a genius to figure out why.

He's going to take them home, just like he brought them here.

Eddie felt the resentment rising up again and he forced it back down with a curse. *Stop being such a goddamned jealous idiot. They need the help, you're not there anymore, and Carson certainly can't handle everything. So quit your bitching.*

Still, he couldn't stop himself from hanging around while Jones held the door open and Carson pushed Sally to the truck. Together, they helped her get into the front seat, and then Carson and Kellie climbed in the back, Carson's face alternating between nervousness and relief. Eddie coaxed Diablo higher into the air and toward his old home, following the Chief's headlights. He tried to imagine what was going through Carson's head. Was he thinking about his mother? Or was he too lovestruck to keep his mind on anything other than the pretty young thing sitting next to him? Carson was a good kid – sensible, intelligent, kind-hearted. All the things Eddie hadn't been. But he was still a teenage boy, meaning hormones could overrule common sense at any moment. Remembering how he'd felt while in Carson's body, he found himself more than a little envious of his brother's new-found happiness.

Don't waste the opportunity, little bro. You never know if you'll get another chance.

From his vantage point a hundred feet up, Eddie noticed

the dark Cadillac in front of the trailer, and the portly bald man standing next to it, before the others even arrived. He let Diablo drift down until they were just above roof level.

Jonathan Lyons? What's our lawyer doing here at this time of night? That nasty feeling started up in his gut again, the same one he'd gotten when he'd seen his mother in the hospital.

"Mrs. Ryder, sorry to interrupt you on what's probably been an already terrible evening," Lyons said, stepping aside as Johnny Ray guided Sally into the house and helped her get situated on the couch.

"Can't this wait?" the Chief asked. He gave the lawyer a nasty scowl that earned him some brownie points with Eddie.

"Actually, I'll only be a moment, but I wanted to deliver this news in person rather than over the phone. I was just getting ready to leave the papers when you showed up."

"What papers?" Sally asked.

"I, um, don't know how to say this, but it appears the insurance policy on the garage...well, it's lapsed." The lawyer looked down, avoiding Sally's eyes.

"Oh, no." Sally's pale face went a shade grayer. "We were counting on that money."

"Lapsed?" Carson looked from his mother to the lawyer. "What does that mean? It's overdue?"

"Not just overdue, son. Cancelled. Apparently, the last three payments were never made, so, at the time of the fire...."

Bullshit! Eddie's mental shout shook the house with thunder, causing everyone to jump.

I paid that goddamn policy every month, even if it meant getting behind on the electric or the phone.

Not only was he sure he'd paid the premiums, he knew exactly where the returned checks and bank statements were – in a shoebox in his bedroom. He kept all the house and work financial documents there because the garage office was always a mess and he'd been afraid of losing important papers or spilling something on them.

"I'm sure Eddie paid them," Sally was saying. "He was very good about paying all the bills on time."

Lyons shrugged. "It's possible there were computer entry errors. But we'd need proof.... If you can bring in the receipts, we'd have a good case against the bank and the insurance company. One I could settle very quickly. But without them...well, it's out of our hands."

The lawyer said goodbye and let himself out, while Eddie fumed by the front window.

They want proof? I'll get them their damn proof. And then I'll make those motherfuckers get on their hands and knees and apologize.

Separating himself from Diablo, Eddie leaped through the window and dove into Carson's body. There was a momentary disorientation, during which Eddie/Carson stumbled, but Eddie regained control just in time to grab the back of the couch before anyone noticed.

"That lawyer is full of shit," he said, the words exiting Carson's mouth before Eddie could stop them.

"What?" Sally turned and stared at him. "Watch the language, young man."

"Sorry," Eddie said, with Carson's voice sounding anything but. "He's wrong, though. The insurance was paid. Eddie told me."

Johnny Ray cleared his throat. "Just because your brother said he did something doesn't mean—"

"Yeah, you would think that," Eddie interrupted the Chief. "I'll show you. I'll prove he didn't mess things up."

Before anyone could say another word, Eddie guided Carson's body down the hall to Eddie's old room, where he quickly located the old shoebox and dumped it out on the bed. Just as he'd known they would be, the insurance bills – complete with the cancelled checks stapled to them – were right in their envelopes. He took them and returned to the living room, slapped the papers down on the table.

"Here you go," he said to Johnny Ray. "Still think Eddie was just bullshitting me?"

Sally started to scold him again for his language, but Johnny Ray cut her off. "Sally, we need to get these to Jonathan as soon as possible. I can take them to his house right now, if you want."

"Yeah, tell that dipshit he'd better straighten things out, pronto."

"Carson!"

"Sorry, Ma," Eddie said. "I'm just sick of everyone thinking Eddie was a piece of shit, and I'm sick of people trying to screw me over."

"Screw you over?" Johnny Ray asked, giving him a quizzical look.

"I mean us. My family. Ah, the hell with it." Eddie shook his head and stormed down the hall. At the last minute, he remembered to veer into Carson's room instead of his own. He slammed the door shut and turned Carson's radio on to a heavy metal station, hoping his tantrum would deter anyone from wanting to come in and talk to him.

Gotta hold it together.

He was letting his temper get the best of him again. Something he'd always tried not to do, especially in front of his mother. Or Carson.

Is it because I don't have a body anymore? That didn't make sense; after all, he had a body at the moment, even if it belonged to Carson. And only the knowledge that his little brother had never broken anything in anger – never thrown a major tantrum at all, in fact – was keeping him from putting his fist through a wall.

An after-effect of dying? Maybe. Something like that had to fuck with your head. But it didn't explain why the anger seemed to be growing stronger every day.

Even now, listening to his mother and Kellie talking in the living room, he felt like destroying something. Or screaming. Or punching someone.

If I keep this up, someone's gonna catch on. Carson, or the little piece of ass he's still not fucking yet. God, what I wouldn't give to stick my—

Stop it! That's not me talking! He slammed his fists into Carson's pillow. *Do what you want to the Hell Riders, but no using Carson's body for anything other than helping the family.*

Except his body – *Carson's* body – was doing its best to betray his good intentions. Just thinking about Kellie Jones had his cock hard as a hammer.

Get a grip. I gotta stop thinking about pussy. I've got more important things to do.

He turned the radio off and let his consciousness exit Carson's body, rising to where Diablo sat waiting. With his mother obviously better, and the financial crisis taken care of, it was time to get back to the real business at hand. The reason he'd come back from death in the first place.

To kill all the Hell Riders.

CHAPTER TWENTY-TWO

A soft knock on the door brought Carson awake.

"Huh? Come in." He sat up, wondering how he'd ended up in his bed. The last thing he remembered was helping his mom into the house and their lawyer, Mr. Lyons, delivering the bad news about the insurance.

"Carson? You okay?" It was Kellie, peeking tentatively around the door.

"Yeah. Why?" The words came out automatically. The truth was, he didn't feel okay. In fact, he felt like crap. His head was all fuzzy, the world seemed out of place, and he couldn't remember going to bed.

Just like the night I passed out at the restaurant. I woke up in my bed that time, too, with no memory of what had happened.

The thought came to him as Kellie entered the room, looking very concerned.

"You were acting kind of...funny before."

From the way she said it, he knew she meant something a lot more serious than 'funny'.

"Funny, how?"

Kellie shrugged. "Not yourself. You were swearing, and then you threw a fit and came in here and slammed the door, started blasting the music. Me and your mom waited a while to see if you'd come out, but you didn't, even after you turned the radio off."

"How long...how long have I been asleep?" He wasn't sure he wanted to hear the answer, but he needed to know.

"Almost an hour. After my dad left—"

"Left? Where did he go?" The last thing Carson remembered was being in the living room and getting the news about their insurance. Chief Jones had been standing next to the couch.

"To the lawyer's house, remember? You found the insurance

records. Turns out they're going to pay for the garage after all. After my dad called and told your mom the news, she went to bed. I hung around, 'cause I wanted to…talk to you."

Normally the idea that Kellie wanted to spend time with him would have had his heart doing the salsa in his chest. Unfortunately, the rest of what she'd said had him too confused to think about romance. He tried to get a grip on his thoughts, but his mind wouldn't focus.

"I…I don't remember any of that. I found them? How? Where? Eddie always took care of that stuff. He…." The words trailed off as a queasy feeling took root in his stomach.

"What is it?"

"Kellie. Remember what we talked about? I think…I think it happened again. No, I'm sure of it."

"You mean, you think your brother came back?"

"Yes. And he took over my body. Possessed me. It's the only thing that makes sense. Think about it. The swearing. The loud music. That's Eddie to a tee. How did he – I mean *I* – seem?"

Kellie frowned. "Really angry. Furious is more like it. You were talking about the papers, and then my dad said something about your brother and you flew off the handle."

"Crap. Eddie couldn't stand the cops, even after your dad helped him out. It wasn't anything personal, he just always felt like the police, and lots of other people in town, had it out for him because of who our father was, and because we were poor."

"That sounds a lot like what you were yelling about."

A shiver ran up Carson's back. "Kellie, we have to do something. If I'm right, then a lot of the weird stuff that's been happening in town is because of Eddie. We have to stop him."

Taking a seat next to him on the bed, Kellie bit her lip before replying. "Carson. Think about what you're saying. Do you really believe your brother's ghost is going around possessing people and making them do things? Making them hurt each other?"

"I do. At least, I think I do. I know I'm not crazy. The only people Eddie's hurt are the Hell Riders. And I'll bet that's because they…." He found himself unable to finish the sentence out loud. *Killed him.*

"What about you? If you're right, he's possessed you twice."

"But he hasn't hurt me, or anyone else, while he was…inside me. I think he only used me to help us, like with the insurance papers."

"Even if that's true – and I'm not saying I believe you – what can we do?"

Carson sighed. "I don't know. But we have to figure something out. I have a real bad feeling about this."

Outside, thunder rumbled in the night sky.

★   ★   ★

Eddie rode Diablo back and forth across Hell Creek, rattling windows and causing people to look up into the sky and wonder how there could be so much thunder on a cloudless morning. Heavy metal music – Demon Dogs, Iced Earth, Priest, Maiden – provided a mental soundtrack to his rage, the tunes cranked up as loud in his head as if Diablo's sound system still worked. He hadn't slept all night, his fury unabated even after he watched Johnny Ray bring the paperwork to Lyons' house. Only several hours of blowing up trees and alligators out in the swamps had eased the pressure growing inside him enough so that he could return to his grave and wait for dawn.

He had big things planned, and he didn't want to use up all his energy.

The moment the sun came up, he'd resumed his aerial laps, his fury growing with each passing hour, searching the town, waiting for his opportunity to—

There.

A motorcycle traveling down the highway, its rider clad in a Hell Riders vest.

Harley Atkins. Eddie recognized the rotund gang member and his bike even from two hundred feet up. Seen from above, Harley resembled a turtle; the vision would have been hilarious if Eddie hadn't already been seething.

"Gotcha, motherfucker." Eddie aimed Diablo straight down and shifted gears, accelerating faster and faster, a supersonic eagle diving at his unsuspecting prey. At the last moment, he eased up on the throttle and slammed himself into his target.

Harley's bike swerved hard left and tilted, the edge of the foot rest skimming the blacktop and throwing up sparks, before Eddie gained control of Harley's body and yanked the heavy bike back up. For a sickening moment it teetered the other way, threatening to dump Eddie onto the highway and turn him into a road pizza, but then it straightened out. Eddie let out a victorious war whoop as he accelerated to ninety miles an hour.

What a rush!

Eddie throttled the bike up even further. With no fear of dying, all that remained was the thrill of the ride, the sheer adrenaline jolt of the speed. He reached up and took off Harley's classic Nazi-style helmet, then tossed it away. The wind batted his face and whipped his filthy, shoulder-length hair. Bugs smashed against his flesh like miniature darts and got lodged in his beard.

Good. The filthier he looks, the better.

Eddie had no care if Harley died on the highway, but he also hoped he didn't. He had bigger plans for the fat slob.

Much bigger.

★ ★ ★

Sitting in his squad car at the edge of town, Wilbur Dennis was splitting his time between watching the occasional car or truck go by and reading the latest copy of *Pistol Digest*. His car was right out in the open, mainly because Chief Jones believed prevention was as good as capture when it came to controlling speeders, but also because there wasn't a damned place within miles where you could hide a car even if you wanted to. Nothing but scrub and swamp once you got more than ten feet from the edge of the road. Not that it mattered. Anyone who traveled through Hell Creek more than once or twice knew there was almost always a radar trap at one end of town or the other. Consequently, speeders tended to be few and far between, especially in the middle of the day.

So it caught him completely by surprise when a motorcycle raced by at close to a hundred miles an hour, its engine roaring like a super-sonic dinosaur. He caught a quick glimpse of black leather and long hair, and then the bike was past.

"Holy fuckin' shit!" Dennis dropped his magazine and hit the switch for the sirens and lights. It was that simple act, that oh-so-slight delay, that saved his life, as the motorcycle executed a crazy, screaming skid, spun around one hundred eighty degrees, and raced back toward town, already doing close to fifty when it whizzed past his front bumper before his car even reached the blacktop.

"Goddamn!" Dennis slammed on the brakes, his brain registering his near-death experience and the middle finger extended in his direction at the same time.

Harley Atkins. He must be drunker than a skunk to try that shit with me. Dennis pulled out and floored the gas pedal, the cruiser's oversized engine growling like a chained lion in response.

As they raced down the highway, Dennis quickly realized he'd have no chance of catching the customized motorcycle. He grabbed his mic and called in the situation. "This is Wilbur. I'm ten miles west of town in pursuit of Harley Atkins. Clocked the bastard at near to a hundred, and then he flipped me the goddamned bird."

"Roger that, Wilbur," came the response. "Johnny Ray's out, but I'm sending Ted your way right now."

"Tell him to be careful. Harley must be wasted. Nearly ran me off the road."

"Heard that loud and clear." The connection clicked off and Dennis laughed. They were gonna put Atkins's fat ass in jail for sure this time. No way he was getting out of this mess.

Up ahead, Atkins slowed his bike, allowing Dennis to close the gap, and then sped up again as he approached the town line.

Almost like he's toying with me, or wants to get caught. Well, it don't matter. His ass is mine.

"Gotcha now, motherfucker," Dennis said, watching the speedometer creep past eighty-five. His hands gripped the steering wheel so tight his knuckles felt ready to split. Truth be told, he hadn't driven this fast since his own days of night-racing hot rods as a teenager, and he was more than a little nervous about blowing a tire or hitting a gator or rabbit that decided to cross the road at the wrong time.

Distant flashing red and blue lights indicated Moselby was coming at them from the north. For a brief second, Dennis thought Atkins might try and slide past the other cruiser. Then the bike went into a long, smoking skid that must've burned the tires to almost nothing and came to a stop twenty yards from the other car, just as Moselby turned his car sideways and blocked the road.

Coughing from the acrid burnt-rubber stench filling the cruiser, Dennis brought his car to a halt and thumbed the loudspeaker.

"Harley Atkins! Step off the goddamn bike and put your hands over your head!"

Once more, Atkins did the exact opposite of what Dennis expected. Instead of arguing, or stumbling around in a drunken stupor, or just sitting there, the overweight biker let the bike fall to the ground and stood still in the middle of the road, his back to Dennis.

Dennis exited his car, gun drawn, and caught sight of Moselby doing the same thing on the other side of the black, oily cloud Atkins had created. Moselby also had his gun out, and Dennis took a few steps to one side, putting himself out of the other officer's direct line of fire. *Just in case.*

"Atkins! Hands up! Last chance, asshole."

Harley turned and looked back, an oddly happy smile on his face, like he was getting ready to collect a lottery check rather than get arrested. Without saying a word, he undid his belt, bent low at the waist, and dropped his jeans. Dennis had time to notice the absurdity of a biker wearing polka-dotted boxer shorts, and then the underwear joined the jeans and Dennis was staring at an ass so fat and hairy it looked like it belonged on a monkey or a bear.

He was so surprised by the comically grotesque sight that it took him several seconds to realize Atkins wasn't just mooning him.

He was taking a shit.

Holy.... That crazy sonuvabitch is dropping a deuce right on the highway!

Moselby shouted something at Atkins, but Dennis barely heard the words. He was frozen in place, watching the turds slide out from between Atkins's butt cheeks and plop onto the blacktop.

No, not the blacktop. They were falling right into the bastard's pants!

Then Atkins looked back again, the crazy smile still plastered on his face, a smile that made Dennis think about the time he'd had to transport a prisoner to the state nuthouse. A lot of the people there had the same smile.

"Hey, Wilbur! Sorry about that." Atkins leaned down and yanked up his underwear and pants, smearing shit up his legs as he did so. "Gonna be some ride back to the station, huh?"

While the smoke slowly rose into the air and dissipated across the swampland, Dennis felt his anger likewise rising inside him as Atkins's words sank in.

I have to put that son of a bitch in my car, and there's gonna be shit smell everywhere.

Not to mention the fact that some of it would probably end up on the backseat, and who would get stuck cleaning it afterward?

Officer Wilbur Fucking Dennis, that's who.

It didn't matter that he had more time served on the force than Ted Moselby. Moselby, that out-of-town bastard, had the higher rank. Which meant his car would remain shit-free.

"You goddamn motherfucker!" Dennis holstered his gun, drew his baton, and charged at Atkins, who just raised his hands and stood there with that stupid grin on his fat face. All his sensibility was gone, lost in a blind rage. Forget Miranda rights, forget due process, Atkins was gonna feel some good old hometown justice.

His first swing took Harley right across his left arm, with a sound like a game-winning home run. Atkins fell to his knees, clutching the broken limb, but that didn't stop Dennis from swinging the baton again. And again.

It never even struck Dennis as odd that Atkins put up no resistance, merely stood there and let himself get beaten. Dennis just kept swinging, not caring where it landed, until Moselby pulled him away. By then, Atkins was on his side, his face bloody, several teeth missing, and livid bruises already forming on his arms and neck.

"That's enough!" Moselby shouted. "Christ, we'll be lucky if he doesn't sue the town after this. Now let's get him in the car. Maybe we can say he resisted arrest."

Together they dragged Atkins's semi-conscious body to Dennis's cruiser and shoved him into the back. And just as Dennis had expected, more than a few shit stains ended up on the door and the upholstery as they maneuvered him in.

While they were attempting to shut the door, Atkins rolled over, leaving another brown stain in his wake, and tried to speak. It took him several attempts to get the words out.

"What a great fuckin' day, huh?"

Then he passed out.

Moselby slammed the door closed and shook his head.

"That is one seriously messed-up individual."

"Yeah, whatever." Dennis climbed into the front and immediately gagged at the stench already filling the car. He kept the windows open on the way through town, but even that didn't help. By the time he arrived at the station, it was all he could do to keep his lunch from jumping out of his stomach.

And there was still the backseat to clean.

CHAPTER TWENTY-THREE

Eddie found himself laughing so hard at Wilbur Dennis's obvious outrage that the lights in the station kept flickering. He forced himself to calm down, not wanting anyone to get distracted from the Harley Atkins show. Act One was finished, and now it was time to begin Act Two.

He'd timed his escape from Atkins's body perfectly, exiting right after delivering his final words to Dennis. No sense in experiencing any more pain than he had to, and Harley's body had been in a motherfucking heap of pain. So much, in fact, that Eddie almost couldn't stand it. It had been a hell of a relief to exit the fat bastard's body and follow the cruiser back to town.

Also, it had smelled awful inside the car. Whatever Harley had eaten that day, it had come out stinking worse than week-old roadkill.

He stationed himself outside the holding cell, watching a semi-conscious Atkins moaning and groaning on his bunk, until Ted Moselby came down the hall. Even better, Johnny Ray was with him.

A two-fer! This is gonna be even better than I'd hoped.

Taking a deep, metaphysical breath, Eddie re-entered Harley Atkins.

And almost screamed.

Even though he'd braced himself for it, he was still unprepared for the extent of Atkins's agony. Every limb shrieked; it hurt to breathe, to move, to even fucking think.

Get a grip. It's only for a few minutes. Besides, he'd been through a lot worse. Once you'd been burned alive, any other pain just didn't compare.

Each movement was an exercise in torture, but Eddie forced Harley's body to stand up and face the two police officers.

"Hey, fuck nuts," he said. The words came out distorted almost beyond recognition, thanks to his missing teeth. Eddie tried to smile but only succeeded in splitting his mangled lips open again. "What's with this cell? It smells like shit."

"Harley, what the hell are you on?" Johnny Ray asked. Eddie almost laughed out loud. The stupid fuck was actually concerned? That wouldn't do. He wanted him mad.

Really mad.

"Hey, Chief, wanna see my Hank Bowman impression?" He unzipped his pants, pulled out his dick, and pissed on the floor, doing his best to aim it at the cell bars. It hurt like hell but it was worth it when Johnny Ray and Moselby had to jump back a couple of feet to avoid the splash zone.

Not surprisingly, there was a strong reddish tint to the piss.

Got yourself a little kidney damage there, Harley. Sucks to be you.

"I think maybe he's finally flipped out," Moselby said. "He was acting crazy on the road, too, like I told you."

"Either that or he smoked some laced weed. PCP or something." Johnny Ray frowned. "Maybe we should send him to the hospital."

Eddie bared his lips and growled at them. He didn't want a trip to the hospital. But if that's what it took to get them to open the door....

He closed his eyes and let Harley's body fall to the floor, landing with a wet thud in his own piss.

"Oh, hell. He passed out again. Open the door, Ted."

Eddie waited until he heard the door open, felt a hand touch his wrist. Then he sprang up, grabbed Moselby's gun from its holster, and pushed his way out of the cell.

"Catch me if you can, dipshits!"

Ignoring the shouts behind him, Eddie ran down the hall and into the station. Every step hurt worse than the last, but he didn't care. Surprised faces looked up as he slammed the door open and waved the gun over his head.

"Look out, look out! Crazy fucker on the loose! I think I'll shoot somebody!" He fired a shot into the ceiling and all the faces disappeared behind desks or chairs.

"Harley! Drop the gun! Now!"

This is it. Time to make a shitload of paperwork for someone.

He turned around, gun still in hand but pointing to the side. "Screw you, ass—"

The twin explosions filled his ears at the same time he felt two mule kicks to the chest. The force of them knocked him out of Harley's body. The sudden absence of pain was so magnificent he cried out in relief, causing one of the fluorescent lights to explode. Below him, the mortally wounded biker stumbled backward and crushed a chair as he collapsed. Johnny Ray and Moselby, both their guns trailing wisps of smoke, approached Atkins's body.

"Goddamn," Moselby said.

Johnny Ray shook his head.

"This is not good."

★   ★   ★

After watching Harley's demise, Eddie rocketed up into an afternoon sky so bright it burned his eyes, his metaphysical self filled to overflowing with energy. He'd possessed multiple people in the same day, and it was like he'd plugged himself into a super-charged battery, jacked his system with a nitrous power booster. Diablo appeared between his legs and together they shot back to earth and raced through town so fast the buildings turned into gray and brown blurs. The sound of shattering glass caught up with him as he spun his ghost cycle in a one-eighty at the end of the street and paused, his laughter shaking peals of thunder from the dazzling blue dome over the town.

Every window from the police station to the end of Main Street was nothing but a pile of broken glass on the sidewalk.

I've never felt so alive! The sensations running through his body were new and yet familiar, like doing coke and whiskey and pot all at once and then multiplying it by ten, but without the disorientation or fuzzy vision.

Pure fuckin' power in the veins, man. This is what people are trying to feel when they shoot up or drop acid.

It was good. No, it was better than good, it was mother-fucking awesome, and he wanted more.

Hey, Hank. Ready or not, here I come for round two.

★   ★   ★

It didn't take long to find Hank. He and Mouse were on the highway, heading from the clubhouse back toward town. Eddie shook his head. The club had wasted no time getting him sprung from jail. Hank's uncle, Caleb Bowman, was an attorney in Homestead and did all the club's legal work for free, in return for VIP status at all the parties. Eddie had seen him at the clubhouse plenty of times over the years, his nose covered in white powder and a sweet young thing or two on his lap.

"Caleb likes to work pro boner!" Ned had cracked at one party, watching his uncle lead guide a girl half his age out to his Caddy.

Eddie's first thought was to use Hank to run Mouse off the road. But he was curious to see where they were going, so he followed them, thinking he might get the opportunity to make a public scene, with the Hell Riders at the center of it.

His curiosity paid off when they pulled into the parking lot of the Wash & Dry Laundromat. Owned by one Rollie Mason, whose daughter, Angela, just happened to be Ned Bowman's old lady. They'd moved in together after high school, and she'd stuck by him even after he got locked away. Now, in addition to running her daddy's business ever since he decided to take an early retirement and drink his remaining years away in front of the television, she handled the books for the club. Now, with Ned in prison, she was his primary go-between, even more so than Hank. She visited him nearly every week at the prison and returned with any orders he needed carried out.

She also spent a lot of her free time at their clubhouse, where she frequently demonstrated that she had her daddy's genes for alcohol tolerance as well has his talent for numbers.

Eddie maneuvered Diablo lower. He had a pretty good idea what would come next. Hank and Angela would go into the back office, leaving Mouse to guard the door. A standard money run, with Hank dropping off the cash from the week's drug sales along with the required cut from any legitimate work any member did. Twenty percent off the top, no excuses. Ned referred to it as union dues; the money was used for various purposes, like maintaining mortgage on the clubhouse and surrounding property, paying bail money, and throwing parties. With everyone in the club working either full-time or part-time jobs, plus Ned – and now Hank in his place – running a decent side business selling coke and pot, the club always had enough cash for its needs.

It was Angela's job to hide it from the IRS.

Eddie had always figured she just mixed it in with the cash from the business. Or kept it locked in a safe somewhere. But no one really knew. The only two people ever allowed in the office with Angela were Ned and Hank.

More than once, Eddie had wondered if the Bowman's were stealing from the club. A little double-dipping he expected; rank had its privileges. But it seemed like a lot more money got brought to the laundromat than the club actually spent.

Now I'll get to see for myself.

Angela didn't look at all pleased to see them, but she nodded for Hank to follow her to the office. Before closing the door, he turned to Mouse.

"Park your ass here and make sure nobody bothers us. Any cops come in, knock twice. Got it?"

"Sure thing." Mouse leaned against the wall and Eddie followed Hank, but not before he caught a glimpse of the self-satisfied grin on Mouse's face.

Like a kid whose father just let him help fix the car for the first time. Fucking suck-ass.

Yeah, and you were just as proud when Ned picked you to watch his back, his subconscious reminded him.

The memory of it made his non-existent stomach churn. He'd been stupid and gullible, looking for someone to take his father's place. And Ned had taken advantage of him. Fucked with his head.

Let's see how you like it, Neddie. You picked the wrong guy to kill. Now you're gonna pay.

Angela sat down behind a cheap metal desk, her dark eyes flashing. "What the fuck is going on? The whole town is saying you've flipped the fuck out. I mean, seriously. Forget that shit with Butch and Jethro. Taking a piss in the middle of a hospital? And I saw a video of you getting your ass kicked by Kristy. I don't have to tell you Ned is off his rocker about all this."

"Yeah?" Eddie fought to control his laughter as Hank's cheeks flushed. "What'd he say?"

"He wants to know what the fuck is going on around here. You losing your grip on those assholes?"

"Hell, no. None of that shit is my fault. Harley thinks we got some bad weed, maybe laced with something. It ain't just me. The whole town's goin' crazy."

"Ned don't care about the rest of the town, or what kind of weed you're smoking. Get your shit together and keep those guys in line or someone else might be wearing that Vice President patch. Got it?"

Eddie snickered as Hank's face went from red to almost purple. Behind his beard, his lips tightened from the effort of holding in whatever he wanted to say, knowing it would get back to his brother and just make things worse for him.

"Yeah, I got it. Loud and clear," he said.

"Good. What've you got for me?"

Hank took a fat manila envelope from the inside pocket of his vest. "Seven grand, give or take. With Jethro in the hospital and Butch gone, we're gonna be a little light for a while until we bring a couple more pledges into the fold."

"Not my problem." Angela dumped the cash onto the desk and counted it. She put aside three hundred dollars and then returned the rest to the envelope. She passed the three hundred to Hank. "Your cut."

"Hey, it's supposed to be four bills."

Angela shrugged. "We're short, you're short. You don't like it, take it up with your brother." She got up and opened a drawer in one of the metal filing cabinets lining the back wall, then dropped the envelope inside. From his vantage point, Eddie saw dozens of others just like it.

"Ah, screw it." Hank stuffed the cash into his wallet, a Playboy billfold attached to his belt by a chrome chain.

"See you next week, Hank."

"Right." Hank exited the office, making sure to slam the door behind him. The cheap wood did nothing to block the sound of him cursing.

Eddie was about to follow Hank when Angela went back to the

filing cabinet, removed the envelope she'd just placed inside, and took a thousand dollars from it. After placing the original envelope back into the drawer, she put two fifties into her pocket and stuffed the rest of the money into a second envelope, which went into the next drawer down.

A drawer also filled with envelopes.

She took an unmarked notebook from the bottom drawer of the desk and made a notation in it. Eddie managed to get a peek before she closed the drawer.

'September 28. $6800. Paid $300 HB.'

Goddamn, I was right. The three of them have been skimming all this time. And with Ned locked up, Angie's double dipping into his share.

Memories of struggling to pay bills or put food on the table, all because he had to tithe part of his earnings to the gang, burned like acid in Eddie's brain.

Sons of bitches. If I'd had just a little of that, we'd have never had to worry about the mortgage or car insurance. Carson could have had new clothes, maybe a better computer. Instead, these three were partying it up behind everyone's backs.

Fuck you, Ned Bowman!

Thunder crashed and the windows rattled with the force of his wrath. Well, they weren't getting away with it any longer.

Fast as lightning, he raced outside and entered Hank just as he was climbing onto his bike. Hank's fury burned just as bright as Eddie's, adding fuel to the inferno raging inside him.

"Hold up," he said, and Mouse looked back at him, his squinting eyes distorted behind his helmet's visor.

"What?"

"I got some business to take care of. Follow me."

Eddie didn't bother checking to see if Mouse was behind him. The little weasel would sooner cut off his own balls than disobey one of Hank's orders.

Angela was just leaving the office when Eddie marched up to her and pushed her back inside. As soon as Mouse joined them, he shut and locked the door.

"You really are crazy, aren't you?" She sounded indignant but not scared.

That was going to change.

"Shut your mouth, bitch." Eddie pulled out the snub-nosed revolver Hank always carried when moving money. It was a tiny thing, meant for an ankle holster or a ladies purse, but it would still do some damage in close quarters. Behind him, Mouse let out a gasp. Eddie knew why. No one, not even Ned's little brother, could possibly be stupid enough to threaten the club president's old lady. It was an automatic death sentence.

Angela's eyes went wide, and she backed away.

"Hank...." Mouse said, the closest he could come to objecting.

"They've been holding out on us." Eddie waved the gun at the cabinet. "Stealin' money right from under our noses. Right, Angie?"

"Ned is gonna kick your ass," she responded, some of her normal arrogance returning. "Put that down and walk out of here, and maybe that's all he'll do."

She ain't lying. Hank will be lucky to get off with just a beating. It doesn't matter, though. Him and all those fucknuts are gonna have bigger things to worry about than Ned Fucking Bowman.

He wished he could visit Ned in person. But that would have to wait. He still wasn't strong enough to leave Hell Creek. So if he couldn't get to Ned in person, he could at least send him a message.

One that couldn't be ignored.

"Fuck him. He can lick my nut sack." It was the same expression Ned had uttered when the lawyers called Eddie to the stand, and Eddie wanted to see if it rang a bell with Angela.

It did. Her eyes narrowed and she started to say something, but just then Mouse interrupted.

"Hey, man, what the fuck? This is insane."

"You ain't seen nothin' yet," Eddie said, as he turned on the old portable radio Angela kept on her desk and dialed around until he located the raucous thunder of AC/DC's 'Highway to Hell.' Humming along, he gestured for Mouse to move next to Angela.

"All right, now let's get this party started." With his free hand, Eddie pulled a fat joint from Hank's vest pocket and lit it up. After inhaling the harsh smoke, he handed the joint to Mouse.

"Take a hit, man, it's good fuckin' shit."

Although he still had a nervous look, Mouse did as he was told and drew in a lungful of smoke.

"Pass it on," Eddie told him, pointing at Angela, who shook her head.

"Screw you." She crossed her arms and ignored the joint.

Eddie leaned over the desk and poked her in the chest with the barrel of the gun. "Smoke it, or you're gonna spend the next hour looking for your nip."

Angela's eyes narrowed, and Eddie had to hold in his laughter as she took the joint and inhaled. He was careful not to take his eyes off her. She wasn't a small girl, and her furious expression told him she was liable to throw caution to the wind and attack him if he gave her half a chance.

The joint went around their tiny, forced circle three more times, and Eddie felt the pot beginning to work its magic on his brain. Had it been his own body, he'd have been totally wasted; it'd been over a year since the last time he smoked, and even before then he'd never been a heavy partier like some of the others. He couldn't afford to be, not with all his responsibilities. But Hank's body was so used to being fucked up that he probably felt weird when he *wasn't* stoned.

Mouse and Angela weren't handling it as well. Mouse's eyes were glassy and Angela was having trouble standing straight.

Oh, yeah. Now the fun really starts.

"Okay," Eddie said, tossing the roach to the floor. "Here's what we're gonna do. Angela, go get the money."

"What? What money?"

"Don't play games. The money you assholes have been hiding from us."

"Screw you, asshole." Angela's eyes narrowed, letting Eddie know he'd guessed right. Ned had his hand deep in the till.

"Wrong answer."

Eddie fired a shot into the wall next. Angela jumped. Mouse let out a girly shriek and then tried to pretend he hadn't. The sound of the report was nearly drowned out by the radio.

"Do it, or the next one goes in your leg." Eddie gave her his best sneer. He hoped that on Hank's face it looked as nasty as it felt.

It must have, because Angela slowly went to the filing cabinet, took a key from her pocket and opened the top drawer.

Her eyes locked on Hank the entire time, she removed the envelopes and tossed them on the desk.

"Keep going." Eddie motioned with the gun.

"That's everything." Her voice trembled as she said it.

"Next drawer. The one with the money you and Ned skim from the takes. Or should I tell Ned how you're pocketing a grand every week from his share?"

Her lips tightened until they almost disappeared. Mouse's eyes darted from Hank to Angela and back, a trapped animal desperately trying to find a way to escape.

The second drawer produced more than forty additional envelopes. He made her open the other two, but they only contained business files.

"Okay. Open them all and dump the money on the floor. Mouse, help her."

Angela frowned, his request not what she'd been expecting. She emptied the envelopes out, packets of wrapped bills creating a pile in front of the cabinet. Eddie found himself gritting his teeth as he watched.

"All right. Now the notebook. You know the one I mean." Eddie motioned the gun at the desk.

"Go fuck yourself." Angela crossed her arms over her chest. "I won't—"

Eddie pulled the trigger again. This time the shot went right into the metal cabinet, leaving a quarter-sized hole in the top drawer. Angela's eyes went wide and the color drained from her face. Her hands shook as she opened the drawer and removed the spiral book notebook. Seeing that made Eddie laugh.

"Sit. On the floor." This time she did as he asked without question, positioning herself on the pile of money. "Good girl," he said, and was rewarded with another killing glare.

"You, too, Rat-boy." Eddie had to say it twice before Mouse realized he was being spoken to. The reference went right over his drug-addled head, but Angela caught it.

There'd only been one person who called Mouse Bates 'Rat-boy' and that was Eddie Ryder. He'd come up with the nickname after Mouse had spilled the beans to Ned one night how Eddie, in a drunken stupor, had let it slip that he'd had a dream about banging Angela.

That slip had earned Eddie, despite his good standing as an enforcer in the Hell Riders, two sucker punches to the stomach while everyone, including Angela and Kristy, had cheered Hank on, and three weeks spent cleaning Ned and Hank's bikes at the clubhouse.

After that, Mouse had always been Rat-boy to Eddie, and although the other riders had laughed when he said it, none of them had ever actually used the term.

"But I don't—"

Eddie aimed the gun at Mouse's head. "Sit your ass down, or I swear to fuckin' God you'll get carted out of here in a body bag."

Mouse quickly dropped to the floor and joined Angela, making sure not to touch her.

Eddie took the notebook and dropped it in Angela's lap.

"Hold it up for the camera and smile." With his free hand, Eddie took Angela's cell phone off the desk and snapped several pictures of them. Then he scrolled through until he found a text from Ned. Prisoners weren't supposed to have access to phones, but money worked just as well behind bars as on the outside, so it couldn't have been hard for Angela to arrange one for him.

Three quick clicks and the pictures were sent.

"Damn. Ned's gonna flip when he sees those." Eddie stuck the phone in his pocket. "Too bad you won't be around for it."

Mouse groaned and shook his head. "You're gonna kill us, aren't you?"

Angela grimaced, and a tear ran down one cheek. Eddie smiled. *Not so high and mighty now, are you, bitch?*

Eddie smiled. "Hell, no. I need you alive. So when the police come and arrest Angie here for money laundering and tax fraud, you can tell them Hank is running the show now. This whole fucking town belongs to me, not Neddie."

"You're committing suicide, you know." Angela's voice held no emotion, as if she was already resigned to her own fate.

Eddie shrugged. "I don't care."

"You'll care when you end up in pieces and fed to the gators."

"Let him try. He already screwed it up once. Turns out I'm pretty hard to kill."

A strange look came over Angela's face and Eddie wondered if she was fitting the pieces together or just confused. Either way, it was time to finish things in the laundromat and move on. He stuffed as much money into Hank's pockets as he could fit, used a roll of duct tape to bind and gag his two captives, and then left them in the office with the music still blaring.

On his way out, he dialed 911 on Angela's phone. "Hello, police? I want to report a crime. Angela Barnes and Rat-boy Bates are in the laundromat on Main Street with a shit-ton of stolen money. You're welcome."

He let some energy trickle through is fingers. The screen shattered and he dropped the smoking phone to the ground. He was tempted to go back inside and put a bullet in each of them, a little murder-suicide to drive Jonesy-boy crazy, but he decided against it.

After all, the fun was just starting.

The killing would come later.

CHAPTER TWENTY-FOUR

Still occupying Hank Bowman's body, Eddie entered Rosie's Diner and took the last empty seat at the counter, right between Clyde Holmes, town doctor and father to Officer Chet Holmes, and Officer Delbert Beauchamps. Hank's basketball-shaped belly rumbled like an idling engine as Eddie breathed in the hot, greasy odors of hamburgers, French fries, meatloaf, fried catfish, and his own personal favorite, gator nuggets.

Damn. When was the last time Hank ate something?

Guess what, Hanky-boy? I think it's time to spend a little of that money we took.

"What'll you have?" asked Jenny Gunderson. Her husband taught science at the high school. Eddie'd always hated him, ever since the time he'd caught Eddie and Sandra making out in the stairwell and gotten them suspended for a week. But as much as he disliked Todd Gunderson, there was no way to hate Jenny. She was possibly the sweetest person in all of Hell Creek, a major reason why Rosie gave her all the best shifts at the diner. It didn't hurt that her looks matched her personality. Not content with making her the nicest person in town, God had blessed her with a face made for television. Maybe not movie-star beautiful, but definitely TV commercial cute. Her pale skin was more suited to sitting under shady trees than frolicking in the surf, but it matched perfectly with her bright blue eyes and fiery red hair.

"I'm feeling mighty hungry, Jen. Gimme two orders of gator nuggets, an order of fries, and a chocolate-peanut butter shake."

"Sure thing." Jenny turned away, and Eddie belatedly remembered that he was Hank to everyone, which explained why Jenny hadn't given him one of her sunny smiles, and why he was currently getting the stink eye from Delbert.

"You're in a pretty fine mood, Hank," Delbert said. His tone indicated he was nosing for information, not making conversation.

Eddie knew why, too. Hank Bowman in a good mood usually meant trouble for someone else. That, or he'd already pulled off some kind of crime or stupid stunt and he knew the police wouldn't be able to pin it on him.

Like when they burned me alive in my own garage. Where were you then, asshole? Probably sound asleep behind the wheel, like always.

The familiar rage burbled up like swamp gas, and Eddie swallowed it down before it could escape. "Yep. Hard not to be in a good mood on a beautiful day like this."

"Ain't that the truth," Clyde Holmes chimed in. "Day like this makes you glad to be alive."

"Yeah?" Eddie paused as Jenny put his milkshake down. "I wouldn't know."

Holmes's bushy eyebrows dipped down as he frowned. "Huh?"

"Never mind." Eddie dunked a gator nugget into some ketchup and popped it into his mouth.

Oh, man! I forgot how good these taste!

In fact, he'd forgotten how good it was to eat anything. Or maybe it was just experiencing the food through someone else. The chunks of cornmeal-battered gator tail were perfectly salty and sweet; the fries were nice and crispy, with a flavor that could only come from old, reused grease. The milkshake was extra thick, so thick it was almost like eating a scoop of vanilla ice cream. And cold! His first sip sent spears of pain across his temples.

How about that. Even an empty-headed shit like Hank Bowman can get a brain freeze from a milkshake.

Eddie had worked his way through three quarters of his supper when he noticed that the diner had grown quiet. He looked up and found everyone staring at him.

"What?" he asked, through a mouthful of fries.

"Ain't never seen anyone attack their food like that," said Clyde. "You're actin' like you ain't eaten in a week."

"Must've been some good shit, give you the munchies like that," added Delbert, favoring him with a disgusted scowl. The half Cajun, half Native American officer had a well-known dislike for illegal drugs of any kind, thanks to his younger brother OD-ing on some bad heroin a few years back. Heroin that Hank and Ned brought into town, although no one could ever prove it.

"Ain't stoned," Eddie said, and then remembered that he actually was. He'd smoked that joint with Mouse and Angela. And who knew what Hank had been doing before Eddie took him over. Hell, people could probably smell him a mile away.

"Yeah, and we all voted Democrat." Someone laughed at Clyde's comment, and the doctor went back to his double cheeseburger.

Screw this.

Eddie finished his shake and dropped two twenties on the counter. "Keep the change, Jen," he told her. Her eyes went wide as she picked up the money.

Guess Hank Bowman's not normally much of a tipper.

Well, tonight he will be.

Eddie spent the next two hours separating Hank from his money. He left ten dollars for a bottle of soda and a pack of smokes. And *goddamn!* but didn't that first cigarette since he'd died taste awesome. He left two thousand dollars in the mailbox for Carson, with a note saying 'in case of emergency.' Then he went to the Saloon, laid the rest of the cash on the bar, and told the bartender to keep buying rounds for everyone until the money ran out.

At around nine p.m., after more shots of tequila than he could count, he decided he'd had enough fun with Hank, marched him into the men's room, and made him piss all over his own pants.

Then he left him passed out and soaking wet between two urinals.

★   ★   ★

The moment Eddie departed Hank's body, all the effects of the alcohol and drugs disappeared, leaving him clearheaded and positively bursting at the seams with supernatural energy.

May the motherfucking Force be with me!

Hovering over the town, he wondered what to do next. He was too charged up to sleep – or whatever his psychic form did when he rested – but he wanted to give the town a chance to spread the word about the crazy shit he'd done all day before he started in on the gang again.

I should check in on Carson and Mom.

Riding Diablo across town, he tried to tell himself he just wanted to make sure his mother was still okay and that his brother hadn't suffered any side effects from his temporary possession. But deep down, he knew there was another reason.

Temptation.

Images and memories kept appearing in his head. Holding his mother's hand. The taste of peanut butter, sweet and salty on his tongue.

Kellie Jones' lips pressed against his in a velvet kiss, her mouth tasting of ice cream and candy.

But I've never even kissed her.

It felt like he had, though. The sensation of it kept coming back to him. Which didn't make sense. He'd always been attracted to older girls, not younger. Girls who liked to get down and dirty, who had attitude. Not sweet, innocent things like Kellie Jones. Were Carson's feelings for her lingering with him, affecting him somehow? Or was it the idea of forbidden fruit, reliving his first time all over again? He'd had his cherry popped at fourteen, two years younger than Carson was now. Best night of his life. Claire Pawling, who'd been three years older than him. A gift from Ned Bowman, for pledging with the Hell Riders.

Either way, you've got to put it out of your mind. She's Carson's girl, and he deserves to experience that prize on his own. And you promised yourself no possessing Carson unless it's an emergency.

At the trailer, he found Carson and Kellie in Carson's room, both of them focused intently on the computer screen.

If that was me, I'd have her on the bed. Why're they wasting time on the computer?

Eddie glided into the room and moved behind them so he could see over their shoulders.

If he'd had a heart, it would have stopped the moment he read the first line.

Signs of possession.

*   *   *

"I give up." Carson leaned back in his seat, stretched his neck back and forth, and then shivered as a momentary wave of cool air caused the hairs on his arms to stand up. He made a mental note to turn down the air conditioner later, so his mother wouldn't get a chill.

"All these sites are about demons. There's nothing about ghosts."

Kellie took a sip of soda and looked at him, her head tilted slightly, which Carson had already learned meant she was thinking hard about something.

"Well, assuming you're right and it's Eddie who's been possessing you, what makes you so sure he's a ghost and not a demon?"

"What?"

"Let's think about this. Maybe Eddie didn't come back as a ghost. Maybe he, you know, went to hell and now he's come back for revenge."

"He's not a demon. He can't be a demon."

"Why not? If you can believe in ghosts, why can't you believe in demons?"

"Because he's my brother!" Carson got up and walked across the room. He felt like kicking something, throwing something, but he held back, afraid Kellie might get scared off by a temper tantrum. He was lucky she'd even stuck around at all, after he'd told her his theory about possession.

"So it's okay for him to come back as a nasty ghost, but not a demon?" Kellie raised one eyebrow, and he realized how stupid his argument sounded.

"It's not just that," he said, his embarrassment calming him enough so he could think again, try to be logical. "Demons are… evil, you know? So far, Eddie's been…good. Not nice, but good."

"You mean when he's inside you."

They'd already discussed the possibility that Eddie might have possessed other people, which would explain the strange way some of the Hell Riders had been acting.

"Yeah. I mean, all he's done is give my mom dinner and save us from losing our insurance money. I don't think a demon would do that."

Kellie's expression turned grim. "If you're right, though, he's also hurt and killed several people."

Carson shook his head. "But maybe that's not being evil. If those are the people who killed him, he might just be after them, and then he'll, I don't know, be at peace. Move on. You know, like in that movie *The Crow.*"

"This isn't a movie. You don't know what he's thinking."

He nodded.

"Then we'll just have to find out."

★　★　★

Eddie was about to take control of his brother again, make him tell Kellie he'd changed his mind, that the whole idea of possession was stupid, when their mother called for Carson.

"We'll talk more in school tomorrow," Kellie said, and then gave Carson a quick kiss and left the house.

As Carson went to see what his mom wanted, Eddie found himself getting angry at his brother.

The stupid shit has a hot piece of ass who obviously wants him, and he doesn't do a damn thing except sit around the stupid computer. If I was him, I'd have her legs up over my shoulders and....

Eddie's internal rage, which had been dampened after his escapades during the day, returned to life and he had to fight the urge to enter his brother, follow Kellie outside, and have his way with her right on the side of the road. Break her in good and hard.

No! That's Carson you're talking about, not some gang-banger.

Eddie held back a scream that he knew would shatter all the windows in the trailer. What was happening to him? He'd been pissed off plenty of times when he was alive, but he'd never, *ever* thought about hurting anyone in his family.

Something's changing inside me. Ever since what happened with Jethro, I—

No. Before that. From the moment I came back, I've been different. Not just stronger. Meaner. I'm always angry. Worse than when I was alive, like the hate is fueling me, making me do these things.

That made him pause.

Am I a monster? Did I really come back as a demon, like Kellie said? Or am I using my powers as an excuse? Was this evil inside me all along, just waiting to come out?

Thinking about it made his head hurt, so he decided to stop. He pushed up and out of the trailer, found Diablo waiting for him. With a roar of thunder that shook the whole neighborhood, he sent Diablo racing toward the swamps while heavy metal music blasted from imaginary speakers. It was time to pay the clubhouse a visit. He felt the need to drink, fuck, and fight.

And not necessarily in that order.

★   ★   ★

Halfway to the kitchen to get his mother a cup of tea, Carson paused. Thunder rumbled outside, but that wasn't the sound that had caught his attention.

For one brief second, he'd been sure he'd heard someone playing "Hellrider" by Demon Dogs.

Eddie's favorite song.

Feeling more than a little chilled all of a sudden, he poured a second cup for himself.

And wished his shivers were just from the air conditioning.

CHAPTER TWENTY-FIVE

On most nights, the Hell Riders' clubhouse was party central for many of the local scumbags and losers. However, when Eddie passed through the newly boarded-over front window, the crowd had a different vibe, with fewer strangers and hangers-on. And it was smaller, too. Conspicuously absent were Hank Bowman and Mouse Bates. Eddie assumed Hank was still home recovering from the abuse his body had taken, and that Mouse was cowering in a hole somewhere, afraid to face Hank after what had happened with Angela. Or maybe in jail. That left Duck Miller and Gary Rock as the only two full patch members of the Hell Riders in attendance.

How many of these assholes were there that night? Just the members, or did Hank bring the prospects, too? Make them get a good look at what happens if you turn your back on your brothers. Maybe it was a big goddamn party, all of them laughing their asses off while I screamed for help.

And not a goddamned one of them ever said a word to the cops.

I should burn the whole place to the fucking ground. Eye for a fucking eye. But not tonight. Tonight I send a message to Hank and every last person in Hell Creek who ever thought it funny to shit on Eddie Ryder.

So who should I kill?

Eddie looked back and forth between them.

Eenie, meenie, miney, moe....

At that moment, a tall blonde with giant eighties-style hair and a tight t-shirt stretched over bra-less tits walked by him. Eddie recognized her right away. Lisa Marie Henderson. She'd been hanging around the club since before Eddie joined, and she'd slept with just about everyone, even Mouse.

But not me. Told me I was too young. That I should come back and see her when I grew some hair on my balls. Then, after he'd hooked up with Sandy, she'd come sniffing around, trying to add him to her list. The memory of her rejection still burning inside him, he'd told her to fuck off. They hadn't spoken since.

The last time he'd seen her had been in the court house. *Sitting in the courtroom with the rest of the hangers-on and cycle sluts who showed up at every party. Cheering Ned on when the guards brought him in. She'd have been more than happy to watch me burn.*

Guess what? Payback's a bitch, Lisa.

He entered her body just as she opened the door to the bathroom. She stumbled for a moment but no one paid any attention. In a room filled with drunks and stoners, she could've fallen on her face and no one would have noticed.

Eddie took a moment to find his balance. Being in a girl was something new. His feet felt too small and the weight of his chest too heavy, all of which threatened to make him tilt forward.

His new body took a breath and he coughed a little as the stink of the clubhouse slapped his face like a piss-soaked towel. It was a wet, greasy smell, composed of pot, cigarettes, booze, fast food, sex, and body odor. In the old days he'd have felt right at home, but either he'd outgrown his *Animal House* phase or his new host wasn't a fan of *eau de pig sty*. Whatever the reason, the barnyard stink had him feeling nauseous. And the intense pressure in his bladder wasn't helping.

Sorry, babe. Gotta hold it in a little longer.

He did an about face and walked back into the main room. About two dozen people were scattered around, slumped on the couches, shooting pool, or just standing by the bar. Plenty of laughter and good-natured conversation filled the spaces between the clouds of smoke, but Eddie sensed something was off. Behind the laughs, behind the glassy eyes, there was a hint of unease, a tinge of fear.

People are spooked, and it's because of me.

The idea of it made him smile.

He aimed Lisa at Gary Rock, who stood by the bar, a whiskey in one hand and a joint in the other. Ignoring more than a few whistles and ass-grabs – he had to keep reminding himself he was in a girl's body – he made his way across the room, walking carefully so he didn't over-balance himself.

"Hey, there." It sounded stupid coming out, and Eddie realized he had no idea how to act like a girl. It felt really weird to be coming on to another guy. At the same time, though, his female body started to react on its own, sending tingling waves of pleasure up through his groin and across his chest.

Is this how girls feel when they're horny?

Gary smiled and Eddie knew right away that it didn't matter how stupid he sounded, he already had the biker hooked and ready to land.

"Hey, yourself. Want a hit?"

Eddie took the offered joint and drew in a deep lungful of smoke. Unlike when he'd been in Hank's body, the pot hit him right away, started his brain dancing in circles. He handed the joint back and blew the smoke out in a long, slow stream. Then he leaned forward and let Lisa's breasts rub against Gary's arm. At the same time, his hand dipped down to Gary's back pocket. Sure enough, he felt the outline of the folding knife Gary always carried, an over-sized blade with a silver skull emblem on the handle. A gift from his grandfather, who'd taken it off a dead German soldier during World War II.

"How about you and me have a little fun?"

Gary downed his shot and took her hand. "Sure thing. I got a room in the back that's just waiting for us."

"Uh, uh." Eddie shook his head. "I'm talking right here." He went to his knees and opened the biker's filthy, grease-stained jeans, pulled them and his equally stained underwear down to the floor. Gary's cock, a short, fat sausage sitting in a thick bird's nest of hair, had already grown semi-hard, peeking out like a shy animal. Fighting against his natural instinct to avoid another man's dick, Eddie put Lisa's face closer to it and then gagged as he caught a nasty whiff of piss and something that smelled of spoiled cheese. A trickle of acidic puke actually rose up, searing his throat, before he forced it down.

Christ, was I the only one who ever fucking showered?

Eddie closed his eyes and slid his mouth over the fleshy tube, which tasted even worse than it smelled, a mix of rancid milk and ass. Overhead, Gary moaned and grabbed the blonde's hair with both hands.

"That's it, baby. Suck that cock."

Telling himself it would all be worth it, Eddie slipped the knife from Gary's pocket. In one swift motion, he flicked the blade open and jammed it into the thick flesh where Gary's cock met his balls. Hot, metallic-tasting liquid flooded his mouth and he started to choke. Gary let out a horrible scream as Eddie continued sawing at his dick with the knife. He tore at Eddie's hair and punched his back, but Eddie hung on like a pit bull, clamping his teeth down hard and whipping his head back and forth while he hacked away.

Gary shouted again and his penis came free, blood splattering in all directions. Eddie rocked back and then his stomach let loose a stream of beer, vodka, and pizza right into the gory hole that was Gary's crotch.

"Aaaah! You bitch!" Gary slapped Eddie's head, sending him sideways onto the floor, where he ended up eye to eye with Gary's deflated dick. "Help! Oh, goddamn! She bit my fuckin' cock off!"

Eddie rolled away from the penis and got to his feet, spitting blood and skin and hair and puke onto the floor. At the same time, Gary's face went pale, pain and blood loss already taking their toll. He collapsed to his knees, his hands pressed tight over his crotch in a vain attempt to stem the red tide running down his legs. A girl screamed for someone to call 911, but everyone else just stared in shock while Gary's life drained out from between his fingers.

His head ringing from the blow he'd taken, Eddie walked up to Gary and kicked him in the face, realizing too late that Lisa was wearing flip-flops. Three of her toes broke when they connected with Gary's cheekbone. Eddie ignored the pain and kicked him again.

Gary reached for her leg, bloody tears running down his cheeks. "I'll kill you, bitch," he whispered.

"Sorry, asshole. You had your chance." Eddie grabbed an empty bottle of Old Granddad off the bar and swung it as hard as he could. It shattered against Gary's mouth and nose, leaving just the neck in Eddie's hand. Glass and broken teeth tumbled across the floor like miniature dice. Eddie took the jagged shard and jammed it into Gary's throat, twisting it back and forth until a new stream of blood burst free.

Standing up, Eddie turned to the stunned crowd. "Now, this is what I call a party! Drinks are on Gary!"

For a moment no one moved. Then one of the prospects, a burly, long-haired ex-con named Frankie Scott, let out a roar. Eddie recognized him right away; he'd done three years for raping a woman in Homestead. Frankie dropped his beer and charged Eddie, who exited Lisa's body right before Frankie's massive fist connected with her face.

How's it feel to be on the other end of the pole, Frankie?

Eddie transferred himself to another woman, grabbed a pool cue, and ran forward, holding the stick out like a spear. With a burst of supernatural energy charging the woman's muscles, he rammed the cue into Frankie's ass so hard it ripped through his jeans and speared his intestines. Frankie fell to the side, his shrieks of pain louder than the music.

Two leather-clad wannabes tackled Eddie, who spread his arms and released a bolt of lightning that knocked the unlucky bikers to the floor and blew out the lights. Chaos erupted in the clubhouse, people punching and kicking blindly at anyone near them. A few of the partygoers ran for the exit. Eddie let them go. They'd spread the word about what happened, which would put the rest of the town even more on edge.

From thirty feet over the clubhouse, Eddie admired the mayhem he'd caused. Fuck the Hell Riders and anyone associated with them. They could all die for all he cared. In fact, they should. Every last one of them.

The only question was, how to top a night like this?

He didn't have the answer to that, not yet, but as he roared away into the heavens, he knew one thing for sure.

He looked forward to trying.

CHAPTER TWENTY-SIX

The following afternoon, Johnny Ray Jones sat at his desk and wondered how much worse things could possibly get. After attending the funeral for Sandy Powell – a somber affair attended by what seemed like half the town, most of them there because Sandy's father held a lot of influence – he'd returned to his office and spent much of the day reading crime reports from the previous night and shaking his head.

It seemed like the whole damn town had gone insane. Three murders at the Hell Riders' clubhouse, including Gary Rock getting his dick cut off. It made Johnny Ray shudder every time he thought about it. And the crazy didn't stop there.

Hank Bowman had flipped out again. He'd apparently robbed the laundromat, at least according to Angela Mason, who was now in jail for a whole list of crimes, starting with money laundering. Then he'd gotten wasted and passed out. When he woke up, he claimed to have no memory of the past six hours. With Harley Atkins' suicide by cop still fresh in his mind, Johnny Ray had opted to have Hank sent to the hospital for blood tests and a psychiatric workup.

If he passes that test, I know there's something wrong with the medical system. Johnny Ray sipped at his iced coffee and then rubbed the frigid cup against his forehead. *Bowman's nuttier than a pecan farm. But the damn hospital will probably say it was a drug overdose and the bastard will get state aid, because addiction is an illness.*

The one big surprise was that Hank hadn't been involved in the crazy shit at the Hell Riders' clubhouse. Of course, they'd done well enough without him. Even now, re-reading papers stained by condensation from where he'd accidentally set his sweating cup down on them, he couldn't believe it had actually happened. Not in his town.

Hoping to make sense of things, he reviewed the facts about the clubhouse murders yet again. He wanted to have something – *anything* – to tell the mayor when they met the following morning.

Lisa Marie Henderson, a party girl with priors for DWI, drunk and disorderly, and solicitation, had killed Gary Rock with a whiskey bottle. Right in front of twenty-something witnesses, several of whom had then beaten her to death. During the resulting brawl, one Frankie Scott, a lowlife scum bag in his own right and kissing cousin to the Bowmans, had gotten himself corn-holed with a pool cue. He'd died on the way to the hospital from internal bleeding. At least ten other shitbags treated for injuries ranging from bruises to knife wounds.

All this on top of Butch Franks' death and the whole Harley Atkins fiasco. How he was going to explain that one to the mayor was still a mystery. All the witnesses in the world saying the biker had a gun wasn't going to make up for Atkins's father being a golfing buddy of the mayor. Not to mention he'd have to account for how Atkins got the gun in the first place.

Damn, I'll be here all day and night going through the statements we got. And it'll be a couple of days before all the blood tests come back.

He decided to take a ride through town to clear his head, patrol a little and remind everyone he was keeping an eye on things. Especially now, with all the craziness happening the last few days, it was important for the people of Hell Creek to know the police weren't hiding with their heads in the sand. As he drove down Main Street, he saw Kellie walking hand in hand with Carson Ryder.

I guess those two are an item now.

Had it happened a week earlier, or even two days earlier, Johnny Ray probably would have been happy – as happy as a father could be, anyway, seeing his sixteen–year–old daughter out with a boyfriend. But Carson's violent outburst the day before had unnerved him. It was more like something Little Eddie would have done. And that had Johnny Ray wondering if maybe Carson didn't have a dose of Big Eddie in him, too, just waiting to come out. After all, he and Eddie both shared the same piece of garbage for a father, and Eddie had inherited plenty of the old man's bad attitude.

Telling himself he wasn't being an over-protective dad,

Johnny Ray swung his SUV over to the curb and rolled down the window, letting in a blast of sauna-like afternoon air redolent with the weighty odors of swamp and hot blacktop.

"Hey, where you two headed?"

On the sidewalk, Kellie and Carson stopped walking and turned his way. Johnny Ray pretended he didn't notice the strange expressions that came and went on their faces, too fast for him to get a real read, before they both smiled at him. Guilt? Embarrassment? The second one would make more sense; after all, teens were notorious for dreading public conversations with their parents, especially if said parent also happened to be the Chief of Police. But guilt was also a strong possibility, although a less comforting one. Who knew how long they'd been dating? Or what they'd been up to.

They're in high school now. Maybe they were headed to some secret place to fool around. Or on their way back from one. These days, did that mean necking? Copping a feel? A blowjob or quick fuck in Carson's bedroom while Sally slept on, unawares?

Who are you to talk? his conscience asked him. *If Sally Ryder weren't sick, you'd be over there right now trying to get her pants off.*

That was different, though. He wasn't in high school, although he'd wanted her just as badly back then, too. If it wasn't for that scumbag Big Eddie....

Johnny Ray slammed the lid down on his inner argument and returned his attention to the kids, who were approaching the car.

"We're going to Carson's, to, um, study," Kellie said, her lie as obvious in her speech as in the way her eyes couldn't meet his.

Not to mention neither of them carried books. You didn't need the observational skills of a cop to know the two of them had something else in mind. However, in deference to his daughter's feelings, he didn't force the subject. A little something he'd picked up from Oprah. She called it giving the kids room to spread their wings. He called it giving them rope to hang themselves. Either way, he felt both proud and irritated for not giving in to his desire to interrogate them.

"Need a lift?"

"No, that's okay. We're gonna grab a soda first. See you later." Kellie gave Johnny Ray a look that nearly broke his heart, because it reminded him too much of the expression his ex-wife would make when he would dote on her too much if she didn't feel well.

"All right, have fun."

"Thanks, Dad."

"Bye, Mr. Jones." Carson lifted his hand in a friendly wave.

Johnny Ray watched them walk down the sidewalk toward Rosie's Diner. Carson seemed the polite, pleasant boy he'd always been, with no sign of anger or rebellion. *Maybe I should cut him some slack. What with his brother dying, his mother getting out of the hospital, and him having to take care of Sally all by himself. Hell, it's a wonder he didn't snap sooner.*

Johnny Ray made a mental note to stop by Sally's place more often, help out more. Take some of the load off Carson's shoulders. If the boy was going to be dating his daughter, the last thing he needed was Carson being so on edge he flew off the handle at the slightest thing.

★   ★   ★

Carson waited until they were well down the street from Kellie's father before bringing up the real reason they'd met after school. "So, we're agreed that speaking to Mr. Gunderson is a good idea?"

During lunch, they'd discussed who would be the best adult to help them. Kellie had suggested Reverend Talbot at the First Gospel Church, because who would know more about demons and possession than a reverend? But Carson had reminded her that Talbot also was notoriously cranky when it came to dealing with kids. Instead, he'd proposed they talk to their science teacher, Todd Gunderson.

"He's friendly, and he doesn't laugh when you say something stupid in class. He might actually listen to us."

"But what's a science teacher know about possession?" Kellie had asked.

Carson had shrugged. "Probably nothing. But maybe he can give us a better explanation than a ghost for what's been happening."

Although he was willing to entertain the idea of a non-supernatural explanation, more and more Carson was becoming convinced Eddie's ghost had to be behind all the crazy things happening in town. The broken windows, the murders, the weird thunder at all times of the day and night.

Ellie had remained doubtful, until the money showed up in Carson's mailbox the previous evening. Nearly two thousand dollars in an unmarked envelope, with a note that read "In case of emergency." Carson had hidden the money in Eddie's closet. He tried to match the handwriting to Eddie's but they couldn't be sure.

The first thing she'd said to him when he got to school was, "Hank Bowman robbed the laundromat yesterday."

That's when they decided to talk to someone. No way Hank, or any of the Hell Riders, would give money to the Ryders.

With the decision made, they decided to wait until after school to speak with Mr. Gunderson. They knew he always stopped by Rosie's Diner on his way home from the school to say hi to his wife, Jenny. Their plan was to meet him there and ask him some questions, the idea being that doing it outside of school would give them more privacy.

However, as soon as they entered Rosie's, their strategy backfired. Three of Kellie's friends sat at the counter. Melanie Parris, Cindy Kolb, and Annette Chadway. He knew them all from school, but none of them had ever spoken to him. They were alternating between looking at their phones, talking, and nibbling on orders of French fries and gator nuggets, a Rosie's special that Carson found especially repulsive. Even worse than peanut butter. Whenever Eddie had brought them home, Carson had to leave the room because just the smell of them made him want to puke.

As they'd expected, Todd Gunderson stood down at the far end of the counter, chatting with Jenny. In order to reach him, though, they'd have to go past all their classmates.

"What do we do?" Kellie asked.

"You go ahead and talk to them," Carson said. "I'll ask Mr. Gunderson if I can speak with him outside. You can meet us out there."

"Okay."

Carson took two steps and his world went black.

★   ★   ★

Kellie paused as Carson stumbled. She was about to ask him if he was okay, but her friend Melanie Parris chose that moment to look over at them. "Kellie! Come sit. We just got milkshakes."

"What the heck." Carson smiled. "We have time. Gunderson's not going anywhere for a while. Besides, I'm hungry as hell." He motioned at the teacher, who was two bites into a big piece of key lime pie. Kellie frowned, but followed Carson to where the girls were sitting.

"Are those gator nuggets?" Carson asked. He reached over Melanie's shoulder and snagged two of the fried treats.

"Hey!" Melanie glared at him. "Rude much?"

"Sorry," Carson said, sounding anything but. He took a twenty-dollar bill from his pocket and put it on the counter. "I'll get the next order. Make it two. Hell, make it the whole 'gator."

"What's the deal, Kellie?" The three girls eyed Carson like he'd just crawled from a sewer. Kellie had hoped things would go smoother the first time they hung out together with her friends, but it was obvious he'd already made a bad impression.

"Carson and I were just grabbing a soda before heading to his house to do our homework." She hoped the girls would get the hint that she and Carson were together and hold back any sarcastic comments.

"No hurry, though," Carson said around a mouthful of fries. "We can shoot the shit for a while. So, who besides me thinks Kellie is hot?"

Melanie's eyes went wide and the other two girls gave nervous giggles. Kellie's face grew warm. She opened her mouth to say something, but no words came out. Was Carson trying to be funny? If so, he was doing a bad job of it.

Does he really think I'm hot?

"C'mon," Carson continued, as if unaware of their reaction to his statement. "You girls always talk about this kind of stuff. Who's popular. Who's pretty. Who's dating who. I mean, I'm a lucky guy, right? Any boy in school would love to get this one alone in a room for a couple of hours." He put his hand on Kellie's waist as he spoke and pulled her close.

Kellie found herself pulling away from him. "I think we should go now," she said, putting as much ice into her voice as she could. Whatever had gotten in to him, they could talk about it later, when Carson was....

Acting like himself again?

Oh, God, it's happening. And at the worst time.

It no longer mattered if he was possessed or just suffering from some kind of mental breakdown. She had to get him outside and away from everyone until he returned to normal.

"Carson, we need to go." She grabbed his hand and tugged.

He wiped his fingers on his shirt and nodded. "Okay." Then he stepped away and stared down the aisle. "Hey, Mr. Gunderson!"

Heads turned toward him at his shout, including Gunderson's. Kellie pulled harder at his hand.

"Eddie says fuck you!" Carson flipped up his middle finger and then let Kellie drag him away. She heard her friends laughing as she led Carson to the door. In any other instance, she'd have been mortified, knowing that in minutes the whole episode would be all over social media and rumors would be flying.

Carson Ryder took a swing at Mr. Gunderson!

Carson and Kellie are doing it!

As bad as all that was, Kellie knew they had bigger problems.

"Eddie says fuck you."

Carson was right! Eddie's ghost, or something, has come back and it's possessing him.

What do I do?

She paused on the sidewalk. There was no way she could bring him to the library. Not only would he make a scene, but then he'd know that *they* knew his secret. She desperately tried to think, while at the same time trying to act as if she wasn't terrified. She couldn't let Eddie's ghost know they were on to him. No telling what he'd do in that case.

Think!

Home. I have to get him home. Whenever he's been possessed like this, he's always passed out afterward. And how would I explain that if it happens in public?

"C'mon, Carson, let's go to your house. We can watch some TV. Besides, your mom is probably wondering where you are."

Carson's eyes lit up in a way she didn't like. It wasn't his usual innocent happy look, the look that told her he really liked her but was too afraid to say it. This was somehow oilier, creepier. She'd seen it before – not on Carson, but on a couple of other boys she'd dated, usually right before they tried to stick their hands down her pants.

The idea of being in a room alone with him suddenly frightened her but she couldn't see a way out of it, now that she'd suggested going to his house. Luckily, it was a long walk to the Ryder's trailer. Hopefully long enough for Eddie to get tired or bored and leave.

Do ghosts even get tired? Who knows why he comes and goes. For all we know, it could be—

Lost in thought, Kellie was caught by surprise when Carson pulled her into a narrow walkway between the hardware store and the empty building that used to be Arlo's Comics before Arlo Hindle found religion and moved to Miami.

"Carson! What are you—"

Carson slapped his hand over her mouth, cutting her off in mid-question. With his other arm he pinned her against the rough wooden wall of the store. Splinters pricked her skin and snagged her hair, and she cried out against his palm. His hand moved down until it was squeezing her left breast. There was no hesitation, no fumbling. It was a hand that knew just what to do, where to touch. An experienced hand.

Kellie's guts churned and burning acid crept up her throat as her stomach threatened to empty itself. Looking into Carson's eyes, she saw nothing but lust. There was no doubt he was going to have his way with her whether she liked it or not.

Something hard pressed against her leg, and she let out a moan before she could stop herself. Although still a virgin, she'd made out with boys before, even gone to second base with a couple of them, so she recognized an erection when she felt one.

Out of nowhere, something Melanie had once said came back to her. They'd been talking about virginity, and Melanie, who'd been dating Kevin Thatch for almost two months at the time, had shared her secret for keeping him out of her pants.

"The best way to avoid sex is to give him a BJ. Once he comes, all he'll want to do is eat and watch TV."

Melanie had demonstrated her technique, using her thumb (which she's said was about right for Kevin). And although Kellie had never even seen a penis except for in pictures on the internet, sticking one in her mouth had to be better than getting raped.

Hoping it wouldn't make Eddie's ghost angry, she forced herself down, sliding out of his grasp, her back scraping painfully down the wall, and went to her knees in front of him. The bulge in Carson's pants was right at eye level, and it looked a lot larger than a thumb. She started to cry, hating what was happening, hating herself for not screaming for help or just punching him in the balls. But that would only hurt Carson or get him in trouble, and none of this was Carson's fault.

Hands grabbed the back of her head and she closed her eyes, dreading the humiliation she was about to go through.

Except nothing happened.

Kellie opened her eyes just in time to see Carson stumble away and fall to the ground.

At the same time, thunder roared through the sky and a chorus of car alarms filled the air with their strident wailing.

CHAPTER TWENTY-SEVEN

Eddie wanted to throw up. Instead, he screamed and sent Diablo barreling through the heavens at full throttle. Down below, people stopped in their tracks and looked up as the ghost bike's violent percussions rocked Hell Creek over and over.

What the hell had he been thinking? How had he gotten so carried away? If the girl hadn't gone to her knees, started crying....

I'd have raped her right there.

What the fuck is happening to me?

It was the same question he kept finding himself asking. Something was wrong, that was for sure. He couldn't blame it on Carson's teenage hormones, couldn't blame it on residual effects from possessing Hank. Even his own anger, so strong it had brought him back from the fucking dead, didn't explain his overwhelming desire to tear Kellie Jones's clothes off and screw her like a three-dollar whore right there in the alley.

I'm changing.

He hated to believe it, but it had to be true. He was turning into someone else, *something* else, and he had no ability to stop it from happening.

Am I really a demon? An evil monster?

He'd thought that once he killed all the Hell Riders and avenged his death he'd be freed from his anger, able to move on to wherever spirits go.

But what if that wasn't the path Fate had in store for him? What if he was doomed to haunt Hell Creek forever, growing stronger and more dangerous every day?

Can't think like that. He eased back on Diablo's throttle and his thoughts slowed in time with the bike. *Gotta stick to the plan. I haven't killed them all, so maybe it's still possible I can finish this and leave Hell Creek forever. Leave this goddamned world forever. That has to be it. In the meantime, I'll just have to be more careful. Control this thing inside me. As long as I don't use Carson's body anymore, I'll be fine. Who cares what I do to anyone else?*

It was time to get back in the game.

Another Hell Rider had to die.

★ ★ ★

The first thing Carson noticed when he woke up was the sting of dirt and gravel grinding against his cheek.

"What…?"

"Lie still," a voice said. Kellie? *No, older. Who?*

He turned his head, saw Mrs. Powell, who ran the Cinema Royale with her husband. *The woman whose daughter Eddie had killed. What's going on?*

"Where am I? What happened?" As soon as he said the words, he knew the answer to his own last question. *Another blackout. Oh, no. That means Eddie was here again.*

"Carson, it's okay. You…got knocked down by a piece of the building."

Kellie's voice. He looked the other way. She was kneeling next to him. Her eyes went wide and then back to normal, and he got the hint.

"The building? What about it?"

"All that thunder," Mrs. Powell said. Her black mourning dress brought back unpleasant memories of Eddie's burial. "It broke windows and some bricks and wood came down and hit you. Kellie ran across the street and got me."

"Oh." Carson pushed himself to his feet. When he got a better look at Kellie, he gasped. Her arms were all scratched, she'd obviously been crying, and her hair and clothes were rumpled and dirty.

Damn you to hell, Eddie. What did you do?

"We should get you home," Kellie said. She thanked Mrs. Powell for her help.

"Are you two sure you're all right? Maybe we should call a doctor."

"No!" He and Kellie said it together. He thought fast. "I, um, was supposed to go right home after school. My mom will kill me if she finds out I was goofing off instead of studying."

Mrs. Powell frowned, but nodded. "Okay. But promise me you'll call a doctor if you have any headaches. You could have a concussion, you know."

"I promise." A concussion was the least of his worries. Compared to getting possessed by your own brother, a head injury was nothing. Even a brain disorder or a tumor would be preferable.

Carson took Kellie's hand and led her away from the theater manager's overly concerned gaze. Once they were out of earshot, he cleared his throat to get Kellie's attention.

"Thanks. For back there. You saved us from a lot of questions."

"It wasn't hard to guess what was happening."

Something in her voice grabbed Carson's attention away from his own problems. "What did he do to you?"

She sighed, and walked in silence for a few seconds before answering. Each footstep was like a punch in Carson's stomach, confirming his suspicions that Eddie had really gone overboard this time.

Then she spoke, and it was far worse than he'd expected.

"Carson, I didn't really know Eddie, only met him once or twice when my dad stopped at the garage, but you always say he was a good brother, that he just fell in with the wrong crowd but never hurt anyone intentionally."

"Yeah, that's right," Carson said, his belly feeling like it might explode.

"If that's true, I think being a ghost has changed him. He was...awful. As bad as any of the Hell Riders. And he did this." She turned so he could see the scrapes on her back and arms.

If she'd told him she'd gotten the scratches and bruises from skateboarding, or falling off a bike, or even getting into a fight at school, Carson wouldn't have thought much of them. The bruises would be gone in a day or two, and the scrapes would fade from angry red to pale pink to nothing at all before a week passed.

But knowing Eddie had done it – *using me! My hands!* – Carson wanted to fall to his knees and puke. He wanted to punch his brother in the nose. He wanted to pull Kellie into an embrace and tell her it was okay, he'd take care of everything.

Instead, he stared at her and started to cry.

Even as he berated himself for doing it — *stop it, she'll think you're a baby!* — the tears grew worse.

And suddenly her arms were around him.

"It's okay. I knew it wasn't you. And they don't hurt, really."

"It's not that," he said, pulling away and sniffing back a nose full of snot. "It's just...he's my brother. I love him. But now...."

Kellie stroked his shoulder. "Now, what?"

"Now I'm starting to hate him."

CHAPTER TWENTY-EIGHT

While hovering over the center of Hell Creek, trying to decide on his next target, Eddie Ryder found inspiration in the unlikeliest of places: the police station.

Johnny Ray Jones was walking across the street, carrying a cardboard tray with four cups of coffee on it.

Isn't that sweet? The boss is bringing coffee to the workers. I should shoot a little lightning up his ass and scare the crap out of him, make him drop the whole damn tray.

He held back, though, still focused mostly on who his next victim should be. Since he was saving Hank Bowman – whom he had finally located in the hospital, one floor down from Jethro Cole – for last, that left only Mouse Bates as the remaining Hell Rider he hadn't fucked with.

Too bad. The one I'd really like to get my hands on is Ned Bowman.

That had proved impossible, though. No matter how hard he tried, Eddie still couldn't break free of the general area surrounding Hell Creek. And with Everglades Correctional Institute way up in Miami, there was no way he could get to Ned.

Or was there?

I can't go to him, but maybe there's a way to bring Ned to me....

Hadn't he seen on TV shows that cops could sometimes get prisoners out of prison for questioning or other reasons? Which meant Chief Jones could take care of his problem for him.

Or rather, I can take care of the problem myself.

A moment later he was sliding into Jones's body. The Chief's hand twitched once, spilling some coffee onto his desk, and then Eddie had control.

Whoah!

Johnny Ray was more than twenty years older than him and he felt it. The differences in how Johnny Ray's body moved, how his reflexes worked, were startling. Even more so than the two girls in the clubhouse. Slower, but more controlled. More deliberate.

Is this how I'd have felt if I'd lived to see forty, forty-five?

A phone rang in the main room and Eddie stopped flexing his fingers. He had to get things done quickly, before a real emergency came up and the Chief was needed.

Leaning toward the door, he called out to Sharon Mays, the weekday dispatcher and part-time secretary and file clerk. "Sharon. Can you ring me the warden up at Everglades Correctional?"

"Sure thing, Johnny Ray," the middle-aged woman answered. A couple of minutes later she said, "Miguel Ramos on Line One."

Eddie saw a button turn green on the desk phone and he pressed it down.

"Warden Ramos?" As he said it, he realized he didn't know if Jones and Ramos knew each other. Had they ever spoken? Were they friendly or just polite?

"Afternoon, Chief. What can I do for you?"

"Well, we've got a bit of a problem down here and I'm hoping you can help." Eddie prayed he wasn't laying on too much of the Southern charm; he had no idea how Jones usually handled official business.

"I'll try."

"You've got a prisoner up there, part of a local biker gang. Name is Ned Bowman. It seems his brother's gone kind of wild, starting a lot of trouble in town. Normally, I'd just lock him up but he's trying to play the crazy card, if you know what I mean, and now he's in the hospital getting evaluated by the shrinks. I think I can get him to admit he's faking it, but I'll need some incentive."

"And you think his brother can provide it." The warden's voice carried more than a hint of skepticism.

"I do. See, it's no secret Ned is still running the show when it comes to the Hell Riders. He does it through Hank and through that girlfriend of his that visits him every week. Hank's scared to death of his brother. If I can get the two of them into a room, just for a few minutes...."

"The point of a prison is to keep people like Ned Bowman locked inside," Ramos said. "Why don't you bring Hank up here?"

"I wish I could. Doctors won't give me permission to move him. I know it's a lot to ask, but Hank and his boys have killed two people and destroyed a lot of property, and I've got the mayor breathing down my neck."

"Hmmm." A strange sound came through the phone, and Eddie realized it was the warden chewing something. Dinner? Gum? The Chief's stomach rumbled, and Eddie almost laughed. After this call, he was going to have himself another nice meal, this time on the Chief's dime.

"All right."

For a moment, Eddie didn't catch on to the warden's agreement. "Jones? You there?"

"What? Yeah, I'm here. Sorry. That's great. I'll send an officer for him tomorrow morning. Thank you, warden."

"Make sure he has all the right paperwork. And don't make me regret this." The connection went dead before Eddie could respond.

Eddie nearly shouted with joy. *Ned Bowman, you're a dead man and you don't even know it!*

Jones's stomach growled again, and Eddie stood up. Time for supper. As he left the office, he stopped at Sharon's desk.

"Do me a favor. I'm having Ned Bowman brought back to town to see if he can scare the insanity plea out of Hank. Dig out the paperwork and give it to Moselby. I want him on the way to Miami at dawn."

"Okay. But Johnny Ray, are you sure this is a good idea?"

Eddie's good mood evaporated like morning fog. "Yes, I'm damn sure! Just do it." He stormed out of the station before the old hag could ask any more questions.

Jesus, Jones needs to learn how to run a tighter ship.

Out on the sidewalk, he paused to consider his options. At Rosie's, the dinner crowd would already be stuffing their fat asses into the booths, eager for their meatloaf and chicken fried steak. It would take forever to get his food. On the other hand, Iron Pete's Pub was only a block away in the other direction.

A beer and a burger. Now that would really hit the spot.

Even better would be letting Johnny Ray wake up in the morning with a nasty hangover and no idea how he got it.

★   ★   ★

Kellie Jones knew something was wrong the minute she walked into the house and found her father asleep on the couch with several empty beer bottles scattered around him. She'd called earlier from Carson's house and left a message saying she'd be eating dinner there and then watching a movie, but her father hadn't called back, which was unusual. And when she'd called at eight for a ride home, there'd been no answer either.

Growing up as the child of a police officer, she knew sometimes his work could keep him at the station for long hours. Accidents, arrests, paperwork. But never to the point where her father didn't call her back at some point, or at least text her, unless there was a real emergency. Except in that case, she'd have heard all sorts of sirens. Which meant something else was going on. And with all the weirdness happening in town, that made her more than a little nervous.

Another part of being a cop's child was the worry that something would happen to her father. Lately, with all the violence happening in town, that worry had grown a few sizes. So, rather than walk home, she'd borrowed Carson's bike for the trip across town.

Finding him home and safe eased her mind; however, the fact that he'd obviously been boozing raised new worries. He'd never been much of a drinker, just a few beers at barbeques or parties. And certainly never while in uniform, or to the point where he smelled like one of the drunks he regularly busted on the weekends.

What the heck had happened?

"Dad, wake up." She poked at him with her finger. He groaned, then opened eyes that were red and watery.

"Huh? Kellie? Whass the matter? Where...?" He sat up, then groaned again as he looked around the room. "How'd I get here?"

"Dad, you're wasted. What's going on?"

"What? Wasted...?" A bleary look of understanding came over him. "How'd I...? I was in my office.... What time is it?"

"Nine o'clock. You weren't answering my calls. I got worried."

"Nine?" He shook his head. "No. It was four-thirty. I went for coffee. Brought it back. That's the last thing I remember."

Kellie's body went cold at her father's words. Memory loss. Abnormal behavior. It could only mean one thing.

Eddie Ryder. Inside my father. He made him get drunk. What else did he do?

"You better go to bed, Dad. We'll figure it out in the morning."

"Huh? Yeah." Johnny Ray stood up, swayed so far to the left that Kellie thought he'd tumble over, and then righted himself. Still leaning slightly to one side, he made his way through the living room and down the hall to his bedroom like he was navigating a maze. A moment later the sound of snoring filled the house.

Kellie hurriedly cleaned up the mess and then texted Carson.

>We've got a real problem.

★   ★   ★

Kellie woke up to the sound of her father calling her name. Her radio was playing a hip-hop dance tune, and she wondered how long the alarm had been going off.

"I'm awake," she shouted, as much for her own benefit as her father's.

"Glad to hear it."

She nearly jumped out of bed at his voice, which came from her doorway. Turning, she saw her father, smiling but looking as tired as she felt, standing there.

"Your alarm's been blasting for ten minutes. I thought maybe you'd gone deaf."

"Sorry." She hit the off button. "I was up late last night, doing homework."

"Uh-huh." His eyebrows went up, a clear sign he didn't believe her. "If you want a ride to school, better get a move on. I've got first shift today."

"Okay."

She got out of bed, her stomach already in knots. What disaster would her father find when he went to work? What kind of mischief had Eddie been up to, besides a drinking binge?

"That may have been all it was," Carson had said the previous night, while they'd been texting each other. They'd spent hours going over

the different ideas they had, continuing their conversation from earlier, at his house. And just like then, they'd ended up getting nowhere. Computer research was useless, not because of a lack of information but the opposite: there were so many websites about ghosts, possession, demons, and poltergeists that they had no idea what to believe and what was pure junk. The one thing that seemed pretty much consistent was that getting rid of a ghost or demon wasn't easy.

Kellie hadn't been satisfied with Carson's ideas on why Eddie would possess her father. If all he wanted to do was drink, why pick him? Why not someone already in a bar?

"Maybe he wanted to embarrass your dad. Make him get drunk in front of everyone. Even though he knew your dad helped him out, he still never really trusted him. Or any other cops. He always blamed the police anytime he got in trouble, said they were out to get him."

It made sense, but it didn't. Eddie had a real grudge against the Hell Riders, and almost everything he'd done up until that point, from what they could tell, had to do with them in some way.

So how does my dad figure into that?

The question had kept her up most of the night, and it continued to hound her as she got ready for school.

She had a feeling that when they found out the answer, they weren't going to like it.

CHAPTER TWENTY-NINE

Eddie could barely control himself as he waited for the patrol car to cross over into the town limits. Nervous energy crackled around him and had the air humming like he'd parked beneath a giant transformer. He'd been up at first light to make sure Jones hadn't discovered the transport orders during the night and cancelled them. Everything seemed fine, though, with Moselby departing Hell Creek for Miami right on schedule. Two hours there, two hours back. Eddie could have waited at the police station for Moselby to return, but he wanted to take control of Ned Bowman the moment the bastard entered the town limits.

The four hours had seemed like a lifetime.

Finally, at just after ten-thirty a.m., Moselby's car came into view. *This is it, Neddy. You're going out with a bang.*

A motherfucking big bang!

Eddie gunned Diablo and swooped down parallel to the police cruiser. Just for fun, he gunned the throttle a few times, creating blasts of thunder that shook the car and startled flocks of birds flying from their nesting places. A group of herons sailed across the road in front of Moselby. One bounced off the front end of the cruiser in an explosion of feathers.

"Jesus!" Moselby jerked the wheel back and forth, trying to keep control of the car as more feathered missiles took flight from the swampy land on both sides of the road.

"What the fuck?" Ned shouted from the back, doing his best to hang on with his hands cuffed behind him.

The car straightened out and Eddie decided to get the game going. He aimed Diablo right for Ned's body and throttled up. The ghostly bike sped forward and passed effortlessly through metal and flesh. As soon as he had control, Eddie released a tiny burst of power, just enough to cause a squeal of feedback from the car's police radio. The car swerved again and Eddie threw himself into the door, smacking Ned's skull against the window.

Moselby righted the car and looked back. "Bowman? You all right?"

Damn. He's too smart to fall for any tricks. Eddie had hoped Moselby would pull over and open the door to check on him. How great would it have been to have Ned drive the police car into town, with Moselby handcuffed in the back? Instead, he'd have to wait a little longer to have his fun.

"I'm fine," Eddie said. "No thanks to you. Where'd you learn to drive, clown college?"

"Shut your mouth." Moselby clicked the radio a couple of times. When it worked normally, he set the mic back in its holder. Eddie figured they had a ten-minute drive into town. Moselby was already on edge. Why not see if he could get under the officer's skin?

"Hey, Ted. How 'bout if we stop for a burger? My treat."

When there was no response from the officer, Eddie kept talking.

"You know I'm gonna cause some trouble while I'm here. Johnny Ray thinks I'm going to be his dog and get my brother to talk? Man, he's got another thing coming. I figure maybe I'll escape and raise some hell, how's that sound? I got some scores to settle, starting with a certain bitch with a big mouth. You still got her locked up? Maybe you can put me in the cell with her, let me have a conjugal bang before I kill her."

Moselby stayed quiet, and Eddie felt himself getting irritated. Time to bring out the big guns.

"Or how about I pay a visit to your wife? What's her name? I'll bet she could use a real man. Or does she get off on the big black dick of yours? Is that it? Wifey likes the dark meat?"

Eddie waited, thinking there was no way Moselby would let that one go. Hell, if someone said that about his woman, he'd—

"You must have me confused with some stupid hick who bought a Crackerjack badge. Hate to break it to you, but in LA even the dumbest meth head has more brains than you. Now sit back and enjoy the ride. After today you won't be seeing the outside for a long time."

"You wanna bet? This is a one-way ride for me, Ted. You and Chief Dumb Ass just don't know it yet."

Eddie leaned back. When he saw Moselby eyeing him in the rearview mirror, he gave him the biggest grin he could make, stretching his lips until they hurt.

As they entered the town proper, Moselby flicked on the radio. "Car twenty here. Approaching home base in five. Backup requested. Our guest is a little feisty."

Feisty? Just fucking wait, asshole. I'll show you feisty. I'll feisty your motherfucking head clean off your shoulders.

*   *   *

"What was that all about?" Johnny Ray Jones asked as he approached Sharon with some papers to be filed.

"That was Ted. He's heading into town with Ned Bowman and wants someone to meet him. Says Bowman's feisty today."

Johnny Ray's hands twitched and he dropped the papers. "Ned Bowman? What the hell's he bringing Bowman here for?"

The look Sharon gave him made him want to check and see if he'd grown an extra head. "Um, 'cause you arranged it with Warden Ramos? Why else?"

"What? I didn't do anything of the sort. Why would I want that piece of crap here instead of locked up?"

Sharon's gaze grew concerned and Johnny Ray started thinking back to the previous night and the missing hours of his life, which apparently included getting shit-faced.

What else did I do?

"How would I know? You spoke to the warden about it and then told me to have Ted fill out the paperwork and handle the pickup. Then you left. Are you feeling okay?"

No, I'm not, you stupid bitch, I'm fucking losing my mind. Don't ask me if I'm okay! He was not even close to okay. He was the opposite of okay, in fact. He felt like screaming. Like kicking over the desk.

Wait. Maybe I'm not crazy. Maybe it's a tumor. Or a stroke. Something's wrong. Gotta play it off for now, act like everything's fine.

"Um, yeah, Sharon. I'm sorry." He gave her a grin. "My mind's a little fuzzy today. I didn't get much sleep."

She smiled and gave him a wink. "I heard you had a liquid dinner last night. I guess even the Chief needs to blow off some steam now and then."

What was she talking about? Had he gotten so shit-faced he blacked out and lost nearly an entire day? How much had he drunk?

"Yeah." His grin felt weaker and he turned away before she noticed. News traveled way too fast in a small town. He didn't need a reputation as a boozer.

"Have them put Bowman in a cell. I'll be out in a few minutes to talk to him."

"You really think he can get Hank to incriminate himself?"

Johnny Ray paused at his office door. "That's the plan." Once he was seated at his desk with the door shut, he tried to look into the black hole in his memory. Use one Bowman against another? It was a crazy idea, and not crazy smart. If anything, Ned would just tell his younger brother to keep his mouth shut.

What the hell had he been thinking?

And he'd gotten Warden Ramos, a well-known hard-ass, to agree to his scheme? That meant he had to see it through or Ramos would be all over him.

Shit. Shit fucking goddamn.

Not even eleven yet, and it was already looking like a very bad day.

*   *   *

Eddie watched Johnny Ray come down the hall and he wanted to laugh until the walls fell down around him. The Chief looked awful.

Cheap beer and tequila will do that to you.

"Howdy, Chief," Eddie said, shaping Ned's lips into a shit-eating grin. "I always wanted to say that. Makes me feel like a cowboy. How you feelin' today, Johnny-boy? Looks to me like you got yourself a bad case of hangover flu."

Johnny Ray glared at him, and Eddie imagined what Johnny Ray was seeing. Ned Bowman had gone to jail a tall, long-haired piece of shit with a pot belly, a bad attitude, and a moustache he liked to call his pussy-tickler.

He'd returned to Hell Creek with a bald head, clean-shaven face, and a body layered in muscle. He'd definitely put his time in prison to good use. Eddie could feel the strength in his borrowed body. It was a body made for violence, something Ned always had a yen for.

Let's see what you're made of, Neddy.

Without warning, he slammed himself against the cell bars, and was rewarded by Moselby and Jones both jumping back a couple of steps.

"Oh yeah, boys, that's the ticket. Got you pissin' in your pants already, don't I?"

To his credit, Johnny Ray recovered quickly. "Speaking of pissing, your brother's been having some trouble with that. Can't seem to keep it in his pants. Now he's under observation at the hospital. The docs are saying he might be a little whoo-hoo." Jones twirled his finger in circles by his temple.

"Why the fuck should I care?"

"We're hoping you might talk to him. Your boys have been out of control. I'm guessing you know about Butch and Jethro."

"And Harley. Don't forget about him. This where you shot him?"

Johnny Ray scowled and Moselby shook his head, a look of disgust plastered on his face.

Eddie laughed. Outside, a peal of thunder shook the town. "You want me to tell Hank to make all nicey-nice? How do you think that's gonna go?"

"Think of it as an episode of *Scared Straight*. Hank gets a look at his brother, shackled and probably somebody's prison bitch. Maybe he thinks twice about ending up there himself." Even as he said it, it was obvious Johnny Ray didn't believe his own words. Hank – and any other Hell Rider – would give their left nut to transform themselves into the badass Ned had become. Even if it meant being locked away for a couple of years. Eddie figured Jones was trying to think fast on his feet, come up with something to cover the fact that he had no idea why he'd arranged for Ned's visit.

Moselby shot his boss a look, one eyebrow raised. "That's why you brought him here?"

Johnny Ray ignored him, continued staring at the person he believed to be Ned Bowman.

"Of course, if you don't get your brother on the straight and narrow, then he'll either end up in the loony bin or up at Everglades with you. You can be butt-buddies together."

"Well, we can't let Hank have all the fun. Tell you what. I'll talk to him on one condition."

Johnny Ray shook his head. "No conditions, Ned."

"You ain't even heard it yet! All I was gonna ask for was something to eat. Your boy grabbed me before breakfast and it looks like I ain't gonna be home for lunch. Least you can do is feed me."

"Damn it."

Moselby looked at Johnny Ray. "What's the matter?"

"Technically, we do have to feed the sonofabitch while he's in our custody."

Eddie clapped his hands. "Yeah, that's what I'm talkin' about. All I want is an order of gator nuggets from Rosie's."

"Gator nuggets?" Johnny Ray smiled. "That's cheaper than the burger and fries you would have gotten. Ted, have Sharon place the order. The sooner he eats, the sooner we bring him to the hospital, and then you can drive his ass back to the pen."

* * *

An hour later, a handcuffed Eddie found himself being led into the hospital room that housed Hank Bowman, who had one wrist and one ankle shackled to the bed. Other than looking haggard from lack of sleep, Hank appeared to be relatively coherent. Part of that stemmed from no drugs or alcohol in the past two days. But Eddie also knew Hank had a crafty side and was probably waiting to see his lawyer before he decided whether to fake an insanity plea or do time in jail.

When Hank saw his brother's face, his eyes went wide.

"Ned? Jesus fucking Christ, what're you doing here? I'm not dying, am I?"

"Oh, for God's sake." Johnny Ray rolled his eyes at Hank. "No, you're not dying, you idiot. I brought him here to talk some sense into you."

"That's right, you ain't dyin'," Eddie repeated. "but you're gonna be, real soon."

Johnny Ray and Ted Moselby both turned and stared at Eddie, who continued as if he didn't notice their expressions.

"Heard you done fucked with the wrong person at the Laundromat," Eddie said, enjoying the terror blossoming in Hank's eyes.

"No!" Hank shouted. "That wasn't me. Who told you that?"

"Oh, I heard it from a little birdie. Or was it a mouse?" Eddie let that sink in, and then went on. "In fact, I hear you been having a lotta problems lately. Takin' things that don't belong to you. Rattin' me out to the cops. Lettin' the club fall apart."

Hank shook his head, his unwashed hair slapping the pillow like a damp mop. "Ned, no, it's not like that. There's shit goin' on in this town, weird things happening—"

"Damn straight there is. I know all about it." He stood up, and both Moselby and Jones went for their guns.

"Sit down, Ned."

"Easy, Chief. I ain't gonna hurt anyone. I just want to make a point." He turned back to Hank. "I know everything. Like how you and Sandy Powell was gettin' it on behind my back. And how you been havin' blackouts lately, and dreamin' about Eddie Ryder comin' for you."

"It's you!" Hank's neck bulged from the force of his scream. He pushed himself up in the bed, trying to put space between him and his brother. "Stay away from me!"

"Yeah, I know everything," Eddie said, raising his voice above Hank's cries. "And I know Eddie's comin' for you. Just like he came for me."

"What the hell does Eddie Ryder have to do with anything?" Moselby asked, but no one answered him.

"Because Eddie's the shit, man. He's the motherfucking devil and he's gonna make things right. Which means it's time for me to leave. Say goodbye to Neddie. I gotta pay a visit to Jethro next. But you can bet your ass I'll be back!"

With that, Eddie turned and sprinted toward the big window that was open to let in the late-morning breeze. Johnny Ray lunged for him but Ned's body was too strong and he knocked him aside. Then the only thing between Eddie and a four-story fall to the parking lot was a piece of heavy screen, and Ned's body went through it like it was paper as Eddie slipped free.

Hovering in the air on Diablo, he watched Ned tumble through the air and hit the blacktop, sending blood and brains in all directions.

With a laugh that rattled the windows, he rose up one floor and entered the hospital again.

CHAPTER THIRTY

Johnny Ray had to shout, "Shut up!" three times at the top of his lungs before Hank Bowman stopped screaming. Two nurses ran in, and they started shouting as well when they went to the window and saw Ned's body down on the pavement.

"What the fuck just happened?" Moselby asked, looking at the smashed, bloody remains of the Hell Riders' founder.

Hank Bowman moaned and pulled the sheets over his head.

His thoughts whirling like house shingles in a hurricane, Johnny Ray just shook his head and stared at the corpse, as if it might rise up and do him a favor by explaining what the hell was going on in his town.

Ned had mentioned Eddie Ryder's name. Why? Guilt over having him killed? That didn't make sense. Ned Bowman wouldn't feel guilty if he ran over his own grandmother. And what was all that shit about Eddie coming for Hank? It didn't make any sense, but at the same time it almost seemed as if Hank knew what his brother had been talking about.

Well, that was one question he could get answered.

"Hank." Johnny Ray touched a hand to Hank's arm. Beneath the starched, stiff sheets, Hank thrashed and shouted for him to go back to where he came from.

"Hank, it's just me. Chief Jones. Why did your brother say those things?" He had to repeat the question several times before Hank stopped crying and answered.

"He didn't, he didn't, it was him that did it."

"Jesus." Moselby joined him by the bed. "One's crazier than the other."

"I'm not crazy!" Hank peeked out from beneath the sheet. His mussed hair, wild eyes, and tear-streaked face were in direct contrast to his statement. "I'm not crazy," he repeated, in a softer voice.

At that moment, a nurse pushed Jones aside and administered a sedative. In the space of two heartbeats, the tension left Hank's face and his eyes drooped to half mast.

"You've got about two minutes before he's asleep," the nurse said.

Moselby crossed his arms and frowned. "He's not going to say anything we can use. His brain is fried like bacon."

"Maybe, maybe not." Johnny Ray leaned closer to Hank. "Hey, Hank," he whispered, "why did Ned say Eddie was coming for you?"

"'Cause he is." Hank's eyes slowly closed but he kept talking, his words beginning to run together. "Already here. Been here for days haunting me at the clubhouse, taking away my memory and making me do things gonna kill me soon then maybe everyone else too he's crazy he's the devil he's...."

The words faded away and Hank's head tilted to one side. He started snoring.

Moselby shook his head. "Told you. It's all those drugs. There's nothing but Swiss cheese in his head."

"Yeah." Johnny Ray headed for the door, his mind awhirl worse than before.

Taking away my memory. Making me do things.

Like what happened to me last night?

★   ★   ★

Unaware of what was happening one floor below them, the nurses were doing rounds as usual when Eddie stumbled out of Jethro's room, dragging the IV pump behind him. The morphine coursing through his veins made his movements slow and awkward, but Eddie managed to stagger down the hall to the stairwell.

"Sorry, gotta go!" he called out, his words garbled by Jethro's swollen mouth and lack of teeth. "Time to make the donuts!"

Two nurses ran to intercept him and Eddie stopped, leaning against the wall so he wouldn't fall over. *Damn, this shit is good!*

"You're not supposed to be out of bed." One of the nurses took him by the arm.

"Sorry, I'm outta here. Got other fish to fry." Eddie yanked the IV needle from his wrist and shoved it straight into his eye. Even through the morphine-induced fog, the pain was incredible and he cried out. Hot, wet liquid flowed down his face and his other eye closed in reaction, leaving him blind.

The nurses screamed and he pushed past them at a run. "You haven't seen the last of me!" he shouted. Then he hit the exit door. The needle rammed deeper, all the way into Jethro's brain, at the same time his hip slammed into the metal bar. The door swung open and Jethro's body, already dying, tumbled down the twelve stairs to the between-floors landing.

Halfway down, his neck snapped and Eddie slipped free, the pain mercifully gone.

"Another one bites the dust," he said, and then gunned Diablo. The stairwell lights flickered and popped, showering sparks onto the twisted corpse.

"Now it's time to set a mouse trap."

★   ★   ★

By the time Johnny Ray finished at the hospital and got back to his desk, there was a shit-storm waiting to rain down on him and its name was Warden Miguel Ramos. Thanks to everyone and their mother having a cell phone and a Twitter account, Ramos had learned about Ned's suicide on the news before Johnny Ray had a chance to call him. And there'd been nothing he could say to defend himself against Ramos's tirade. He'd screwed up, plain and simple. Had they known Ned was suicidal — not to mention batshit crazy — he'd have had two more men with him.

Except according to the prison records, Bowman's problems tended more toward a bad attitude and a big mouth. No signs of depression or psychological problems, other than his rampant anti-social tendencies.

In the end, it was the lack of any warning signs that kept Ramos from bringing charges of negligence against the Hell Creek police force in general, and Johnny Ray in particular.

"You're damn lucky you went by the book," Ramos said, his voice still loud enough even at the end of the phone call that Johnny Ray had to keep the phone two inches from his ear. "And I'm gonna want a detailed report. And don't think I won't go through it with a magnifying glass. If I find one thing that even hints you screwed up—"

"You won't," Johnny Ray told him. And he wouldn't, because for the first time in all his years as Chief he was going to fudge the hell out of an official report. There'd be no mention of Eddie Ryder. No talk about people coming back from the dead. Nope. Ned accused Hank of stealing money from the club and then jumped out the window. Plain and simple, case closed, end of story. And he'd send the damn thing off himself, so Ted Moselby would have no chance to see how his own statements had been modified.

After emailing the documents to Ramos's secretary, he spent the rest of the afternoon dealing with the load of standard paperwork that accompanied any prisoner suicide or death. He was signing the last pages when someone knocked on his door.

"Come in." He prayed it was Sharon with a cup of coffee from Rosie's. Or two. Instead, the door opened and Kellie stepped in, Carson Ryder trailing behind her.

"Hey, Dad. Busy?"

"Hi, Chief Jones."

"Hi, kids. Yeah, I am busy. Think you can fend for yourself for dinner tonight?" He took a twenty out of his wallet and handed it to Kellie. "My treat. Grab a burger or some pizza. And do your dad a favor. Wherever you go, have them send something over for me."

"Okay. Thanks. When do you think you'll—"

"Hey, Chief?" Wilbur Dennis gave a perfunctory rap on the door frame and stuck his head in. "Angela Mason is making a big stink in her cell. Says it wasn't Hank who tied her up at the laundromat, it was Eddie Ryder, of all people. Only he was pretending to be Hank. She wants to talk to you."

Johnny Ray's stomach felt like it was about to hit the floor. He heard Kellie gasp, and he looked over at Carson just in time to see him turn white.

"Oh, for Christ's....Tell her I'll be down there in a little while. Jesus."

"Okay. She must've been smokin' some wicked shit. Oops, pardon my French, kids." He waved and disappeared.

"I'm sorry you had to hear that, Carson. But don't pay any mind to it. It seems like some of the Hell Riders are trying to use your brother's name as part of some stupid plan to avoid doing jail time for their crimes."

"Why would they do that?" Kellie asked. Next to her, Carson sat down and hid his face in his hands.

"I don't know, honey. They're crazy, for one thing. Angela, Hank, Jethro. Even Ned. That's what happens when you do as many drugs as they do."

"Ned?" Carson looked up. "He said something about my brother, too?"

Not wanting to divulge too much about the case – or subject the boy to any more misguided talk about his brother – Johnny Ray opted for a watered-down version of the truth. They'd know soon enough anyway, from people talking in town.

"He mentioned Eddie's name today before he...killed himself. I think it was a code word for Hank, to keep up this farce they're running."

"He killed himself? Why?" Kellie asked.

I wish I knew. "Like I said, he was nuts. Maybe high. The tox screens aren't back yet. Ted said he was acting weird in the car, and even when I talked to him this morning, he wasn't all there. Whatever it is, Jethro Cole must have been on it too. And Hank."

Johnny Ray stopped. The last thing he should be talking to the kids about was an ongoing case. "Just forget all about this stuff, okay? Get your dinner, do your homework, and I'll see you later tonight." He reached out to ruffle Kellie's hair, then drew his arm back, not wanting to embarrass her in front of Carson.

"Okay, Dad. Love you." She turned and headed for the door.

"Bye, Mr. Jones. Thank you for dinner." Carson's words were polite, but there was something in his voice that caught Johnny Ray's notice.

He's afraid. Something he did, like maybe with my daughter? Or is it because of all this talk about his brother and the Hell Riders?

With a tired sigh, Johnny Ray returned to his paperwork and hoped the kids remembered to have his dinner sent over.

CHAPTER THIRTY-ONE

Before they reached Rosie's Diner, Carson pulled Kellie onto a bench. "It was Eddie. He killed Ned."

"I know." Kellie's face was a mask of fear. "And Jethro. But what can we do?"

"We have to stop him, and there's only one thing I can think of. A séance."

"What? Are you serious?"

He nodded. "Yeah. We call his spirit to us, and then we make it go away for good."

"No." She shook her head. "That will just leave us open to getting possessed. It's too dangerous."

Carson waited for an elderly couple to walk past before speaking. "He can possess us any time he wants. But if we do the séance right, maybe he'll be under our control, instead of the other way around. Or maybe I can just talk to him, tell him to stop, that he's gone too far. He'll listen to me."

"Your *brother* would have listened to you, you mean. It's not Eddie anymore, remember? He's a ghost, or a demon. Something supernatural. And he might not be sane anymore."

"I know." It hurt Carson to admit it; just hearing her say the words made him want to tell her to shut up, to stop talking about his brother that way. But he couldn't deny Eddie was acting crazier than the people he was taking his revenge against.

Still, if there was a chance they could make him stop, or send him back to wherever he'd come from....

"I have to try it. Will you help me?" He didn't look at her, afraid of what he'd see, what he'd hear.

No, Carson, I won't. You're as crazy as your brother. I'm not risking my life for—

"Yes."

Yes? "Wait, what? You will?"

She put her hand on his, and his heart soared.

"Of course I'll help. I think you're probably nuts, but you're also right. What else can we do?"

"Okay, but we have to be careful. He could be watching us, listening to us. So it should be you who looks up the information and gets what we need. He hasn't, you know, taken you over yet, which means he probably won't be spying on you or anything."

"That makes sense, I guess. I'll go get started. You should go home, too. Check on your mom. Act like nothing's wrong. In case...."

"Yeah. Send me an email when you think you've got all the information we need."

"Okay." She leaned forward and kissed him.

His lips tingled all the way home.

★   ★   ★

At the same time Carson and Kellie were sharing a kiss, Eddie hovered near the ceiling inside the Hell Riders' clubhouse, where Mouse Bates was busy telling a group of prospects and hangers-on that both Bowman brothers were totally fucked in the head, and that Ned probably committed suicide because he was afraid of Angela flipping to the feds.

"Or maybe," he added in a sly voice, "Hank pushed him out that window, and the cops just aren't telling anyone the real truth 'cause they couldn't stop it."

The handful of wannabes standing by the bar nodded in agreement. Most of them hadn't been around when Ned ran the gang, but they'd all seen Hank's temper, had heard about the crazy shit he'd done lately. It didn't seem all that strange that he'd kill his own brother over a piece of tail. Or to take over the club. Jethro's suicide made more sense. He'd crossed Hank, and he knew he was dead meat the moment he left the hospital.

Eddie waited until Mouse stopped speaking and then slid into his body, which twitched once, spilling some beer onto the floor and everyone's boots. No one said anything. Any one of them, including some of the girls, could have broken Mouse in two with one hand, but he wore the colors, which meant he could piss on their feet all night long and they couldn't do a thing.

Not if they wanted to wake up with all their teeth.

That rule was something Eddie intended to take advantage of before he sent Rat-boy to the big mouse trap in the sky.

He raised Mouse's beer. "With everyone else dead or in the hospital, that leaves me in charge. So whattya say we have ourselves a party?"

The group raised their beers and cheered.

"Party!"

"Fuck yeah!"

"Let's do it!"

"All right. You." Eddie pointed at Moshpit Elardo, a burly kid who was only fifteen, but already had the Hell Riders' emblem – a flaming skull with red eyes, devil horns, and a Nazi-style biker helmet – tattooed on his arm, meaning he stood one step away from getting his colors. "Go get some food. Gimme two orders of gator nuggets from Rosie's and a bunch of pizzas. You." This time he selected the biggest, meanest-looking prospect of the bunch, Vinny June. All the June offspring – four boys and three girls – were a little wacked, and Vinny, the youngest, was following in his siblings' footsteps. He had a lazy eye that always drifted to the left and hair that looked like it hadn't been combed in a month. He also stunk like a wet coon dog, but then bathing had never been important to any of the Junes. Including the women.

"What, Mouse? You want me to get some booze? Or some babes?" Vinny's eagerness to please was almost pathetic, coming from someone who could wrestle an alligator and probably win.

"Naw, I want you to put on some better music. Charred Walls of the Damned. Demon Dogs. Powerwolf. Some good hard shit."

Eddie poured himself another beer and chugged it down, letting the foam spill over his chin and down his shirt.

"Let's get this motherfuckin' party started!"

★　　★　　★

Two hours later, Eddie's head was buzzing, his stomach felt like it might erupt at any second, and things were starting to get blurry. He'd never realized Mouse had such a low tolerance for booze.

Time to get down to business, before I puke. Or pass out.

Eddie moved around to the back of the bar, where there was always some kind of gun stashed away, just in case of trouble. Hopefully, the cops hadn't confiscated it after the last shooting. Sure enough, a sawed-off shotgun rested under a loose floorboard. His intention was to put a scare into everyone, send them scurrying back to town with a message that Mouse had flipped out and shot up the place. Whoever came back would find a very dead Rat-boy.

Except the minute he raised the gun, his whole plan fell apart.

"Yo, motherfuckers!" he yelled, bringing the shotgun up to his shoulder and pointing at the center of the room. "Who wants to die first?"

Something hard and heavy smashed into his shoulder at the same time an explosion of noise filled his ears. The force of the blow slammed him into the bar and then he bounced off and fell to the floor, his whole body racked with pain.

What the...? Someone shot me!

Instinctively, Eddie left Mouse's body and rose into the air. From his new vantage point, he saw Moshpit in the hallway that led to the bathroom, a long-barreled revolver in his hand.

Mouse Bates lay on the floor, blood pouring from a fist-sized hole in his shoulder. Moshpit stood statue-still, his eyes comically wide. Eddie knew why. He had to be thinking he'd just signed his own death warrant by shooting someone who wore the colors.

Life's a bitch and then you die. Shoulda stayed in school, asshole.

Eddie aimed himself at Moshpit and dove forward. The minute he had control, he pointed the pistol at Mouse and pulled the trigger three more times, blasting Mouse's head into pieces. The other prospects backed away as Eddie dropped the pistol and picked up the shotgun.

The room spun around him, shapes and colors distorted and melting together. Eddie dimly understood that Moshpit was wacked out of his mind on something a lot stronger than pot or booze.

"Fucking messed things up!" The words seemed to come in slow motion. Something moved and he pulled both triggers. Vinny June fell over, hands clutching a gaping wound in his stomach. Another distorted shape approached him and Eddie swung the shotgun like a baseball bat, catching his attacker right in the face. The other two recruits tackled him. His head hit a table as he went down and a burst of white filled his vision.

"Fucking bastards!" he shouted. "You can't hurt Eddie Ryder! I'm the fucking devil!"

He grabbed blindly at his attackers and channeled all his rage and pain into neon-red bolts of lightning that exploded into thunderous fireworks where his flesh touched theirs.

The bikers flew through the air like two comets, their shirts aflame, their screams lost in the twin detonations from Eddie's burning hands. One of them crashed through the bar, wood and alcohol igniting into a giant fireball. The other one hit the ground and skidded across the floor, flames trailing behind him, until he came to rest against a wall. His frantic cries grew louder as the fire spread across his body and he rolled around on the floor in a desperate attempt to put himself out.

Holy shit! Eddie looked at his hands and gasped. They were nothing but charred sticks, all the skin and muscle burned away. He tried making a fist and the blackened bones crumbled into charcoal nuggets.

Then the pain hit, the reaction delayed by shock and the drugs Moshpit had taken. Eddie cried out and dropped to his knees, so overwhelmed by his agony that all rational thought disappeared. His other hand disintegrated and he fell to one side, unable to balance himself on his two stumps. His senses overloaded, he didn't notice the heat on his back until it morphed into something else, a suffering so sharp and intense that it surpassed the white-hot torture in his arms. For a moment he was back in his garage, the walls aflame and laughter filling the air.

It's happening again!

He tried to leave but his mind was paralyzed by the pain, just like the last time. The fire engulfed him, even worse than his first death, because he knew the worst was yet to come.

And then there was only the crimson supernova of insanity.

★ ★ ★

Eddie woke up to a blessed absence of pain. The sky was dark around him, the ground a hundred feet below. Diablo growled happily between his legs, motor thrumming. He looked down, saw the Hell Riders' clubhouse engulfed in flames. Two fire trucks were at the scene, pumping swamp water onto the building, although it was far too late to save anything. Then he noticed a second set of flames, in the grassy area next to the parking lot. Flames that spelled out words.

EDDIE WAS HERE

Did I do that? He didn't remember. Everything after catching fire was gone, leaving nothing behind but a haze of red. Somehow, though, it seemed right. Time to let everyone know he was back. Fuck them all. Why should he hide? What the hell could they do to him anyhow?

Maybe he couldn't leave Hell Creek – not yet, anyway – but he sure as shit could make the town his own.

PART THREE
RECKONINGS

Feeding and flowing through rivers of red
Clouding my vision and the thoughts in my head
Seeds of misery planted inside me
My demons are guiding me
From below they are spawning
They're tearing and clawing
Waiting to be set free
Destroying my body and leaving me torn
Not willing to die, every day I'm reborn

'Guiding Me,' by Charred Walls of the Damned

★　　★　　★

A demon escaped from bowels of Hell
To see his face it is Death's knell
Hearts stop from his slightest gaze
Entire towns his fury will raze
Hell Rider!
Burning through the night
Hell Rider!
Coming for you

'Hellrider,' by Demon Dogs

CHAPTER THIRTY-TWO

Kellie jerked awake at her desk, her sleep broken by the haunting wail of police sirens somewhere in town. She'd been lost in a nightmare world where prehistoric beasts surrounded her house, howling their blood lust, while she and Carson pushed furniture against the doors to keep the monsters outside.

Just a dream, she told herself, although that didn't stop lingering shivers from creeping up and down her back. She glanced at the time on her computer screen. Only nine-thirty. It seemed later, in part because the dream had felt so long, but she'd only been asleep for a few minutes. Piled next to her were pages of information on how to safely perform a séance. She hadn't realized there were so many rules for contacting spirits, and even more for keeping evil entities from hurting you when you called them.

Maybe I should watch more scary movies.

She'd also been trying to find information on how to control or banish an evil spirit or ghost or demon. That hadn't gone as well. There were so many different kinds of demons and spirits, and so many different spells and precautions, it was impossible to figure out which ones they needed. Especially considering they had no idea what Eddie was. In the end, she'd tried to simplify the list down to a handful of things they all had in common. Even then, the list ended up being almost a page long, and many of the items were completely useless, because they were either illegal to obtain – where was she supposed to get the eye of a corpse or a candle made of human fat? – or totally impractical. As in, who had blood from the spirit's firstborn just lying around? Eddie didn't even have a firstborn, at least not that she knew of. And where in town would she find someone to sell her a goat to slaughter?

Which left only a few items they had a chance of actually obtaining without getting arrested. Holy water. Candles of various colors. A lock of hair from the dead person. A picture of the person. Sea salt. The blood of a virgin.

Well, that last one will be easy enough. Kellie pictured herself running a knife across her wrist and cringed.

Hopefully we don't need too much. Like maybe I can just stick a pin in my finger.

She wondered what Carson was doing. Was he still up? Waiting for her to text him about her research? Fragments of her dream came back, and she had a sudden urge to make sure he was okay. As she was sending the text message, more sirens loosed their undulating cries through the quiet of the night.

What's going on?

And does it have anything to do with Eddie Ryder?

★   ★   ★

"Screaming thunder faster faster! Ride the highway I'm Hell's master!"

Sonic explosions followed Eddie as he bellowed the words to the Demon Dogs' 'Hellrider' and aimed Diablo straight up into the sky, the moon his unattainable target. He knew he'd only get a mile or two up before the invisible tether tying him to Hell Creek halted his progress, but the exhilaration of rocketing through the atmosphere gave him a thrill he never grew tired of. It made doing a hundred miles an hour on the highway seem like coasting through a parking lot.

After leaving the scene of the clubhouse fire he'd traveled to the other side of town and lit a second blazing message, torched it into the highway in letters ten feet long with a single thought, right in front of the sign that read 'Entering Hell Creek, population 4,340'.

EDDIE LIVES!

After reading it, he'd thought maybe it sounded too much like the title of an Iron Maiden CD, but then he'd decided he didn't give a flying fuck. People would figure out the truth soon enough. He'd make sure of that.

Why should he settle for only Hank Bowman being frightened to death, when he could have an entire town trembling before him?

What did they ever do for me? Used my garage? Big fuckin' deal. Not like they had a lot of choices. And how many people would bother to give me the time of day when they saw me around town, even after I went straight? The cops still gave me the stink eye, like I was gonna screw their wives and rob the bank. The same goddamn bank that wouldn't let me refinance my loans when business got slow.

It wasn't just the Hell Riders who needed to be taught a lesson. All those people who never helped him or his family, who treated him like a second-class citizen? It was time to show them they messed with the wrong person.

Fuck yeah.

But first he had to check in on Hank Bowman.

★　　★　　★

Handcuffed to his hospital bed, Hank didn't resemble in any way the nasty, don't-fuck-with-me badass he'd worked so hard to become. His face was pale, his eyes sunken, and his body oddly misshapen under his hospital gown, which didn't hide his pot belly and skinny legs the way jeans and oversized t-shirts did.

He looks like a big fat spider waiting to be squashed.

Eddie stood in the back corner of the room while the Hell Riders' vice president – *now president, although not for much longer, cocksucker –* languished in a drug-assisted slumber. Despite the sedatives, it wasn't a peaceful sleep. His limbs twitched constantly and he kept moaning and tossing his head from side to side. Eddie pointed a finger at one of the tiny lights built into the base of the wall and it popped with a miniature burst of sparks. Hank's moans grew louder and then subsided. Eddie popped another light, and was rewarded with the same response. He was about to move on to one of the ceiling lights when the door opened and a nurse wheeled a tiny cart into the room.

The nurse proceeded to check Hank's blood pressure, take his temperature, and get an oxygen reading from his finger. Through it all, Hank slept on. Eddie waited until she'd marked the numbers on Eddie's chart before entering her body. Then he shut the door to

Hank's room and approached the bed.

"Wakey wakey, Hank," he said, patting Hank's cheeks. At first there was no response other than an increase in his movements and his eyelids fluttering a few times. Eddie prodded him with a finger, with zero effect.

"What the hell did they give him?" He didn't have all day; someone was bound to come in to see why the nurse hadn't continued her rounds.

Time for a jump start.

He pulled off the sheet and tugged down the top of Hank's gown, exposing a forest of sweaty, matted hair. Touching the nurse's finger to Hank's chest, he channeled a burst of energy. Hank's body convulsed and his eyes flew open. The stink of burnt hair filled the room and Eddie laughed at the sight of a blister forming above Hank's heart. A similar burn decorated the nurse's fingertip.

"Wha—?" Hank struggled to focus, his eyes still glazed and his pupils dilated from the drugs.

"Hello, Hank. Hope you had a nice sleep." Eddie slammed his hand over Hank's mouth, pressing down with all his weight. With his other hand, Eddie traced a fingernail down Hank's arm, the one handcuffed to the bedrail. Energy crackled and a long, red welt rose up. By the time he reached Hank's wrist, the nurse's fingernail had melted and the tip of her finger was black and smoking.

Hank's screamed but the muffled sounds carried no weight. He beat weakly at Eddie with his free arm, still more sedated than awake.

Eyeing the blistered flesh on Hank's forearm, Eddie laughed as an idea came to him.

"You killed me," he said, pointing the nurse's ruined finger at Hank. With no more effort than thinking of it, the finger burst into flames. "You know what it feels like to burn to death, Hank? You're gonna find out."

"MMMmmm unnnnh!" Hank jerked from side to side and he kicked his legs.

"Oh, yes, you're going to burn. But not today. This is just a little taste."

Skin hissed and hair sizzled as Eddie traced letters across Hank's chest. The edge of the gown smoldered, adding to the stink filling the air. Hank bit into the nurse's palm and screamed through his clenched teeth. Blood ran down his face and into his mouth and his cries turned into choking coughs. His unchained hand clawed at Eddie's arm, fingernails gouging deep scratches.

When he was done, Eddie leaned back to admire his handiwork. Blistered flesh spelled out the message.

EDDIE LIVES.

"Tell everyone, Hank. Tell them who did this to you. I want them to believe. You hear me? I'm gonna destroy this whole fucking town! Tell them! Tell them Eddie Ryder was here!"

The ceiling lights exploded and sparks flew from the monitor on the nurse's cart. Hank screamed again, and this time his voice carried as Eddie left the nurse and her unconscious form fell to the floor.

Eddie shot through the hospital wall and sent Diablo racing across town, his laughter filling the sky with thunder. Far below, people craned their necks at the sudden din. Seeing them made Eddie laugh even harder.

"Just wait! You're all gonna wish you never fucked with Eddie Ryder!"

CHAPTER THIRTY-THREE

Carson was halfway through his math homework when his phone chirped, signaling an incoming text from Kellie. It caught him by surprise; he hadn't expected to hear from her until morning. For a split second, until he started reading the message, he thought maybe she just wanted to say hi.

>R U OK? Lots of sirens in town.

She's thinking Eddie's causing trouble again.

That made him wonder if their relationship would continue after they solved the problem of Eddie. Without the drama and excitement, would she still be interested in him?

She didn't have to text you at all, idiot. She could have just told you everything in school tomorrow. Plus, she asked if you're okay. That must mean she cares, right?

Unsure how he should be feeling, he responded back.

>I'm ok. Thanks. Just studying.

>OK. Looked up séances. Wanna talk about it?

>Yes. But not 2nite. In case…u know who is around.

>Right. ;)

A ghost emoji followed, and then a scared face.

Carson smiled as he typed.

>TTY, ok? ☺

Her answer was just as brief.

>K. C U tomorrow. XX ☺

Carson's heart did a double-beat and that by-now-familiar tingling started up in his stomach. He found himself smiling as he read the last line again.

Kisses and smiley face! I—

Sudden thunder shook the trailer. Carson gasped and dropped his phone. He jumped out of his chair and looked outside, positive it was Eddie's motorcycle rattling the windows. A second crash followed, only this one was dimmer, higher up in the sky. Flickering heat lightning accompanied the rumbling. Embarrassed by his reaction he sat down again, waiting for his heart to resume a normal pace.

Get hold of yourself. It was one thing to believe in a ghost or demon, another to think that a motorcycle could come back from the dead as well.

Oh yeah? What about the strange thunder in town lately, and the broken windows? That all started happening the same time as Eddie's return.

With no logical answer forthcoming from his brain, Carson found himself unable to concentrate on his studies, thanks to a jittery feeling in his chest that slowly grew stronger as the night wore on.

★   ★   ★

Eddie stormed across the skies in a fury. He'd gone home to see how his mom and Carson were doing. They were his only links to his old life, and a piece of him didn't want to let that go, wanted to still feel some connection to his family. To be human. Even if it was just in spirit.

Instead, he'd arrived just in time to see Carson reading a text message from Chief Jones's hot piece of ass daughter. It hadn't said much, but he'd seen enough to have a good idea of what they were planning, considering the stuff they'd been searching on the computer the last time.

A séance. They're planning a fucking séance. To contact me, for sure. And why would they want to do that?

Because they want to stop me. To get rid of me for good.

The thought of it made his blood boil – or would have, if he'd had blood. Who the hell were they to cock-block his only chance for revenge? Especially Carson. He should know better, should realize that Eddie was doing it partly for him and Mom, so that no one would ever bother them again.

Can they really stop me?

Sudden fear dampened his fiery rage. He slowed Diablo to a coast. What if they did call him into the real world? The fact that they believed in his existence at all, were looking for ways to destroy him, was bad enough. Could they trap him somehow? Send him somewhere else, cast him away forever? If anyone could do it, he'd bet on Carson. The kid was too damn smart for his own good. The more he thought about it, the more likely it seemed they'd find a way.

I need to find out more.

Except he couldn't go back to Carson's room – he'd already seen that Carson was playing it smart, not committing any of the details to paper or even to his phone.

Is that because he knows I might be watching him?

Another frightening possibility. Not only were they aware of him coming and going, but they knew, or at least suspected, he could take over peoples' bodies. Including Carson's.

If someone did that to me, I'd sure as hell want them dead and gone.

This is different, thought. I have a job to do. For them. For what they did to me. And I can't let anyone stop me, not even him.

With watching Carson out of the question, there was only one other choice left.

It was time to pay Kellie Jones a visit.

★   ★   ★

Kellie was asleep when Eddie arrived at her window, her still form visible in the ghostly blue light of her laptop's screensaver. He kept Diablo's throttle to a low growl, not even loud enough to rattle the glass. The thought of entering a sleeping person made him hesitate a moment; he didn't want to be stuck inside her until she woke up.

Shit. Gotta try. I need to know what they're up to.

Sliding off Diablo, he passed through the window and into Kellie's still form softly as a summer breeze. There was a moment of pure blackness, and then he opened his eyes and saw the ceiling above him in the dark room.

Eddie sat up, marveling at the strangeness of her body. His skin prickled with goosebumps and every sense seemed amped to the max. The flowery smells of perfume and shampoo filled his nose and the sheets were cool against his flesh. He felt filled to the brim with energy, like a cat ready pounce. Even more than when he'd been inside Carson, this body felt ready to leap into the air, do somersaults and handsprings.

He took several deep breaths, forcing himself to calm down. *You're in control.* He repeated the words several times. The last thing he needed was to get distracted and have Kellie's body react the wrong way, at the wrong time.

He swung his legs out of bed and sat up. Every muscle seemed to vibrate, ached to move. Other sensations appeared, a weird anxious feeling in his chest and lower belly. Even his nipples were tingling.

Speaking of which...

He walked over to the mirror and lifted up Kellie's shirt. Ran one hand across her breasts, wondering if Carson had felt them yet. Or if anyone had.

How far have you gone with my little brother? Has he done this? He squeezed one breast harder, was rewarded with an electric jolt of pleasure that ran down to between his legs.

You like that? Maybe I should do more. Take this body out for a test drive? Pay Carson a visit and see what—

An image of Carson's face rose up in his mind, splashing cold water on the sudden lust coursing through him.

Christ! What the hell are you thinking? That's your brother!

Eddie let the shirt fall back down and moved away from the mirror. *Not what you came here for, dude. First things first. Find out what this bitch knows.*

There'll be time later for fun and games.

He got up and went to her desk, where he shuffled through the papers and notebooks until he eventually found what he was looking for tucked between her math and chemistry textbooks. A cold rage took hold of him when he saw what she had hidden.

Printouts that explained how to conduct a séance. Detailed descriptions of ghosts and spirits and even demons. Worst of all, a list of things that could be used to bind and control supernatural beings.

"Goddammit!" Eddie threw the papers on the bed. Even his own brother was turning against him now, just like everyone else. All his life, people had looked down on him. Told him he wasn't worth shit. Told him what to do, how to dress. Threatened to lock him away if he didn't get his act together.

And now they were trying to control him in death, too.

"Ain't gonna happen, bitches." Eddie picked the papers up. He was ready to burn them right there, but what good would that do, except tip the little shits off that he knew what was going on. Besides, they probably had everything saved in their computers or on their phones. Better they think he didn't know he'd found out their stupid plans.

That way he could really surprise the hell out of them.

He sat down at Kellie's desk and read through the printouts again, doing his best to memorize the unfamiliar terms. Then he put the papers in order as best he could remember and tucked them back in place.

Kellie's cell phone chose that moment to give a soft chime and he jumped, knocking a couple of school books to the floor. Cursing under his breath, he quickly put the books back on the desk, grabbed the phone, and hurried to her bed. A few heartbeats later his caution was rewarded when Chief Jones's sleepy voice called out.

"Kellie? You still awake?" Floorboards creaked and the bedroom door opened partway. Eddie bit his cheek to keep from laughing as Johnny Ray looked in, said his daughter's name once more, and then softly closed the door and returned to his own bed.

Eddie counted to fifty before sitting up and checking the phone. Maybe it was Carson, with more information about their plans to bind him.

It wasn't. Instead, it turned out to be a picture message from one of Kellie's girlfriends, showing her at a party in someone's house. He recognized her face; she'd been the bitchy one at Rosie's, the one who'd been looking down her nose at Carson just for grabbing a few gator nuggets. Like her shit didn't stink. Beneath the picture it said 'U should be here'.

"Fuck you." Same old crap, different person. *I'll bet no one invited Carson to the party. Just like I never got invited to anything when I was a kid. Can't have trailer trash like the Ryders at your house.* Eddie tossed the phone onto the bed and prepared to leave Kellie's body. Then a thought hit him.

Wait. It's only a little past midnight. Jones had his chance to party. Why not let his daughter break some rules?

He picked up the phone and typed in a message.

>Where r u?

★   ★   ★

The party was in full swing when Eddie arrived. He'd grabbed a t-shirt off the floor in Kellie's room and then tip-toed out of the house. From there it was just a fifteen-minute walk to the party, which was happening at the house of a senior whose parents were away.

Hip-hop music blasted from the open windows and a few teenagers stood outside, smoking or pissing or both. Eddie noticed a couple of guys eyeing him as he passed, and he wondered if it was because he hadn't bothered putting on a bra or because no one expected to see the Chief's daughter at a party.

Inside, he barely had time to grab a bottle of beer before a dusky-skinned girl with beads strung in her dark hair ran up to him, her eyes glazed over and a red plastic cup in her hand.

"Kellie!" the girl squealed. He recognized her as Melanie Parris, the same girl who'd texted Kellie earlier. "You came! Ohmygod, I can't believe it! Kellie Jones at her first after-hours party!"

"Yeah." Eddie swigged some beer and burped. "Why not? You only live once, right?"

"You know it! C'mon, let's dance!" Melanie tugged at his arm, spilling her own drink, something red and fruity, in the process. It joined dozens of other stains on the living room carpet. Eddie laughed to himself.

Ooh, someone's parents are going to be mighty pissed when they get home.

"No dancing for me. This music sucks." He pulled his arm away.

"What?" Melanie managed to look hurt and befuddled all at once. It was a look he'd seen on many girls at many parties. The kind of look where he knew he could get her into a bedroom or bathroom easy as pie, and have her pants off with just a few sweet whispered words.

She was hammered.

It made Eddie want to grab her and kiss her.

Not yet. Keep it in your pants for a while.

"This hip-hop is bullshit. I wanna hear some real music." Eddie headed for the sound system, which was a satellite radio connected wirelessly to speakers throughout the house. He hit the menu button and scrolled through until he came to the classic metal channel, aptly named Graveyard. He punched *Enter* and was rewarded with the burning guitar solo from Judas Priest's 'Painkiller'.

"Now this is the shit," he said to nobody in particular. Melanie had already wandered off and the only people standing nearby were two jock types wearing the orange and blue jackets of the high school football team.

"Hey, what happened to the music?" someone called out. A chorus of groans and shouted obscenities followed. Eddie turned and saw a bunch of kids staring at him with angry looks.

"You can hear that dance crap anytime," Eddie said to them, raising his voice over the thundering chords. "This is real party music. C'mon, let's drink!" He raised his beer to the crowd and chugged the whole thing down. Kellie's stomach, unused to alcohol of any kind, immediately started gurgling and churning, which made Eddie laugh out loud. He wondered how she'd like waking up in her own puke later.

"Change it back, bitch!" an older girl yelled, stepping forward. One of her friends immediately pulled her to the side and told her to shut up. Eddie couldn't hear what they said after that, but he imagined she was being warned not to start trouble with the police chief's daughter.

This is too fucking cool. I've got a free pass to do anything I want.

His first thought was to start a fight; just walk right up to the biggest, baddest girl at the party and slug her in the face. Maybe bust a few of Kellie-bitch's knuckles in the process. Then he saw a couple making out in the kitchen and a better idea came to him.

Maybe if I can do something to break Carson and Kellie up, they'll be too upset to worry about me. All I have to do is make him think his girl cheated on him.

Changing direction, Eddie headed back to where the two football jocks were filling up their beers from a keg. Pushing in between them, he took a beer from the taller one's hand and chugged it. This time getting the whole glass down was harder. His stomach sloshed like an over-inflated water balloon. But he didn't stop until he finished it. Then he wrapped Kellie's arms around the boy's waist, leaned up, and kissed him. The jock froze for a moment, and then jammed his tongue into Eddie's mouth.

For a brief second, Eddie thought he might puke at the idea of kissing another guy. It was like having your mouth invaded by a giant slug, and he wondered if he'd kissed that badly when he'd been alive. It didn't help that the jock's breath tasted of beer and cigars.

Then Kellie's body responded to the physical sensations and the grossness of the situation faded away. A tingling feeling ignited between her legs and a series of shivers ran up her back as the jock pulled her closer and placed a strong hand on her ass.

Eddie let himself give in to his new body's desires, felt himself getting lost in them. The sensations were almost overwhelming, threatening to cast all conscious thought aside.

Damn. It's not so bad being a girl. I should have done this sooner.

Pain and pleasure blossomed in Eddie's left breast as the jock's fingers squeezed and pinched it through the thin cotton of the t-shirt. When he realized Eddie had no bra on, jock-boy smiled and slid his hand under the material. The moment his fingers touched Kellie's nipple, Eddie found himself moaning.

"C'mon, let's find a room." The jock took Eddie by the hand and led him through the crowd. Several guys whistled and cheered. Eddie let himself be led, still dizzy from his lust. They ended up in a small bedroom with plain white furniture and a twin bed in one corner. A guest room, Eddie figured, as the jock guided him into a sitting position on the bed.

As if by magic, the jock's pants and underwear were suddenly on the floor and he was tugging Eddie's jeans down. Eddie helped, wriggling out of them and then pulling his shirt off so he was only in his panties. The guy climbed onto the bed with her and started kissing her again, his hands roaming all over her body.

The bedroom door flew open, flooding the room with bright light and dance music.

"Oh, my God! Kellie! What are you doing?"

Eddie looked up and saw Melanie standing in the doorway, her eyes as wide as if she'd seen a ghost.

If you only knew, Eddie thought, and then decided to really start some trouble.

"He tried to rape me!" Eddie pointed at the jock. "He made me take my clothes off and then he was all over me."

"What? She came on to me. She wanted it."

"Bullshit." Eddie grabbed Kellie's jeans and pulled them on. "All I did was kiss him. That doesn't mean I wanted to fuck you."

"No! She's lying!" The jock looked back and forth between the two girls. Belatedly, he realized Kellie was fully dressed and he was standing with his pants around his ankles. "I swear. It wasn't me. It was her."

"Perv!" Melanie pushed him out of the way and grabbed Kellie's shirt. "C'mon, let's get out of here."

As Eddie went past the still protesting jock, he flipped up his middle finger. "Fuck you, douchebag. Next time keep your hands to yourself."

Then they were past him and back into the party, which was still going strong.

"Hey, everybody!" Eddie yelled, pointing towards the bedroom. "There's a guy in there jerking off!"

Dozens of faces turned in time to see the poor jock belatedly trying to find his pants. People crowded around the door, attracted to the misery of a peer the way sharks are drawn to blood. A few took out cell phones and started taking pictures.

He'll be on YouTube before he gets his zipper up. Eddie laughed and two of the speakers blew out in a squeal of feedback.

Melanie led the way to the back door. Eddie followed in her wake, pausing just long enough to grab a bottle of white wine off the kitchen counter.

"I can't believe that asshole," Melanie said, once they were in the relative quiet of the back lawn and heading for the road. "Fucking football players think they own the whole world."

"Forget him." Eddie held up the wine. "We can have our own little party."

"Kellie, what's gotten into you? I love it!" Melanie took the bottle and drank a long mouthful, then handed it back to Eddie, who chugged several gulps, the cheap wine turning into a burning river of acid as it went down his throat.

"Can't a girl cut loose once in a while?" Before Melanie could answer, Eddie grabbed her by the shoulders and pulled her into a hard kiss. There was a moment where the other girl tried to push away, and then it was gone as she crushed her soft lips against Eddie's and their tongues started a wild dance together. Unlike the jock's, Melanie's tongue was smooth as silk and flavored with wine and strawberry. It was a kiss that might have gone on forever if Eddie hadn't slipped his hand between them to squeeze a plump breast.

"Wait!" Melanie pushed away. "We can't do this. I'm not...I'm not into that."

"Could have fooled me," Eddie said, running his hand down her arm. She backed away further.

"Kellie, this isn't like you at all. I think maybe someone spiked your drink. Maybe they gave you roofies. Oh, God, maybe I drank some, too! What if we've been poisoned? Should we go to the hospital? Should we tell—"

Eddie couldn't take it anymore.

"Jesus Christ, shut the fuck up!"

He slapped her across the face. Melanie's head rocked back and her teeth clacked together, miraculously missing her tongue.

Melanie put a hand up to her cheek, which even in the dim light of the street lamps was already turning bright red. Her eyes went wide, then narrowed to slits as anger replaced surprise.

"You bitch! Fuck you, Kellie Jones." She turned and stomped her way down the street, leaving Eddie alone and laughing with the half-filled bottle.

"Damn. I was hoping for a girl fight. Well, no sense wasting good booze." He tipped the bottle up and chugged the remaining wine down. He had just enough time to toss the bottle away before his stomach rebelled and he puked up wine, beer, and half-digested chicken fingers all over his pants, sneakers, and the sidewalk.

"Fucking-a. That should make for interesting breakfast conversation tomorrow in the Jones house."

Twenty minutes later he was back in Kellie's room. He got into bed fully clothed and pulled the covers over himself.

"Good night, sweet thang."

An instant later, he rode Diablo into the night.

★   ★   ★

Eddie parked Diablo a thousand feet above Hell Creek, pondering his next move. He was bursting with energy; it seemed like he gained more and more with each body he possessed. Or maybe the younger ones charged him more. Whatever the reason, he knew he couldn't waste it.

Maybe now it's time to bust free from this shit hole.

So far he'd had no luck with the mystical barrier that confined him to Hell Creek. He figured he just wasn't strong enough yet to bash through the invisible wall.

That's going to change tonight.

Tonight he felt like he could smash his way through the center of the fucking Earth, blow the planet to bits. Nothing was going to stop him.

He rode Diablo all the way to the north end of the town limits, past the last houses, until he reached barren land and the barrier wouldn't let him move another inch forward. Then he aimed himself south and, with the barrier pressing against his back, let Diablo go full throttle, racing through the night faster than he'd ever gone before, faster than *anyone* had ever gone on a bike before. Houses and buildings turned into gray, elongated blurs below him, Main Street reduced to a darker gray stripe through their center.

By the time he shot past the trailer housing his mother and Carson, he knew he had to be doing more than two hundred and fifty miles per hour. Then there was only swamp and open road. Four seconds later he reached the south end of the town limits.

And hit a solid force so hard his supernatural form seemed to fuse with the pseudo-metal of Diablo, crushing each non-existent bone inside him and driving steel spears into every piece of his body. He had time for one long scream and then his mind shut down.

★   ★   ★

A ground-shaking explosion of sound shattered the pre-dawn darkness, rattling windows and setting off car alarms. Children cried out in their sleep and adults sat up in their beds, wondering what had happened. To the few people still awake in Hell Creek at that hour, it was just one more occurrence of the weird heat thunder that had plagued the town all month, and most of them didn't even pay attention to it anymore.

In his bed, Carson moaned and rolled over but didn't wake.

CHAPTER THIRTY-FOUR

The next day at school was not a good one for Carson. He arrived early, thinking Kellie would want to talk before homeroom. Except she wasn't on her bus. When she didn't show for first period, he started to worry. As soon as class was over he texted her, but got no answer. He considered calling, but on the off chance she was sick or something, and resting, he decided to wait.

By lunchtime, he couldn't take it anymore and called her cell. It went straight to voicemail.

The rest of the school day dragged on. He barely heard anything his teachers said, spent most of his time either secretively checking his phone for messages or staring into space, wondering what could be wrong with her. He considered asking Melanie or Cindy if they knew where she was, but they weren't in school, either. Dozens of possibilities drifted through his thoughts, ranging from a stomach virus to Kellie trying the séance on her own and ending up getting devoured by a demon.

The moment the final bell rang, he hurried down the hall and out the doors and then ran all the way to her house. By the time he arrived, he was gasping for breath and so covered in sweat that road dust had turned to mud on his neck and arms.

He was all set to march up the steps and pound on the door when he saw Kellie sitting on the front porch.

Crying.

"Kellie? What's the matter? What happened? Is everything okay?" He mentally kicked himself for his stupid question. *Of course everything isn't okay. She's bawling her eyes out.*

Kellie shook her head but didn't answer. Tears ran down her cheeks and a handful of used tissues on the floor next to her showed she'd been at it for a while.

Not sure what to do or say, Carson sat down and tried to put a hand on her shoulder, a gesture he figured might be comforting. Instead, she jerked away.

"Don't touch me!"

Had he done something to upset her? Try as he might, he couldn't think of what it was, but that didn't surprise him. In TV shows and movies, guys were always doing dumb things without realizing it. Why should he be any different? He certainly didn't have much experience with relationships. He stood up, figuring it would be better if he left her alone.

"No, don't go." Kellie snuffled back snot. "I just don't want to be touched right now."

"Okay." Carson sat down again, making sure to keep some space between them.

"Carson, something happened last night. Something bad. I did bad things. Or maybe I didn't. I don't know. I...I can't remember."

A cold chill crept over Carson, even though the day was hot and sunny. "You don't remember? Do you think...do you think it was Eddie?"

She shook her head, paused, and then shrugged her shoulders. "I sure hope so. I don't want to think I could have ever done what I did, not on my own. Either way, though, it doesn't matter. Everyone thinks it was me and I can't prove it wasn't." Kellie hid her face in her hands, leaving Carson to wonder exactly what it was that had happened. How bad could it be?

He asked.

And when she told him, he knew the answer to his question.

Bad. Very bad.

⋆　　⋆　　⋆

Up to that point in his life, the hardest thing Carson ever had to do was comfort his mother after Eddie's murder. That had been a terrible time and he'd always figured nothing could ever be worse, other than his mother dying before he graduated high school, meaning he'd have to go live in a foster home where he'd probably get beat up all the time by the other kids.

But leaving Kellie alone on her porch was pretty close. He

couldn't stay, because he had to get home to check on his mother and get her dinner ready. Kellie refused to leave, saying she just wanted to be alone so she wouldn't have to deal with anybody. And Carson understood that; after what she'd been through, it would be impossible to act like nothing was wrong around other people. But he also worried that his leaving would make things worse. More than once while telling the sordid details of her night − all relayed to her by Melanie and other people who'd been at the party − she'd stopped, unwilling to go on because she thought that when he heard the whole story he'd never want to be around her again. As if *that* would ever happen. But it was how she felt, and he respected that, even if he didn't agree.

In typical high school fashion, rumors were already flying. If Carson had hung out with a different crowd he might have heard them. Not that it mattered. Kellie's phone was blowing up with comments, people saying she'd passed out in bed with a guy, that she'd offered to do the whole football team, that she'd been wasted on ecstacy and ran through the party naked.

All she really knew was that she'd been in a room with someone and freaked out when he got naked, and then she'd tried to make out with Melanie. She'd woken up in bed with puke all over her clothes and no memory of anything.

Carson had done his best to convince Kellie it wasn't her fault, it had to be Eddie who'd done those things, and that he didn't think any less of her. But he was pretty sure she didn't believe him. And as bad as he felt for her, all of his emotions were currently crushed under the weight of his hatred for his dead brother. If it had been possible to kill Eddie for good right then and there − douse him with holy water, drive a stake through his heart, cast his soul back to hell − he'd have gladly done it without a moment's hesitation.

Instead, he had to act like nothing was wrong in front of his mother, fix her dinner, and make sure she took her medications, all while seething so badly inside it took every ounce of his control not to scream and punch the walls and kick furniture over.

As soon as he could, he escaped the house and called Kellie to check on her. They'd been texting each other every fifteen minutes or so, with a secret code. If either of them responded wrong, the other would know Eddie had possessed them.

"I'm on my way," Carson said. "Jello."

"Meet me behind the house," she answered. "Pizza."

Carson shoved his phone in his pocket and got on his bike, hoping that even if Eddie saw their messages, he wouldn't figure out the code was their favorite school lunch foods.

Kellie's house was a ten-minute ride, and during that time Carson went over their plan in his head again and again, trying to find any possible flaws. Before leaving Kellie earlier in the afternoon, they'd agreed that the only way to be sure Eddie wasn't watching them while they conducted their séance was if they knew he was up to trouble somewhere else. That trouble could be anything, but they figured it was a safe bet that if something strange or violent was happening in town, Eddie was involved somehow.

Which was why he and Kellie planned on spending the evening with one of her father's old police radios, a handheld unit the size of a sneaker. As soon as they heard a police call that sounded like Eddie's doing, they'd immediately start their séance.

Seated on an old blanket in Kellie's backyard, the radio crackling sporadically between them, a warm breeze delivering the soft scent of roses from the garden and fresh-cut grass from the neighbor's lawn, Carson was almost able to forget why they were there and imagine them on a romantic date instead. In fact, the temptation to put his arm around her was so strong he actually found himself about to do it more than once and had clench his fist to keep his arm still. He was afraid that if he touched her she would flinch, and then the spell would be broken. As much as she'd insisted earlier that she just wanted to be alone for a while, and that she didn't want him to think bad of her, he worried there might be something else wrong. That she might not want to be around him right now because he was Eddie's brother.

What if he was right? Would things ever go back to the way they were? Could they? He wasn't sure, but he hoped destroying the monster Eddie had become would be a good step in that direction, that maybe it would remove some of the distance between them.

Maybe they could even be boyfriend and girlfriend.

The radio spat out static again, drawing his attention.

"Chief, we've got a disturbance reported at nineteen Palomino Trail Road. That's one-nine Palomino."

Kellie bit her lip as she turned the volume up on the radio.

"On my way. Who called it in?"

"Neighbor. It's Jenny Gunderson's place. I tried calling, but no answer."

"Okay. I'll be there in five. Send Wilbur as backup."

"My brother didn't like Mr. Gunderson," Carson said.

Kellie nodded. "Remember what happened at Rosie's the other day?" She put the radio down and grabbed the brown paper bag sitting next to her.

"I think this is it."

CHAPTER THIRTY-FIVE

Eddie's slow return to consciousness brought no relief from the throbbing agony in his head or the total darkness surrounding him. How long he'd dwelt in his semi-awake state, he had no idea. Minutes, hours, days – there was no way for him to tell. Eventually, the pain subsided to a steady ache, worse than a hangover but not quite as bad as the time he'd slipped on some grease in the shop and fallen head-first onto the arm of the pneumatic lift, resulting in a concussion and fifteen stitches.

What worried him more than the pain was the blindness.

Had he finally overdone it? Had his attempt to leave Hell Creek driven him from the Earth, left him trapped in some kind of limbo, awaiting his final judgment? Or was he somewhere else, a place where the mind just floated through empty space forever?

He tried flexing his arms and legs, felt more than a little relief when it resulted in a sensation of movement, although he could tell he still had no physical form.

Which means I should be able to move my whole body, then.

He tried it, commanding his self to rise up. His incorporeal body responded, and an instant later he found himself rising through the ground to hover above a place that by now was as familiar to him as his own bedroom.

His grave site.

That explained the darkness. Back to where it all started. Or ended. Or started again, depending on how you look at it. Grave site, birth site, wish I may, wish I might.

I wish I could kill someone tonight.

Why, I think I will, stank you very much.

He laughed, but the sky stayed silent, his supernatural battery drained to near zero from his breakout attempt. He let himself slip back down to the ground, resting atop the sprouting grass of his plot.

So peaceful. Relaxing.

To the west, the setting sun was minutes away from dipping below the horizon, telling him he'd been out for an entire day. Wide strokes of deep purple and red painted the clouds, and the nearby gravestones cast long, darkening shadows across the neatly manicured lawn. Too weak to move, Eddie watched the sun complete its journey, finally sinking out of sight in a blaze of color. When the first stars of the evening made their appearance in the not-yet-black sky, he tried to stand up, but couldn't muster the energy to do so.

Can't stay here forever. Got a job to do. He couldn't quite remember what that job was — something about revenge? — but he knew he had to do it. Knew the memory would come back as soon as his strength returned.

Need to recharge.

That meant finding someone he could possess, draw strength from. Somebody he didn't give two shits about. But they also had to be close by, because he didn't think he could move his body very far. Maybe the night watchman? Or a gravedigger? Someone had to still be around. Otherwise he'd be stuck in the graveyard all night.

Just then, two circles of light came around a corner and quickly resolved into the headlights of a car heading for the exit.

A car Eddie recognized from the several times he'd worked on it at his garage.

Todd fucking Gunderson.

Just thinking the name sparked the embers of his anger, although he couldn't recall why he hated the man so much. Just that he did.

It took all his remaining strength to push himself up and glide into the car as it went past. The slight breeze threatened to send him spiraling off to the side but Eddie managed to keep himself on course and slip into Todd Gunderson's body. It wasn't his most graceful entry; Todd's hands jerked the wheel hard to the left and the old Volvo clipped two headstones before Eddie got control and guided it back onto the path.

Having solid form seemed to bolster his energy levels a bit, and except for a couple of brief dizzy spells, he managed to make it back to the Gundersons' house without any trouble. Grateful to find the place empty, he went into the bedroom and immediately fell asleep.

Eddie woke to the sound of a woman's voice in the other room calling, "Todd? Are you home?" He glanced at the clock, and saw with some surprise he'd only been asleep for an hour. Yet he felt ten times better. So much so that when Jenny Gunderson walked into the bedroom, he immediately felt himself growing hard. And jealous.

How did a wuss like Todd Gunderson manage to snag a piece of ass like Jenny?

It was just another part of Eddie's life that didn't seem fair. Girls like Jenny would never date someone like Eddie. Oh, sure, they'd sneak around and enjoy a fling with a 'bad boy,' but a serious relationship? Never. Not in a million years. No, they preferred men they could wrap around their fingers, men who would gladly fork over their paychecks and let themselves be led around by their dicks. A stuck-up bitch like Jenny Gunderson wouldn't know what to do with a real man.

But she was going to find out.

"Todd? What are you doing home so early?" Jenny asked, tossing her purse on a nightstand. "I thought you were going back to the school after the cemetery."

"Changed my mind," Eddie said, sitting up and giving her his best smile. "I decided there was a better way to spend my night."

She gave him a curious look. "Better how? Don't you have to be there for the Science Club meeting?"

"Let's just say being surrounded by all that death made me realize we have to enjoy life while we have the chance." He got off the bed and walked toward her. Although she didn't back away, something in her posture changed, letting him know that she'd never experienced her husband acting in such a forceful manner.

Of course not. He's a pussy.

"Todd, what are you—?"

He stopped her words by grabbing her, pulling her close, and smashing his lips against her mouth in a violent kiss. She tried to pull away but he pushed her against the bedroom wall hard enough to rattle the perfume bottles on her dresser. Pinning her tight with one hand against her shoulder, Eddie slid his other hand down to her chest, gripping a breast as he shoved his tongue into her mouth.

He'd figured she'd quickly change from surprised and frightened to hot and horny. After all, it was her husband, at least in her mind. And it had probably been a long time since she had it good and rough, especially being married to Goody-Goody Gunderson.

Eddie increased the pressure of his fingers on her breast, was rewarded with a moan against his tongue.

That's more like it. Now she's—

His whole body exploded with pain as Jenny rammed her knee into his balls. He released her and stumbled back until he hit the bed, then he collapsed to the floor, groaning and retching while his hands gingerly cupped his balls.

"What the hell is the matter with you? Why would you do something like that?" Tears ran down Jenny's face as she shouted at him.

"Fucking goddamn sonofabitch!" Eddie pushed himself to his feet, doing his best to ignore the stomach-wrenching ache between his legs. "You fuckin' bitch. Is that how you treat your husband? Maybe you need to learn some manners."

He raised his fists and took a step forward, but before he could reach her, Jenny turned and ran out of the room. Eddie followed as fast as he could, each step sending darts of pain through his balls and into his stomach. He wondered if he'd even be able to get it up when he caught her, decided it didn't matter. It would be just as much fun to slap her around and then let Gunderson suffer the consequences.

He rounded the corner into the kitchen and found himself facing what looked like a wooden hammer covered in pyramid-shaped points.

"One more step and I'll pound you like last night's chicken." Jenny stood on the other side of the counter that divided the kitchen and dining room, her angry tone all the more menacing for the weapon she wielded. Not that Eddie cared.

"Give it your best shot," he told her, taking one step and then another. "Ain't gonna stop me from fucking the shit out of you tonight."

He braced his hands against the counter as she raised her arm, prepared to duck one way or the other when she swung the hammer at his face.

She slammed the mallet straight down onto his left hand, crushing flesh and bone between the wooden points and the counter top. Eddie screamed as fire raced up his arm. He jerked his hand away, the top already red and swollen. Beads of blood sat inside the triangular depressions the mallet had left in his skin.

"Goddammit!" He dove across the counter and grabbed her shirt with both hands. Jenny swung the mallet again but her balance was off and the edge of it only struck a glancing blow against his arm. Before she could rear back for another swing, he yanked it out of her hand and tossed it across the kitchen. Jenny cried out for help and he silenced her with a fist to the mouth, a solid blow that rocked her head back and left her so dazed she crumpled to the floor when he let go of her.

Eddie rounded the counter and paused, considering his options. *What to do, what to do? Drag her into the living room or just give her the old sausage right on the kitchen floor?*

Fuck it. Why waste time? He unzipped his pants, paused when her cell phone rang.

I doubt it's for me. He laughed at his joke, causing the lights to flicker, and finished stripping his pants off. Then he knelt down next to Jenny, eager to get a look at the tits he'd admired for so many years from across the counter at Rosie's. She moaned but didn't wake up as he tore her uniform blouse open, exposing a heavy white bra that annoyed him. He'd expected something more feminine. Lace, with little slits for the nips to poke through. Not a grandma bra. It didn't matter, though. He thumbed the clasp open and pulled the two halves away, getting his first good look at the breasts he'd fantasized about since he'd been Carson's age.

One of them had a three-inch square piece of medical gauze taped to it.

Frowning, he carefully peeled the tape up and folded the

bandage back, revealing a freshly stitched, semi-circular wound with some black, crusty blood scabbed around the sutures. More dried blood stained the inside of the gauze.

What the hell?

Eddie leaned back, his erection shrinking as he stared at the bruised flesh surrounding the stitches. She might have just had a mole removed, but remembering her reaction when he'd made his first move on her, he didn't think so.

Breast cancer? Jenny Gunderson? It didn't seem possible. She was too young. But the more he thought about it, the more sense it made. A biopsy. That explained why she'd been so cold when he'd made his first move on her. Why else would a wife turn down her husband?

Now she thinks Gunderson is a Grade-A asshole, the kind of limp-dick who'd force himself on a woman going through a cancer scare.

Eddie's guilt vanished, replaced by manic glee. The whole situation kept getting better. Not that Jenny deserved cancer, but she'd sure as hell be kicking Gunderson out to the curb when she woke up.

All thoughts of raping Jenny disappeared, a new plan taking shape in his head. A plan that would have Gunderson's good name smeared across the front page of the newspaper all week, and him left suffering from the humiliation of it.

Pants still bunched around his ankles, Eddie shuffled into the kitchen and dialed 911.

"Something's wrong at the Gunderson house," he shouted, then hung up. He went into the living room and turned on the stereo as loud as it would go. When the phone rang, he hit the green button and cried out.

"Help! Help!"

Eddie dropped the phone, the voice on the other end lost in the music. While he waited for the cops to arrive, he grabbed a beer from the refrigerator and made a ham and cheese sandwich. He was enjoying some of Jenny's delicious homemade cookies when the first red and blue lights lit up the windows.

Time to rock out with my cock out.

Eddie threw open the door, still naked from the waist down.

"Howdy, Chief!" he called out, waving a cookie in the air. "C'mon in and have a beer!"

"Put your hands up and step outside." Jones's amplified voice echoed off the nearby houses, drawing neighbors onto porches like moths to a bug zapper.

Eddie gave Jones a big smile and raised his hands. He was preparing to walk down the steps when invisible claws dug deep into his essence and tore him from Gunderson's body as painfully as if he'd been gutted alive.

His screams followed him as he flew across town.

CHAPTER THIRTY-SIX

Carson and Kellie had wasted no time getting to work on their séance. With no idea of how long Eddie would be distracted, they knew they needed to hurry if they wanted their one chance to stop him from succeeding.

On the ground next to each of them was a bottle of holy water and a baggie of sea salt. Carson placed five lit candles, each with a drop of Kellie's blood on them, in a rough circle around their blanket and then used the salt to draw a circle around the blanket. At the same time, Kellie took the final object, a plastic doll, from their bag of supplies. It was a cheap GI Joe knockoff Carson had found in the back of his closet. After deciding that Eddie needed to be dealt with in a decisive manner, they'd reviewed the different tactics detailed in Kellie's research and chosen a spell to bind his spirit inside an inanimate object as the safest – and most permanent – solution.

While Carson finished the preparations and sat down, Kellie unfolded a piece of paper and chanted the words written on it.

"Eddie Ryder, we command your spirit to hear us.

Eddie Ryder, heed our call.

Eddie Ryder, we command your spirit to appear to us.

Eddie Ryder, show yourself."

While she repeated the spell, Carson joined in, at the same time sprinkling holy water over each of the candles. After four repetitions he began to feel more than a little foolish. Nothing was happening, which is what he should have expected. After all, if conducting a séance was something anyone could do, there'd be people all over the world trapping ghosts and demons and—

With a sound like a balloon exploding, a semi-transparent image of Eddie's face appeared over their heads.

Carson let out a shout and dropped the bottle as more of Eddie's body took shape.

"Use the salt!" Kellie screamed, grabbing a handful and tossing it at the candles.

Eddie's face grew more distinct and his mouth opened. No sounds came out, but Carson knew his brother well enough to recognize he was angry.

Very angry.

Carson picked up his own baggie, never taking his eyes off his brother's ghostly form, and sprinkled it over the candles on his side of the blanket. When they were done, Kellie handed him the plastic doll and started reading from a new sheet of paper.

"Eddie Ryder, we bind you with salt and flame. You cannot harm us. You cannot disobey us. You are ours to command. Speak now, and tell us why you haunt this plane."

There was another loud *pop!* and suddenly Eddie had a voice.

"—fuckers! I'll make you pay for this! Let me the fuck go!"

Carson's stomach twisted. Eddie's voice was as real as if he were alive, so real you could almost forget the way his body disappeared just below the waist, or how the rest of him faded to wispy smoke around the edges. Unexpected tears burst free as Carson's sorrow and grief pushed past his recent hatred of his brother.

"Eddie!" he cried out, reaching up with his free hand.

"No!" Kellie tried to slap his hand away, but it was too late. Eddie's insubstantial fingers touched Carson's, igniting a fireworks of bright white sparks inside the circle.

Carson shouted in pain and fell onto his back. Eddie's mocking laughter filled the night air.

"You stupid fuck! This ain't no movie, little brother. Let me the fuck out of here or I swear I'll make sure your little whore gets ass-raped by the whole football team the next time I take her out for a spin."

Carson's momentary grief shattered at Eddie's words, and he cursed himself for being so stupid. Even though his fingers felt like they were on fire, he grabbed the doll with both hands and held it up. "Fuck you, Eddie. Say hello to your new home. Now, Kellie!"

Although Carson had skipped several steps in their plan, Kellie was ready. "Eddie Ryder, we bind your soul. Eddie Ryder, we bind your thoughts. Eddie Ryder, we bind your heart."

Each time she spoke his name, she cast a handful of salt at his image. Although the salt passed right through him, something in it affected him and he cried out in pain, his features twisting and mutating like a wax figurine on a hot sidewalk.

After Kellie tossed the final handful, Carson thrust the doll forward into Eddie's swirling body. For one brief second, Eddie's diaphanous form froze in place, human smoke made somehow immobile by magic.

Then it disappeared into the plastic doll so fast Carson hardly had time to register what had happened before it was over.

"Did you see that?" He waved the doll at Kellie. "It was like a genie going into a lamp. He—"

"Holy water!" Kellie screamed, pointing at the bottle.

"Oh!" Carson dropped the doll and scrambled for the holy water he'd tossed aside earlier. He opened it and poured the blessed water over the doll, while they both chanted, "I bind you, Eddie Ryder," three more times.

After that, neither of them spoke for several heartbeats.

Carson finally broke the silence. "Is that it?"

Kellie shrugged. "I don't know. That was the only binding spell I could find that didn't include all sorts of herbs and potions we'd never be able to get. It's supposed to be a spell that wizards and high priests used back in ancient times. It's for binding demons inside a person. That was as close as I could find, and I just substituted the doll."

"Well, as long as it—"

The world disappeared in a white, soundless explosion. Carson screamed, but no sound reached his ears.

Then even his thoughts were gone.

★　　★　　★

Eddie's first thought was to shoot lightning bolts down on the two unconscious figures below him, just let loose with explosive energy until nothing remained of the whole goddamned yard but a smoking crater. He actually had his hand raised in the air before he remembered it was Carson down there, and as much as his little brother had hurt him – physically *and* emotionally – with his betrayal, they were still brothers. And nothing came before family. So instead, he vented his anger into a nearby swamp, blasting several holes in the soft earth and setting a dozen trees on fire before his fury used itself up.

Even after he regained control of himself, the whole episode still had him straddling the line between enraged and total insanity. Not that he was aware of his mental state. He only knew he was so far beyond pissed off he didn't have words to describe it.

How Carson and his goddamn girlfriend had managed to even temporarily cage him was beyond comprehension. Two teenagers with nothing but some candles, some salt, and a spell from the internet? It shouldn't have been possible. But they'd done it, stolen him right the fuck out of Gunderson's body and pulled him across town, trapped him in some kind of supernatural bird cage, and then stuffed him into a fucking plastic doll of all things.

He couldn't let it happen again, no way, no fucking how. He had to keep Carson and Little Miss Bitch Titties apart, at least until he finished taking his revenge on Hank and the rest of the town. But he'd have to be careful so that he didn't hurt Carson in the process.

At least not any more than the little shit hurt me.

Once he figured out what to do, it was just a matter of waiting a couple of minutes for Carson to wake up and then slipping inside and taking over. He was tempted to leave Kellie lying there on the burning blanket, but he figured he shouldn't deprive Carson of his one chance for pussy, so he grabbed her ankles and dragged her over to a section of lawn that was well away from any of the flames.

Then he started walking toward town.

⋆ ⋆ ⋆

Johnny Ray Jones was heading back to the station when Sharon Mays' voice came over the radio.

"Chief, we have an 11-25 out near the corner of Main and Hyacinth. Possible arson. Fire truck's already on the way. Are you still in the area or should I send Delbert?"

Johnny Ray slammed his palm against the steering wheel and cursed. He was less than a mile away from Hyacinth. What he really wanted to do was get started on the paperwork for Todd Gunderson's arrest – which was going to be another pain in the ass on top of all the other shit that needed his attention – but his conscience wouldn't allow it. It would take Delbert Beauchamps ten or fifteen minutes to get to Hyacinth Street from the station.

"No, I'll handle it," he told Sharon. "I'm almost there right now."

The one good thing about taking the call was that from Hyacinth it was only a hop and skip to his own house. Assuming it was just a brush fire, he could duck in and check on Kellie before heading back to the station. Maybe even change his sweat-soaked shirt and grab a snack, since it looked like he'd be stuck at his desk until at least midnight. If not longer.

Christ, at this rate I should just put a cot in my office.

Johnny Ray was still two blocks from Hyacinth when he saw the reddish-orange glow of flames down the street. His first thought was that some kid had lit garbage cans on fire. It wouldn't be the first time that'd happened.

Then he got closer and saw there were small fires randomly burning in the gutters on both sides of the street. None of them were larger than a basketball in diameter, but there had to be at least twenty of them lighting up the night.

He was so focused on the fires that he didn't see the person walking down the center of the road until it was almost too late. Johnny Ray slammed on the brakes, sending the SUV into a screeching skid that ended up with the driver's door only an arm's length away from the figure, whom he belatedly recognized as Carson Ryder.

His nostrils and throat burning from the pungent, skunk-like stink of charred rubber, Johnny Ray opened his window and leaned out.

"Carson? What are you doing here?"

The boy didn't answer, just stared straight ahead, a dazed look in his eyes. His hair stuck up in all directions and dirt coated his face.

Jesus. He's in shock. Johnny Ray's first thought was to get the kid to the hospital. He was halfway out of the car when he noticed something in Carson's hand.

A box of long-stemmed matches.

Remembering Carson's violent outburst a few days earlier, and thinking he could be wacked on PCP or something, Johnny Ray slowed down and approached the boy with one hand hovering near his gun. "Carson, are you okay, son? You can talk to me. What happened?"

Carson opened his mouth, but instead of speaking, he started to sing.

"Burning fire, in the night. Demon flames, Hell's alight. Rock on, Chief." Carson raised a fist, his forefinger and pinky extended in the classic devil horns.

Then his eyes closed and he collapsed onto the road.

Johnny Ray groaned and reached for his radio as the first fire truck rounded the corner, siren crying.

I really hope this whole day is just a bad dream.

Then another thought came to him.

Kellie!

CHAPTER THIRTY-SEVEN

Eddie waited until the ambulance was on its way to the hospital before re-entering Carson's body. It hadn't taken the EMTs long to revive him, and Eddie'd been afraid Jones might decide to just drive him home instead of getting medical help. But it turned out there'd been no reason to worry. The moment a groggy Carson told them he had no idea what had happened, Jones shook his head and told them to get him to the hospital as fast as they could.

Now the EMT sat less than three feet away, fiddling with some type of machine hooked to Carson's arm. It pleased Eddie to no end that Roscoe Jackson was the tech who'd gotten the call.

The very same Roscoe Jackson who, while drunk in Homestead bar one night, had called Eddie's father a no-good piece of shit. "Town's better off with him gone."

Despite all the times Eddie had said the very same thing, to himself and to Carson, he flew into a rage and attacked Roscoe, hammering at him with both fists while the EMT cowered on the floor, his arms protecting his face. Only the fact that Eddie had been wasted on tequila and Budweiser and missed with half his punches had saved Roscoe from any injury. That, in turn, had kept him from pressing charges on Eddie after the bouncers pulled them apart and the cops arrived. When Carson had asked him why he got into the fight, he'd given an honest answer.

"Only family gets to talk shit about family."

"Hey, Roscoe," Eddie said, just loud enough to be heard over the ambulance's motor.

Jackson looked up, surprised to see his patient so alert.

He's gonna be even more surprised in a second.

"You know who you are?" Jackson asked.

"Sure. I'm Super-Dog, woof woof!" Eddie crossed his eyes and stuck out his tongue at the barrel-chested, acne-faced man, who to his credit didn't get flustered.

"You're in an ambulance. Do you remember what happened to you?"

"Yep." Eddie leaned forward and then raised his voice to a shout. "Hell Rider! Chrome and steel forged in Hell! Hell Rider, hear the tolling of death's bell!" Still screaming the lyrics to his favorite metal song, he tried to throw a punch at the EMT.

And discovered his arms were strapped to his sides.

"What the fuck? Let me go, you motherfucker!" Eddie struggled against the canvas bonds but couldn't free himself.

The EMT picked up a clipboard and made a note on a chart, then took a syringe and injected something into Eddie's arm. Less than a second later, Eddie felt a heaviness come over him.

Perfect! Now Carson will be useless for hours. And without him around, that little bitch of his won't dare do anything to stop me.

Grinning in anticipation, Eddie left Carson's body behind and headed into town. He had a few scores to settle before it was time to finish off Hank for good.

And I haven't forgotten that you're on my list, Roscoe. I'll be back for you in a little while.

★   ★   ★

The Hell Creek Theater occupied the southeast corner of Main Street and River Road. When Eddie and Diablo arrived, the blazing red marquee lights announced that the current showing was a double feature: *Ascent of the Dead* and *Buzzsaw*. Eddie checked the giant clock on the town hall tower, saw that it was almost ten-thirty.

Second movie's already started, I'll bet.

He'd chosen the movie theater because Denny Powell, Sandy's fuckhole of a father, owned it. And Denny Powell always had a bug up his ass about Sandy dating Eddie. Thought Eddie wasn't good enough for his little girl.

Wonder how he felt when she started dating Hank? How'd that grab you, douchebag? At least I didn't get her killed. Or at least I wouldn't have, if she and her boyfriend hadn't killed me. Come to think of it, someone probably would have killed her sooner or later 'cause of her fucking around. Did you know your daughter was a hoe? I sure didn't, but I guess I was the only one. Great big fucking joke on me.

Fuckin' bastards.

Gritting his non-existent teeth, Eddie glided into the building. As usual, Powell was in his office, counting the night's sales and entering the information into his computer. Eddie took up a spot across the room and let a trickle of energy flow from his fingers. In response, the lights flickered and sparks flew from the computer's CPU.

"What the fuck?" Powell jumped up and stared at his dead computer.

"Should have been nicer to me," Eddie said, even though Powell couldn't hear him. "Now it's time to join your cheating slut of a daughter."

Eddie took control of Powell and walked him down to the projection room. Unlike the newer theaters in Miami or Homestead, with their state-of-the-art digital systems, the Hell Creek Theater still used an old-fashioned reel-to-reel projector. Eddie was intimately familiar with its workings, having spent more than a few nights banging Sandy on the floor of the projection room on those rare occasions her father took a day off and Sandy had to cover for him. More often than not, they'd have to stop in the middle of what they were doing so Sandy could switch to the second reel.

Steeling himself, Eddie stuck his hand directly between the lamp and the film strip. There was a sizzling sound and the smell of roasted pork quickly filled the air.

The pain was a thousand times worse than he'd expected and he cried out as the super-hot glass melted his skin. Bolts of lightning flashed through the room. The walls caught fire and the projector exploded, sending metal shrapnel through the air. Several pieces hit Eddie in the arms and chest, but he never felt them over the horrible agony in his hand.

In the theater, the screen went dark and people started yelling to "turn the movie on!"

Fighting to keep himself anchored in Powell's body, Eddie

staggered out the door and down the short staircase that led to one of the balconies.

"Movie's over, assholes!" he shouted. "Eddie's back in town!" Several movie-goers looked up and pointed. A woman cried out, and Eddie noticed his clothes were on fire. Laughing, he raised his arms and began singing as loud as he could.

"I am the wrath of Hell
Engine tolling death bell
Riding fire through the night
Demon raging fear your plight
Hell Rider!"

Screaming the last word so loud it shattered all the ceiling lights, Eddie launched himself off the balcony in a flaming swan dive.

He let Powell's body fall halfway to the seats before he left it.

★　　★　　★

Kellie Jones heard someone calling her name. She tried to see who it was but couldn't. Everything was black. The voice in the darkness grew louder, more urgent. She smelled smoke and panic rose up inside her. *Fire!* Something was on fire, but she couldn't see what. Hands grabbed her shoulder and shook her, and she realized she couldn't see because her eyes were closed.

She opened them and saw her father's anxious face staring down at her.

"Dad?"

"Kellie! Thank God. Are you all right?"

Kellie pushed herself up into a sitting position. A quick bout of dizziness came and went, and she leaned against her father's arm until she was sure it wasn't coming back. A nearly full moon gave off just enough light to turn the yard a ghostly gray and her father's face into a pale mask.

"What...where's Carson?" She glanced around, noticed the charred blanket and burned grass off to one side. The candles were lumps of wax, the papers with her spell nothing but ashes already scattering in the mild breeze.

Something changed in her father's face, and she knew he had bad news about Carson. "Tell me."

He shook his head, not in denial of her request but in regret over his next words.

"He's...he's not well, Kellie. He had a breakdown of some kind. I found him down the road from here. He was incoherent, and he'd been lighting fires. I tried to talk to him but he just passed out. He's in the hospital now."

"Oh, no." *Eddie again. He did something to Carson.* She stood up. "I have to see him right now."

"No." This time when her father shook his head, it was an order. "It's going to be a while before he's allowed any visitors, and then the first one will be me. I haven't even told his mother yet. I might have to arrest him for arson."

Kellie opened her mouth to argue, then stopped. What could she say? That Carson hadn't really done those things, that he'd been possessed by his dead brother's ghost? A ghost that planned on killing more people? She'd end up in the hospital too, in a white room with padded walls.

"Okay, Dad. I think maybe I should go lie down for a while."

"Wait." He put his hand out. "Not so fast. What happened here?" He indicated the burnt lawn.

"Um, Carson and I...we were out here...just reading magazines and talking. Enjoying the night. We lit some candles so we could see. I must have fallen asleep."

Her father gave her a look so disapproving it felt like it held physical weight. She knew her resolve would melt under the force of his gaze, so she hurried away before he could say anything else.

The fact that he let her go without saying anything told her how badly he was hurting from her lying to him.

I hate doing it as much as he hates me doing it. But what choice was there? Hopefully he'd go back to work soon and she could sneak over to the hospital and help Carson escape so they could destroy Eddie Ryder forever.

After that, her father could punish her as much as he wanted.

CHAPTER THIRTY-EIGHT

Emma Sanchez paused on the way back to the ambulance to adjust the gun strapped to her ankle. She knew most EMTs didn't carry firearms, but ever since the night a coked-up Butch Franks had tried to rape her behind the Dairy King she'd always made sure to keep her gun with her. Roscoe Jackson, her usual shift partner most nights, knew about it, and the reason she carried it. He didn't approve, but then he was big enough that he didn't need a weapon if he encountered trouble.

And Emma had a feeling there was going to be trouble.

If not tonight, then soon.

They'd just dropped off Carson Ryder, who she'd always thought seemed like a nice enough kid. In the summers he sometimes cut her lawn for extra cash. She'd never have suspected him to be a druggie or an arsonist, but according to Chief Jones it seemed like he might be both. The kid certainly appeared to be wacked on something. It was just another strange occurrence in a long list of weird things happening in Hell Creek lately, things like windows breaking on their own, thunder and lightning in clear skies, and people killing each other – and themselves – for no logical reason.

It all made Emma very thankful for her gun.

"Hey." Roscoe stood by the back of the ambulance, smoking a cigarette. "Everything come out okay?"

Emma rolled her eyes. He said the same thing every time she went to the restroom, even if all she needed to do was splash some water on her face or wash her hands.

If he ever gets married, he'll drive his husband crazy.

Of course, the odds of Roscoe getting married – unless he moved out of town – were pretty slim. Hell Creek had its good points, but being tolerant of gays wasn't one of them. In that respect, the town was still mired in the 1950s.

"Sure did." She smacked his arm as she went past. "Damn near blew the toilet off the wall."

Roscoe made a sound that was half cough and half laughter, and she smiled, happy to have shocked him with her comeback. That would teach him. Maybe next time he'd think of something new to say.

She was about to open the passenger door when a strong hand grabbed her arm and swung her around so hard she slammed into the side of the ambulance.

★   ★   ★

Still hyped to the max after the rush of sending another asshole to an early grave, Eddie returned to the hospital to check on Carson and found Roscoe and his partner catching a smoke outside the Emergency Room.

Fuck, yeah. Perfect timing.

Let's see how he likes the taste of pussy for a change.

He slid into the hulking EMT and came up behind the Spanish-looking girl who was getting ready to open her door. She wasn't much to look at – fat in the ass and about ten years too old for Eddie's taste – but then all that mattered was having Roscoe wake up dick-deep in something other than a man's Hershey-hole.

Eddie slammed her against the side of the ambulance and smashed his lips against hers, cutting off her shout before it left her throat. Holding her in place with the weight of his body, he tore at her uniform with his hands, ripping the shirt and bra away so violently they left red welts on her skin.

The EMT screamed into Eddie's mouth and he punched her in the chest, knocking a gush of air from her lungs. She tried to bring her knee up into his balls but he had himself wedged too tightly against her for it to do any damage. Her fists beat against his arms, and then they dropped to her sides, allowing him unimpeded access to her half-naked body. He bent down, sucking one fat brown nipple into his mouth.

Something hard poked him in the ribs. He slid one hand down to push away the annoying object, felt cold steel against his palm.

Fire and pain exploded in his stomach.

★　　★　　★

Emma watched Roscoe stumble back, his expression a combination of surprise and anger. A dark stain was already spreading across the front of his blue shirt. He raised his hands to her, and she felt a terrible guilt at having pulled the trigger.

Oh my God, what have I done? What—

Roscoe's mouth opened and his hands clenched into fists.

"You fucking bitch! I'll kill you for that."

Even bleeding and in obvious pain, Roscoe Jackson was an imposing figure as he stepped toward her, a giant mountain of a man who looked fully capable of carrying out his promise and then having a beer or two before his wound got the better of him.

Her finger moved on the trigger before she even thought consciously about doing it. She fired another shot into his belly. When he still refused to go down, she put one into his chest.

Only then did Roscoe fall, a slow collapse much like a tree toppling from a chainsaw's attack.

No longer afraid, but still cautious enough to keep the gun trained on him, Emma knelt by her dying partner as he tried to speak through the bloody foam bubbling over his lips.

"You killed the wrong guy, bitch."

His eyes closed and his last breath gurgled out, leaving Emma with nothing but unanswered questions and a murder weapon in her hand as people came rushing out of the emergency room.

CHAPTER THIRTY-NINE

Kellie hadn't intended to fall asleep, but at some point during the night she'd passed from faking it right into the real thing without realizing it.

The sound of sirens brought her awake.

Something big is happening.

Even in a small town like Hell Creek, when you grew up as a cop's daughter you learned early on not only how to tell the difference between police, ambulance, and fire sirens, but how to differentiate between ordinary occurrences and major events. A single siren or two meant an accident or a brush fire. A cacophony of different wails and howls meant something unusual was going on – a multi-car pileup on the highway, a building on fire on Main Street.

What sent Kellie running to her window was not only the fact that she heard four separate emergency tones – which indicated fire trucks from Homestead were providing assistance – but that the majority of the sirens seemed to emanate from the center of town. The reddish-orange glow coloring the sky confirmed her fears.

Hell Creek's business district was on fire.

She didn't even bother to check if her father was still home. There was no way he'd be anywhere other than on the scene. Instead, she grabbed her clothes off the floor and got dressed.

This will be the best chance I have to get Carson free.

It never crossed her mind that she might be heading right for Eddie's target.

★   ★   ★

Kellie hid her bike behind a dumpster at the back of the hospital. Her original plan had been to sneak in through the emergency entrance, thinking the ER would be so busy she could get in without being noticed. Her route into town had taken her within two blocks of the fire, close enough to feel the heat and taste the black poison of burning plastic and rubber. Despite the efforts of six fire trucks, flames still turned the night sky bright as day and towered well above the rooftops of Main Street's buildings. From what she'd seen, at least three buildings were already lost causes and several others close to joining them.

She came around the corner of the hospital and realized she needed to rethink her plan. Ambulances and police cars jammed the bay. Hospital staff and emergency workers ran back and forth, shouting at each other as they wheeled or carried victims into the hospital.

Oh, God. There were people in those buildings. Damn you, Eddie Ryder!

More than ever, she knew they had to stop Eddie as soon as possible. Which meant getting Carson free. She detoured through the parking lot and headed for the main entrance, hoping that in all the confusion she could slip past the guards.

'The entire lobby was empty, including the front desk.

Things must be worse than I thought.

Kellie leaned over the desk to grab the registration book, grateful that the hospital hadn't switched over to a computerized visitor check-in system. She looked up Carson's name and found his room was only two floors up. She took the stairs rather than the elevator and ended up entering the hallway only four doors down from Carson's room.

There were no guards by the door, but she knew there might be one inside. Without a window in the door, there was no way to tell.

Only one way to find out.

She pushed the door open just enough to peek inside. The ceiling lights were off but the usual assortment of tiny wall and floor lights, together with the sunset-orange glow of the fire illuminating the windows, allowed her to see well enough. Carson was in bed, asleep. An empty chair sat beneath the window. Unless a guard was standing or sitting to one side of the door or the other, the room was empty.

Kellie said a prayer for good luck and stepped through.

No one was there.

"Carson!" She said it in a whisper-shout as she hurried to the bed. He woke up immediately.

"Kellie? What are you doing here?"

"Getting you out. We have to stop your brother. He's out of control. He lit a big fire in town."

"I know, your father accused me of doing it."

"Not those little fires." Kellie shook her head. "I'm talking a big fire. Really big. Right on Main Street. Look." She pointed out the window, where flames and smoke were visible between the black shapes of buildings.

Carson gasped. He tried to get out of bed but had to stop, thanks to his wrist being handcuffed to the railing.

"Hang on a sec." Kellie took a key from her pocket. "One of my dad's spares. I had a feeling I might need it." She opened the handcuff. Carson jumped out of bed and then had to grab her arm for support.

"What's the matter?" Kellie asked.

"I think...I think they must have drugged me. I feel kinda messed up in the head. Dizzy."

"Maybe you should stay here." She didn't want him to; the last thing she felt like doing was fighting Eddie Ryder alone.

"No, it'll pass. I need to move around, that's all. Can you find my shoes?"

"Sure."

By the time she located them at the back of the closet, Carson was standing on his own. His face remained sickly pale, and his eyes had dark shadows underneath like he hadn't slept in a week. But he walked to the door without wobbling or pausing.

They took the stairs back down to the main floor, Carson following Kellie's lead as she explained the situation in the ER and how they needed to use the front door in order to get away unnoticed. Everything was fine until they got to the main entrance.

And found Kellie's father standing there.

★   ★   ★

Eddie located Johnny Ray Jones just as the Chief entered the hospital.

Guess what, motherfucker? Gonna pay for turning my family against me, and for all those times you busted my ass when I was alive.

He was about to enter Jones's body when he noticed the traitor and the bitch approaching the doors. He paused, hovering above their heads.

Probably talking about me. Now I can find out what they're up to.

★   ★   ★

"Kellie, what the hell is going on?"

Kellie Jones froze at the sight of her father. What was he doing at the hospital? Why wasn't he at the fire?

Carson spoke up. "She came to get me, Chief Jones."

"I can see that. Like I don't have enough problems without you running loose again. For all I know, you're the one responsible for all this." He waved his hands around, indicating nothing in particular and the whole town in general, but Kellie knew he meant the fire and the resulting injuries.

"It wasn't Carson, Dad."

"Sure. Just like it wasn't him who lit that fire in my yard, or the ones on the street? I've got ten people dead and twice that many in the ER, so I'm through playing games, boy."

"It's true, it wasn't me." Carson stepped forward, putting himself between Kellie and her father. "It was Eddie, and we have to stop him."

Kellie groaned. She knew her father wouldn't believe a story like that. His next words confirmed it.

"Eddie? Your brother? Now I know you're guilty, and crazy as all hell on top of it."

"But Dad—"

Jones cut his daughter off. "Don't 'Dad' me. We found Eddie's name burning outside another arson scene, down at the Hell Riders' clubhouse. And someone shouted it in the movie theater just as the fire started there. It doesn't take a genius to add two and two. Carson's been lighting fires all over town in some twisted response to his brother's death."

Just then Officer Delbert Beauchamps joined them.

"Chief, I got a doctor to take care of Wilbur. Says he's got some pretty bad burns on his arm but he'll be okay. Gonna be out of commission for a few weeks, though."

Jones turned to Carson. "Now one of my men is hurt, too, thanks to you. Del, take these two to my office—"

"*Chief Jones!*" his radio interrupted. "*We got a problem. The fire's spreading. It's almost here at the station. I'm evacuating everyone.*"

"God-fucking-dammit!" Jones glared at Carson and then looked back at Delbert. "Change of plans. Take them to the courthouse and then meet me at the station. We have to help Sharon."

He bolted out the door, leaving Kellie and Carson with Delbert. She looked at his heavily lined face and knew it was a lost cause to try and explain things to him, but she tried anyway.

"Del, you have to let us go. None of this is Carson's fault. It's his brother, Eddie. He's come back from the dead. I know that sounds crazy but it's true. We think we can stop him, if it's not too late."

Delbert stared at her for so long she thought he might be in shock from her story. She didn't blame him. Anyone hearing her would think she was a candidate for the nuthouse.

Then he surprised the hell out of her.

"I believe you."

Carson let out a gasp that Delbert ignored as he kept speaking.

"Too many strange things happening in town lately. Ain't normal, and nobody in town's responsible, no matter what your father says. I grew up with stories of ghosts and possession. My gram always told us the spirits were everywhere, all around us. Good ones and bad ones."

"Can you help us?" Carson asked.

Delbert's eyes narrowed. "The Chief ordered me to do something. I'm supposed to follow orders. But if something were to happen on the way to the courthouse, like say I see someone who needs my help, and you two happened to run off…well, I can always say the most important thing is to save lives."

"Thank you." Kellie gave him a hug. She'd always been a little afraid of the tall, heavily muscled officer who rarely smiled or talked. Now she wished she'd gotten to know him better.

"C'mon, Kellie, we have to get going before it's too late." Carson grabbed her hand and pulled her toward the doors. They'd only gone a few steps when she stopped.

"Wait here. I have to tell Delbert something."

★　　★　　★

Eddie felt a moment of indecision when Chief Jones left the hospital. Should he follow through with his original plan and put Jones through some nasty paces, or make sure Carson and Kellie didn't have any more surprises in store for him? In the end, it was hearing how Jones didn't believe Eddie was back that made up Eddie's mind.

Fucking dumbshit hick cop. The evidence is all over your goddamn town and you can't see it! Guess they won't be filming CSI: Hell Creek *anytime soon. Well, if you need proof, then I'll give you some.*

Eddie raced ahead to the police station, where Sharon Mays had BJ Flood and Price Bay, who ran the Army-Navy Store down the block, helping her move valuable files and evidence into the fireproof walk-in safe that had come with the building, which had been a bank back in the sixties. Eddie zeroed in on Sharon and was just getting a feel for her body when Jones came in.

"Thanks, Sharon. What's left to move?"

Eddie dropped the box Sharon had been carrying. "What's left? I'll tell you what's left, fuck-face. Burning this whole town to the goddamn ground!" Eddie bent down and put his hand against a wall socket, let some of his energy flow out.

And then he found himself floating up to the ceiling as Sharon's pacemaker turned into a lump of red-hot plastic and metal that burned a hole right through her heart before it cooled.

Holy shit, that was fucking AWESOME!

Before Jones or the other two men had time to react to Sharon's sudden death, Eddie swooped into BJ Flood's body and pointed at the body on the floor, just as Jones came out of his shock and knelt down to check Sharon for a pulse.

"Goddamn! Did you see that? We shoulda taped it. Put it on the internet and make a million bucks."

Jones looked over at him. "What the hell is wrong with you?"

"Not me, Chief Dumb Ass. You. How stupid can you be?"

Jones' mouth opened but no words came out. Eddie laughed, setting the lights to flickering, which only made him laugh harder, until the entire office resembled a dance club.

"Hey, Jonesy, adouchebagsayswhat?" Eddie asked, speaking at doublespeed.

"What?" The police chief still had the look of someone doing their best village idiot impression.

"Exactly." Eddie turned and grabbed Price Bay, who'd been standing there just as dumbfounded, and let his power surge through BJ's fingers into his partner's neck. Sparks flew and smoke filled the air as all the hair on Price's body caught fire. Price screamed and Eddie did the same, his hands and arms burning like he'd stuck them in hot coals. But he didn't let go, not even when his flesh melted right into Price's and the other man's eyes exploded like two miniature water balloons, spraying hot fluids across the room.

Only when he felt BJ's heart begin a stuttering dance step did Eddie turn the juice off, but by then it was too late. He had just enough time to smile at Jones and speak a final sentence before death forced him out of another body.

"Hey, Jonesy. Now do you believe in ghosts?"

CHAPTER FORTY

Carson took Kellie's hand as they left the hospital grounds. "What was that all about back there?"

"What?"

"You and Beauchamps."

"I gave him a message. For my dad. In case something…you know, happens. To us."

Carson frowned. Something in Kellie's answer was off. The words made sense but her tone….

She's lying. But why?

Two immediate thoughts came to his mind: *Is it really her or Eddie?* followed by, *If it isn't Eddie, why the secret?*

And either way, could he still trust her?

What choice did he have?

"I need to go home," he said. "My mom…I have to check on her. Make sure she took her medicine. Plus, with all the fires and everything, she's gonna be worried."

"Okay."

It was a half-hour walk to the trailer. Carson kept a careful eye on Kellie the entire time, but everything she said seemed normal, and her actions seemed her own. From what he could tell, she wasn't possessed.

Maybe she was telling the truth. Or maybe it was something so personal she doesn't want to tell you.

Was that it? Had she delivered a goodbye message to her father, a final 'I love you'?

Does she think she's going to die?

It made sense. There was no telling what Eddie would do to them, or what might happen to them in town. No one was safe while Eddie remained on the loose.

Which was why Carson had to stop him. He'd come up with a

plan in the hospital but he hadn't told Kellie yet because he knew how she'd react. She'd say no. He'd have to convince her, though. Without her help, it wouldn't work.

And Eddie would keep on killing.

When they arrived at his house, the lights were all off except the one over the front door.

"Wait here," Carson whispered. "I'll check on her and come right back."

A quick peek into his mother's room revealed that she was asleep and her oxygen line in place under her nose. He checked her medicine case, saw that she'd taken everything for that night. He poured her a fresh glass of water and left by the bed, along with a blueberry muffin from the refrigerator and a note saying not to worry about him, he'd explain everything in the morning.

Then he tiptoed back outside.

"She's fine," he said, in answer to the question on Kellie's face. "Let's go. We have to get some things from your house."

"What things?"

"The salt and holy water. We're going to bind Eddie again."

Kellie shook her head. "Carson, that didn't work the last time. What makes you think it will be different now?"

"Because this time we're going to bind him into a body and then kill him before he can escape."

"What? You can't do that." Kellie stopped walking, turned to face him. "You'd be killing whoever's body he was in. That would be murder."

"I know." Here came the part he dreaded telling her. "That's why it has to be me."

"No! I won't let you do that. There has to be another way to stop him." She crossed her arms, her face angrier than he'd ever seen it. In a way, it made him feel good.

It meant she cared.

"Kellie, look." He took her by the shoulders and turned her toward town. A hazy red glow occupied the entire horizon, as if a city from hell hid just out of sight. Instead of chirping insects and gentle bird calls, the night screamed with the frantic cries of sirens and alarms, and the blaring of car horns.

"All that death and destruction, it's because of Eddie. My brother. He'll keep on doing it, too. You know that. He'll kill everyone in town. My mother. Your father. I have to stop him, and I can't do it without you."

She stared at him for several moments, her lips tight, a single tear tracking down one cheek. Finally, she nodded.

"Okay. I'll help you."

She took his hand and they started walking again. Carson wanted to thank her, to tell her that he didn't want to die, that if there was any other way he'd choose it.

He stayed quiet, though.

Because he was pretty sure she was lying again.

And if she was, they were all in big trouble.

Eddie Ryder had no idea he'd gone completely insane. He couldn't remember feeling any other way, couldn't conceive of a time when he didn't burn with the twin desires of revenge and domination. In the tattered remnants of his mind, the town trembled at his feet and he planned to keep playing with his new toys until the game was over.

Then he'd move on to the big leagues.

Since leaving Johnny Ray Jones in a state of total confusion, he'd spent the next three hours picking people at random and forcing them to do his own version of the funky chicken. First, he'd made a volunteer fireman drive a fire truck right into the bank. Then, while people scrambled around, trying to free the truck and still keep fighting the fires that raged up and down Main Street, he switched bodies and had the fire chief from Homestead walk down the road to Rosie's Diner, break into the back, and start up the deep fryer. Once it came up to temp, he cooked a big batch of gator bites and ate them while watching the reports of the fires on the news. After he finished, he plunged the fire chief's hands into the hot oil.

Bored with the fires, he'd possessed every housewife on Cypress Street, one after another, and had them leave their houses buck naked and stand at the end of their driveways. Since each one passed out after he left their body, the street was soon littered with rows of naked women and angry, frantic husbands trying to cover them with coats and blankets. He only stopped when he took over a woman who'd been in her kitchen getting a glass of water. As he pulled her nightgown over her head, he caught sight of a calendar on the refrigerator.

And saw it was September 19th. In a moment of clarity, a memory came to him.

I joined the Hell Riders on September 20th. That's tomorrow.

Thinking of the Hell Riders reminded him of Hank Bowman.

That's perfect! I'll kill him tomorrow. It'll be my anniversary present to me – the end of the old Hell Riders and the beginning of the one true Hell Rider.

Eddie broke the glass and cut open the woman's palm, savoring the sharp pain as blood welled up. Dabbing a finger in the blood, he left a message on the white door of the refrigerator.

Hell Rider. Comin' for you!

CHAPTER FORTY-ONE

Carson's first thought when he opened his eyes was that Eddie had possessed him again. An unfamiliar ceiling looked down at him and the couch he lay on was too soft and fresh-smelling to be his own.

Oh, God. What did he make me do this time?

"Carson?"

Kellie's voice. Why…? Then he remembered. They'd gone back to Kellie's house and gathered the remaining holy water and salt from the lawn. The paper with the spell on it was gone, burned in the fire Eddie had caused, but it was a simple matter to print another copy and then practice it until they had it memorized. The candles were gone, melted into blobs of wax, and Carson hoped they weren't a vital part of the spell because from what he'd seen on the news nothing in town would be open in the morning.

By then it'd been well after midnight, and they decided the best thing to do was catch a few hours of sleep and then try to find Eddie.

The last thing he remembered before dropping into an exhausted slumber was Kellie giving him a long, tender kiss good night.

A goodbye kiss. If my plan works, I'll be dead before the day is over.

The thought of it made him want to cry, and only Kellie's sad smile as she came into the Joneses' TV room the next morning enabled him to keep his tears inside. He could see she was trying to maintain a brave front for him, but she couldn't hide the fact that his impending death weighed just as heavily on her.

Gotta pretend everything's gonna be okay.

"Hey. What time is it?"

"A little after nine. Guess you were tired. You hungry?"

He was, but he shook his head 'no'. He hadn't intended to sleep so late; they'd wasted a lot of time.

"We should get going. Eddie—"

"Isn't anywhere, from what I can tell." Kellie held up her phone. "I've been checking the news every fifteen minutes. No more fires or...anything else since last night. Maybe demons need to rest, too."

Carson frowned. Something she'd said.... "What do you mean, or anything else? What else did he do last night?"

He knew it had to be bad from the way she paused before answering. "He killed a bunch of people. A fireman from Homestead. Mr. Powell and some others at the movie theater. And...he did something to Mr. Gunderson. Made him hurt his wife."

"We've got to find him right now!" Carson made a fist and then didn't know what to do with it. He felt helpless. Useless. And he hated that feeling, despite being well acquainted with it from gym class, from having a dying mother, from having a brother who always ended up screwing his family – first by getting in trouble, then by dying.

And now he's going to destroy the entire town. Way to go, Eddie. Real good memories to leave me with.

"We need to eat." Kellie took his hands in hers, looked into his eyes. Her calm was cool water washing over his fire, dampening his anger so he could think clearly again. "We might not have the chance later, and I'm hungry. Then we'll take care of Eddie."

"Okay," he said, believing her even though it seemed an impossible task. "But how?"

She smiled. "Simple. Instead of looking for him, we just make sure he comes to us."

★   ★   ★

The morning of Eddie Ryder's ultimate revenge dawned warm, clear, and less humid than most September days in southern Florida, but Eddie never noticed.

He was too busy being insane.

At some point during the previous night – he couldn't remember when – he'd run out of ideas for people to use and things to destroy. He'd spent some time – again, he wasn't sure how long – blasting holes in the highway and blowing up alligators in the swamps. He'd only stopped when his energy ran out.

With exhaustion came some momentary breaks in his lunacy. Faces had appeared in his head without bringing on red rages. *Carson. Mom.*

After resting for a few hours at his grave, he'd ridden out to the old house just as the sun's first glow appeared on the horizon and looked in on her, seen her sleeping. Out of long-ingrained habit, he'd checked her nightstand to make sure she'd taken her medicines.

And saw the note Carson left.

Ma,

Don't be scared that I'm not here when you wake up. I had some important things to do. Things that will make this town normal again. I'll explain everything when I get home. In the meantime, be sure to take your medicine.

I love you,
Carson

BACKSTABBING BASTARD! Seeing evidence of Carson's continued treachery had sent Eddie into another fit of madness. He'd roared off into the sky, an invisible comet trailing fire and thunder as he headed back toward the conflagration that was the center of town. He never noticed the sparks landing on the lawns and roofs below him like molten fire seeds.

Or the flames that sprouted from them.

★   ★   ★

Carson and Kellie arrived at the hospital just before eleven, after a harrowing walk through a town that seemed more like a war zone. They'd both been stunned by the amount of damage Eddie had wrought in only one night.

"Are you sure this is going to work?" Carson asked. Her plan seemed deceptively simple. Maybe too simple.

"Absolutely." Kellie's voice sang with confidence. "We know he wants to kill Hank. That means he'll have to come to the hospital. He's also mad at you and me. So either he'll take over Hank and come after us, or he'll use one of us to go after Hank. Whichever he does, we have him trapped."

Carson shook his head. "That's all well and good, but we need him inside *me*. If he takes you over, I sure as hell won't bind him to you. And if he takes over Hank, he could beat the crap out of both of us before we finish the spell."

"You don't have to kill me, or Hank. Just knock me out and Eddie will leave, go to another body. We'll do the same to Hank. We'll keep knocking people out until Eddie goes into you."

"I guess." He still wasn't sure about it. It also wasn't pleasant contemplating his own death sentence. Something Kellie didn't seem to mind talking about, which struck Carson as kind of odd. Not that he thought she didn't care if he died.

But something's going on. She's been acting weird all morning. Too cheerful. She's not telling me everything.

What could it be? They'd practiced the spell again just to be sure they had every word right. Then they'd sprinkled the last of the holy water on Carson's clothes and arms and poured the salt into his pockets. That had been Kellie's idea. She'd thought that by already having the salt and holy water on him, it would make casting the spell that much faster when Eddie took him over.

They'd even spent some time making out after breakfast, right on the living room couch where her father could have caught them if he'd come home. Those fifteen minutes had probably been the best in Carson's entire life, and while he hated the fact that he was going to die a virgin, at least he could go knowing he'd felt a girl's breast. His hand still tingled from the memory of it.

Of course, that only made him want to live even more.

However, try as he might, he couldn't think of any other solution.

"So, should we go inside and wait by Hank's room, or just hang out here?" Carson pointed to a bench next to the main doors.

Kellie's body did a weird twitch and then she gave him a smile that was most definitely not pleasant.

"How about you eat shit and die, traitor?"

Then her foot connected with his balls and all he knew was stars and pain.

★   ★   ★

The nearby windows shook from Eddie's laughter. Carson lay curled on the ground, his hands clutching his nuts and a puddle of vomit near his mouth. Eddie toed him with one foot and Carson let out a moan.

"Get up, you little pussy. What the hell do you care about your balls? You never let a girl get near them anyhow."

"Leave her alone." Carson's words came out in halting gasps. "Take me instead."

"No way, little bro." He prodded his brother again, harder. "Making your own squeeze kick the shit out of you is too much fun. Now get the fuck up or this whole building is coming down."

Just to make sure Carson believed him, he released a small energy blast and shattered the glass doors of the hospital. Inside, several people screamed.

Carson, strings of drool still hanging from his lower lip, rolled over and got to his knees. Tears ran down his cheeks.

"You're an asshole, Eddie. Why are you doing this? You killed the Hell Riders. Now go away and leave the rest of us alone."

"What the hell do you know about anything, you little piece of shit?" Eddie drew back his foot and Carson cringed. "I could kill you right now. I could burn this whole damn town down. And maybe I will. Maybe that's why I came back. *I'm the motherfucking Angel of Destruction, riding wings of fire to start a new world!*"

Eddie shouted the lyrics so loud Kellie's throat cracked at the end from the force of it.

"This isn't one of your stupid songs, Eddie." Carson stumbled and groaned as he stood up, but he stayed on his feet. "Go back to hell or wherever you came from."

"Bite me. Hey, what do you think?" He squeezed Kellie's hands over her breasts. "Pretty nice, aren't they? You get to touch them yet, you little wuss?"

"Fuck you!" Carson slammed both hands into Eddie's shoulders, sending Kellie's smaller body against the bench. He drew back his fist, prepared to knock her out like they'd planned.

"Carson Ryder! Move another inch and I swear I'll shoot you."

★ ★ ★

Johnny Ray Jones had only been a block away from the hospital when the call came in that someone had just set off a bomb in the lobby. With everything that had gone on in town the past forty-eight hours, he'd thought nothing would surprise him when he got there.

He'd been wrong.

Pulling up, he'd immediately seen Carson and Kellie. Although he couldn't hear them, it was obvious they were arguing. And then the sonovabitch actually hit Kellie. Knocked her down.

No one did that to his daughter, especially not a crazy fuck like Carson Ryder.

Although the threat to shoot him had sprung from his mouth, Johnny Ray knew better than to pull his gun on a kid, especially in broad daylight in front of dozens of witnesses. He unsnapped it, but instead of drawing it he took out his Taser and aimed it at Carson.

"Daddy!" Kellie sprang up from the bench and ran over to him. Wrapped her arms around him in a big hug. "Thank God, you saved me!"

"It's okay, sweetheart." With his free hand, Johnny Ray patted Kellie's head. To Carson, he said, "You. Sit down on the bench and put your hands in the air."

"Oh, Daddy," Kellie murmured into his chest. "You're such a fucking dick."

Surprised by Kellie's words, Johnny Ray didn't notice her pulling his gun from its holster until she'd already stepped away and aimed it at Carson.

"Kellie! No, don't—"

The rest of his words disappeared as the gun went off.

A second later, Carson screamed and fell off the bench.

★   ★   ★

Eddie couldn't see the expression on Johnny Ray's face as he took the cop's gun and aimed it at his brother, but he was sure it couldn't be more priceless than the shocked look Carson gave him just before the bullet hit home. Eyes wider than Eddie'd ever seen them, his mouth hanging open like a nutcracker waiting for a pecan, Carson would have been right at home in a slapstick horror movie.

The only thing that spoiled the moment was seeing the little prick holding his arm when he hit the ground.

Damn bitch's hands are too small to aim properly. I'll take care of that.

Holding the pistol in both hands, he walked toward Carson, who was crying and shouting, "Ow! Ow!" over and over. Blood dripped from between his fingers.

Eddie pointed the gun at Carson's chest. "Sayo-fucking-nara, little bro. Let this be a lesson to you. Never—"

Something hit him from behind, knocking the air from his lungs and sending the gun flying.

Shit. Forgot about Jones.

Then his head hit the concrete.

★   ★   ★

Talk about a cluster fuck. Johnny Ray Jones stood in the ER, watching the doctors tend to Carson's arm and Kellie's head.

"You're going to be fine," a doctor said to Carson. "The bullet only grazed you. A few stitches and you'll be as good as new."

While the doctor sutured Carson's wound, one of the nurses who'd examined Kellie approached Johnny Ray. "It's just a bump, Chief Jones. She was perfectly coherent when she woke up. I doubt there's a concussion, but we'll keep her here for a few hours to make sure. If you want, we can run a head CT as well."

"Please." Johnny Ray tried to see past him, where Kellie was now sitting up and talking to a nurse. She looked alert, but there was something in her face....

Fear? Confusion? Embarrassment? It's so hard to tell with teenage girls what the hell's going on in their heads.

He realized the doctor was still staring at him. "Can I talk to her now?"

"Of course. I'll go schedule—"

KABLAM!

Compared to all the noise and destruction of the previous night, the explosion wasn't loud, but it startled everyone all the same. Johnny Ray's instincts took over and he immediately went into action.

"Stay here!" he yelled at the doctor, and then ran out to the ambulance bay. He didn't know exactly where the detonation had occurred, but it had come from somewhere outside the building and the bay was the closest exit.

Shouts from around the corner sent him to the front of the building, where the flaming, upside-down wreckage of an SUV sat right in the drop-off circle by the hospital's entrance. Through the smoke and fire, the words *Police Chief* were still visible on the doors.

My car...? How...?

Kellie!

Johnny Ray rushed back into the hospital. He didn't know how the car was related to his daughter, but he knew down to his core, in the center of every bone in his body, that she was in trouble.

Big trouble.

★   ★   ★

The moment he heard the explosion, Carson knew it had to be Eddie causing more problems. He slid off the bed and hurried to the next curtained area, where they'd taken Kellie.

And nearly ran into her halfway there.

"I didn't mean to—"

"I'm so sorry—"

"It wasn't me—"

"I know."

They hugged each other and, for Carson at least, everything was okay again. The pain in his arm didn't matter. It had been Eddie, not her, who pulled the trigger. As far as he was concerned, she didn't even have to apologize because there wasn't anything to forgive.

But there was something they had to do.

"This is our only chance," he said, reluctantly pulling away from her.

"Hank's room." Kellie pointed at the door that led to the main hospital. "Now, while everyone's occupied and before Eddie comes looking for us again."

They'd only gone two steps when the door opened and Kellie's father shouted at them to stop.

Then every piece of glass in the ER shattered.

★   ★   ★

Eddie had been about to take over Kellie again when she mentioned Hank's name. He paused, trying to decide who he should kill first.

Traitor friend or traitor brother?

It should have been an easy decision, but his mind wasn't focusing properly. Jagged fragments of heavy metal songs filled his head until it felt like he'd wedged it between the speakers at the loudest headbanger concert ever. His body vibrated with energy, as if all the electricity in the hospital had been poured into him by some unknown force, turning him into some kind of human engine that threatened to explode at any moment.

No, not an engine. A fucking nuclear power plant.

Then Chief Jones entered the room and Eddie burst into laughter. Random energy escaped like super-charged electrical farts, shattering glass and shorting out medical equipment.

Yes! Kill all three of them now and save Hank for last.

He saw a face he recognized, a man moaning from the shards of glass embedded in his arms and chest. *I know you, motherfucker. You were the cocksucker who called me beef jerky in the morgue. Let's see how you like getting burned to a crisp.*

He dove into the man's body.

The pain was as sharp as the glass causing it, but Eddie drowned it in a billion-decibel music mix that shielded his brain from the worst of it.

"Sweet home Ala — Fire flowing through my veins — Devil gonna get ya — Highway to hell — Voices within the walls — Seasons don't fear the — Hours of execution I must repeat — Hell Rider, riding through the night!—"

He turned and faced Chief Jones. "Hey, Chief Suck-my-dick! Check this out!"

Eddie opened his mouth and let loose the music in his head. Carried on waves of supernatural energy, it exploded from the wall speakers positioned throughout the hospital.

*"Dark clouds from above, bring darkness and doom
Effortlessly shattering, what lies in its course
A deafening roar, it feels no remorse!"*

The music rose in volume until it turned into an ear-splitting wail of feedback. Jones ran to Kellie and Carson, wrapped his arms around them as if he could protect them from the aural barrage. A second later the speakers in the ER blew.

The supernatural din grew even louder. Dark lines appeared in the walls as the wiring inside them superheated.

*"Wrath of Satan
Reigns o'er all!*

Evil consumes the meek
People cower in the field
As vengeance he does seek
Hell Rider!
Taking their souls
Hell Rider!"

Flames sprouted from the walls, filling the air with smoke. Screams from elsewhere in the hospital were evidence of similar occurrences on every floor.

"Jesus!" Jones pushed the children toward the door. If he could get them outside—

"Close, but you still don't have a clue, do you?" Eddie let out a laugh and the ceiling bulbs popped and sparked, sending the ER into a gloom lit only by the emergency lights and lines of fire.

Eddie aimed his hands at the closest wall. White-hot bolts of lightning shot from his flaming fingertips and danced across the paint, blistering and melting it. When the smoke cleared, jagged letters spelled out a single sentence.

Eddie Ryder lives!

"What in the fuck is going on?" Jones asked, speaking to no one in particular.

"I tried to tell you—" Carson began, but Eddie cut him off.

"You tried to tell him, but he was too stupid to believe you, little brother. Chief Jones, I am the re-in-fucking-carnation of Eddie Ryder. Do you believe me now? I've been the one fucking with your town, asshole. Me! Not my dickless little brother, not your prissy-ass daughter, and not those fat fucking Hell Riders. Me! Eddie Goddamn Ryder! And there isn't a thing you can do to stop me."

"Guess again." Jones lifted his hand and fired his Taser.

Eddie smiled as the twin electrodes sailed out and struck his chest. He could have fried them in the air, but his present body was getting too painful to control anyhow.

As the unconscious orderly twitched and fell to the floor, Eddie switched hosts, taking over a gray-haired doctor who'd been watching the events unfold.

"Sorry, Chief, over here now. Did Carson forget to mention I can be anyone I fucking wanna be?" He picked up a scalpel and tilted it back and forth. "Gonna have to cut you up now, Chief."

Jones stepped in front of the children and drew his gun. "One more step and I'll shoot."

Flipping the blade from hand to hand, Eddie shook his head. "No you won't. You shoot me and you kill this person, while I simply move on to somebody else. Don't believe me? Ask Ned Bowman or Mouse Bates when you see them in Hell." He took another step, scalpel raised in the air.

The sound of the gun firing and the sudden eruption of pain in his leg happened simultaneously. His left leg collapsed and he fell to the floor.

Gritting his teeth against the pain, Eddie glared at the Chief as he came closer.

"You fucking shot me? See how you like shooting your own daughter."

Eddie flung himself out of the doctor and into Jones. The force of it, violent and fast, caused Jones to drop the gun. Quickly recovering his balance, Eddie picked up the pistol before Carson could grab it.

"Looks like you two are gonna take a trip to never-never land together. Who's first?" Eddie swung the gun back and forth from Carson to Kellie and back again.

Before he could pull the trigger, the ER doors burst open and two EMTs wheeled a stretcher in. A nurse ran alongside, calling out vital signs.

"Thirty-eight-year-old female suffering from chronic emphysema aggravated by smoke inhalation. Oh-two sat eighty-one and dropping. BP one hundred over eighty-eight. Acuity level two."

Eddie froze at the nurse's words. *Thirty-eight? Emphysema? No, it can't be....*

Ma?

He stopped the stretcher and looked down.

It was her.

"Ma!" He grabbed her hand and squeezed.

Her eyes opened. Although her voice was muffled by the oxygen mask covering it, he understood her words.

"Johnny Ray?" Her hand tightened against his. "Johnny, take...take care of Carson for me. He needs a dad."

Before Eddie could respond, the EMTs wheeled her past and into a curtained room.

"This is all your fault!" Carson ran up and punched him. "You heard the nurse. Smoke inhalation. You lit the fires, Eddie." Carson held his arms wide. "You wanna kill me? Go ahead! I don't give a shit anymore. Me, Ma, all those people in the theater. Is this why you came back?"

From behind the blue curtain came a high-pitched whining sound.

"She's coding!"

CHAPTER FORTY-TWO

Is this why you came back?

Something in those words broke loose a piece of sanity from the mountain of Eddie's madness. A singular clarity of thought that cut through all the bug-fuck crazy like the sun boring a hole through dark thunderclouds.

I wanted to get revenge for my death. That's all.

So finish it and leave Carson alone. He's not responsible for you dying. Only the Hell Riders are.

"Carson, listen." Eddie dropped the gun. "I'm...I'm not me anymore. My brain's all fucked up. I...I'm changing into something, something dangerous. Take Kellie and Ma and get the hell away from here. As far away as you can. This is.... I think this is the last little piece of the real me left. Something big and black is eating the rest of it. I love you, Carson. I don't think we'll get the chance to talk again. Tell Ma I love her, too. Don't try to stop me. I don't want you to get hurt."

He pulled Carson into a quick but strong hug, and then left Chief Jones's body.

It was time to end things.

* * *

Carson gasped as Chief Jones let go of him and collapsed onto the floor. "Eddie...."

"Carson!" Kellie's voice. He turned to look at her.

"Hurry! Hank's room!"

He looked back at the curtained room hiding his mother. That's where he should be. Not giving up his life to kill the demon that used to be his brother.

"Carson! Only you can stop him."

Goddammit! His hatred of Eddie returned. Now he was even preventing Carson from his last chance to see his mother. But someone had to put an end to things.

"Let's go." He took Kellie's hand and they raced for the stairs.

They arrived at Hank Bowman's room just in time to see a nurse pass out next to the bed. Hank's hands and feet were untied, and he was scooting himself into a sitting position before the nurse even hit the floor.

"Say the spell!" Kellie shouted.

"What? He's not inside me yet! And Hank isn't—"

"Just do it!"

Kellie launched into the spell they'd practiced. Trusting that she knew what she was doing, Carson joined in.

"Eddie Ryder, we bind you to this body with salt and holy water. Eddie Ryder, we bind you to this body with salt and holy water. Eddie Ryder—"

Eddie's manic laughter rang out from Hank's body and every fluorescent light on the entire wing exploded. He pointed at Carson, who ducked, expecting a bolt of lightning to the chest.

"You're damn lucky there's a part of me that still doesn't want to kill you. But that part's getting smaller, little brother. I think this is your last chance to grab your fuck-buddy and get the hell out of here before I get really pissed."

His finger moved a couple of inches to the right and then lightning did fill the room, three neon-bright zig-zag lines that left blue and red after-images in Carson's vision.

Behind them, the entire wall burst into flame.

None of it stopped Kellie's chanting and Carson hurriedly started reciting the spell again, embarrassed into action by her bravery.

Eddie's finger swung in her direction, thumb and forefinger cocked in the time-honored caricature of a gun. "You're starting to annoy me, bitch."

A loud explosion caused Carson to cry out, and he ran to Kellie, afraid Eddie had blown her guts out.

Then he noticed she was not only still standing, but still speaking the binding spell. Movement by the door caught his attention, and he saw Chief Jones with a gun in his hand.

Across the room, Hank went down to one knee.

Carson turned as Eddie shouted at them in Hank's voice.

"You fucking cock-sucking sonovawhore! You shot me again! Goddamn, that fucking hurts!" He had his hands pressed against one leg, blood already dripping from between his fingers.

Without skipping a word, Kellie kicked Carson in the leg and motioned for him to keep reciting the spell. He started up again, wondering why she was so intent on finishing it. Did she think they had a chance of trapping Eddie in Hank's body without salt or holy water?

"Eat shit and die, Eddie Ryder." Chief Jones aimed the gun at Hank's chest.

"Not today, dickbag." Eddie lifted his hands and incandescent darts of energy sprayed out from every finger, blasting fist-sized holes in the walls, ceiling, and floor. A ceiling tile fell on Kellie's head and she cried out. Carson threw up his arms to protect his face from tile and wood shrapnel that bit and stung like a thousand wasps. Jones fired his gun, but the bullets exploded in mid-flight, never reaching their target.

Then Eddie stood up and ran, using Hank's body like a battering ram to bowl over Chief Jones before speeding out the door.

★   ★   ★

Eddie's thoughts were in turmoil as he slammed open an emergency door at the back of the hospital and ran across the parking lot. His leg screamed with every step, which only added to his confusion as he limped toward Main Street.

Should have killed them all—
No! Carson's family! Can't hurt family—
"Speeding through night, hell's fire eyes alite!"
Fuck them. They tried to hurt you—
"You got another thing coming!"
Doesn't matter—
Does matter—
"Dark walls that surround my mind—"

"Hell Rider, gonna drive right over you!"
The bitch made him do it, can't blame—
Shot me! Motherfucker shot me!

Through it all, one thought stood out clear, a single star in the endless dark insanity of Eddie Ryder's mind.

It was time for Hank Bowman to die.

And he needed to die the same way Eddie had, roasting like a pig on a flaming spit.

On Main Street, smoke still rose from the smoldering ruins of the movie theater and surrounding buildings. Eddie aimed Hank's body for them and ran faster.

★   ★   ★

"Are you okay?" Carson knelt next to Kellie as she brushed chunks of fiberboard from her hair.

"Yeah." She gave him a weak smile. "Good thing those ceiling tiles aren't hard."

You're lucky, Eddie. I'd have killed you with my bare hands if you'd hurt her.

He helped her up and they went to Chief Jones, who sat on the floor, trying to catch his breath.

"Dad! Are you—"

He waved them off. "I'm fine. Just had the...wind...knocked out of me. Where'd he go?"

"I don't know." Kellie looked at Carson, who shook his head.

"I have no idea where he's going. But he left a trail." He pointed to the drops of blood on the floor. They led out the door and down to the stairwell. "We can follow him."

"Only for as long as he stays in Hank's body," the Chief said. Seeing the surprised looks on Carson and Kellie's faces, he nodded.

"Yeah, I believe you now. After what I've seen today, I'd probably believe you if you told me Bigfoot was robbing stores on Main Street."

"So what do we do?" Kellie asked.

Carson bit his lip and tried to think. Where would Eddie

go next? And why hadn't he just left Hank's body behind, instead of....

"I know what Eddie's doing," he told them, as it all became clear in his mind.

"What?" Kellie and her father asked in unison.

"He stayed in Hank because it's Hank's time to die. That's why he came up here in the first place. First Hank, and then... then the rest of the town."

Chief Jones groaned and pushed himself to his feet, a worried look on his face. Carson knew how he felt. Once Eddie finished with Hank, there'd be no stopping him.

Kellie, however, surprised the hell out of him by laughing.

"That's perfect."

★   ★   ★

Eddie stood in front of Earl's Chevron on the corner of Main and Pahayokee and smiled.

This is it. Say good-fucking-bye, Hanky-wanky.

There'd been nothing left of the movie theater and adjoining buildings when Eddie reached them, but it didn't matter. He'd remembered the gas station only two blocks away, the perfect place for Hank to go up in flames.

A calmness had come over him as he limped-jogged down the soot-covered sidewalk, dragging his blood-soaked leg like a stubborn child. The arguing thoughts in his head had given way to two simple, repeating sentences.

Hank's gonna die.

I'm a fucking god.

Hank's gonna die.

I'm a fucking god.

Now even they had disappeared, overtaken by the sheer joy of knowing that in a few moments he'd be sitting on Diablo, watching Hank Bowman scream and cry in agony as his body melted away.

See how you like it, fuck face. Now you're gonna know what I felt.

Like everything else on Main Street, Earl's was closed, thanks to the fires. Eddie neither noticed nor cared. He hobbled to the nearest pump and placed his hands on it.

Ooh, Hank, this is gonna hurt so bad!

Summoning up as much of his power as he could, Eddie started counting.

Five...

Four...

Three...

Two...

One....

Die, you cocksuckingfatassfuckingpieceofshit!

With a triumphant shout that shattered the windows of every building on the block, he let it all out in a single blast.

A second later, his war cry turned into agonizing screams.

★　　★　　★

Carson didn't know whether to hug Kellie or be mad at her as she explained what she'd done.

"Yesterday, outside the hospital, when I told you I had to give Delbert a message for my dad? I kinda lied. What I told him was to get salt and holy water and sprinkle them on Hank's body."

"What? You mean...?"

She nodded. "That's why we had to say the spell. We trapped Eddie inside Hank, and he didn't know it."

Chief Jones looked confused. "But how did you know Eddie would be inside Hank?"

Kellie shrugged. "We figured that sooner or later he'd want to kill Hank. I just hoped he'd go after him before he came after me and Carson. That almost backfired."

"But why?" Carson couldn't understand it. "We had a plan. He would take over my body, and then—"

"Then what?" Kellie glared at him. "I'd kill you? No way I was gonna let that happen. I love you, and I—"

"You love me? You mean—"

Sudden bright light from the windows interrupted him. Before they had time to even move, the floor shook and a sound louder than anything Carson had ever heard battered his ears.

★   ★   ★

The pain was at once unimaginable and all too familiar as the intense heat seared Eddie's lungs and the flames turned his flesh into boiling liquids. He kept waiting for his escape, to rise out of Hank's body and end the nightmarish torture, but it didn't happen.

In the end, his mind finally crumbled and he was back in his garage again, blindly struggling to find Diablo and cursing the Hell Riders for their murderous deed.

CHAPTER FORTY-THREE

"Good night, Ma. We'll see you tomorrow." Carson gave his mother a kiss and stepped away from the hospital bed.

In the hallway, Kellie and Chief Jones waited while he shut the door.

Three days had passed since Eddie's death in the fire, during which time Carson had gradually accepted that they'd really killed him, that his brother's vengeful spirit was finally gone. He'd been staying at Kellie's house while his mother recovered, but the doctors had said she'd be released in a day or two, which meant things would finally be getting back to normal.

In the aftermath of the gas station explosion, after emergency helicopters from Miami doused the fire with flame-retardant chemicals so the firefighters could get in, a few charred bones, partially fused to pieces of metal and plastic, had been found. Chief Jones had told a small lie to the coroner, saying he'd seen Hank Bowman running toward the gas station with some kind of homemade explosive in a box. As a favor to Carson and Sally – and to keep his paperwork from sounding insane – he'd also made sure to put into the official record that Hank and the Hell Riders were the source of all the fires and explosions in town over the last few days.

The Bowman family buried Hank's few remains in Homestead the day after the fire, their second funeral in less than a week, in a plot right next to his brother. Just like Ned's burial, it was attended by a handful of relatives and no one from Hell Creek.

Since Hank's death, there'd been no thunder or lightning in Hell Creek, and no violence or vandalism of any kind.

Holding Kellie's hand as they walked to the elevator, Carson allowed himself his first real smile in what seemed like weeks. His mother was alive, the prettiest girl in school was in love with him, and the town was safe again.

Maybe Kellie is right. It's time to stop worrying. Time to move on. Time to live.

EPILOGUE

Eddie woke to the sound of voices.

Help! Help me!

Who the fuck—

Where the hell—

Who is that?

Ned? Ned, I can't see—

Hank? Fuckin' A, are you dead too?

Dead? No, I....

Shut the FUCK UP, both of you!

Ryder? What the fuck are you doing—

His laughter rumbled out. Weak, but that would change.

Boys, I've got good news and bad news....

★   ★   ★

Arvis Keel nearly jumped out of his skin as violent thunder boomed in the cloudless twilight descending on Homestead Cemetery. Before he had more than a moment to wonder at the unexpected disturbance, a second rumbling took over, a sound much more familiar to him.

A motorcycle? And a loud one at that, one of them custom choppers I'll bet. Sounds pretty close.

But the gates are closed. Locked 'em myself.

He took a flask from his pocket and sipped at the sweet bourbon while he pondered what to do. Call the police? Check for trespassers himself?

Then a second engine revved, this one deeper, more powerful. Almost angry.

A third joined in.

Arvis shut the door to the utility shed and hurried for the

caretaker's office. Three bikes meant trouble. He'd seen motorcycle gangs plenty of times before, in Homestead and on the nearby highways. You couldn't live in the area and not see them. And he knew one thing for sure: you didn't mess with them.

He was halfway to the office when the lights blew out and music blared from the evening sky.

"Hell Rider
Never ending, life eternal
Judgment day approaching
World left black and smoking
Wheels of death descending
Destruction never ending!
Hell Rider!"

AFTERTHOUGHTS

So Admire the heroes, the endangered ones
Follow the inspired, under the rising sun
Take care of the wounded, battles they have won
Brave ones saving lives, honor deeds they've done
Admire the heroes, shut out the dark souls

'Admire the Heroes,' by Charred Walls of the Damned

ACKNOWLEDGMENTS

As always, I want to thank my wife, Andrea, and my mom for being my biggest supporters. Having people in your corner is vital to the success and mental health of any writer. And to my dad, who I will always miss. Wish you could have read this one, you'd have liked it.

Special thanks go out to the people who made this book possible: Don D'Auria, Mike Valsted, Maria Tissot, and Nick Wells at Flame Tree Press, along with Nik Keevil for the fantastic cover to this book.

My writer friends who've helped in one way or another with getting this book completed, including Joe McKinney, Tim Waggoner, Jeff Strand, Jon Maberry, Lisa Morton, Stephen Owen, Shaun Jeffrey, Theresa Fuller, and the late, great, Rocky Wood.

My fabulous beta readers (Rena Mason, Patrick Freivald, Erinn Kemper, James Chambers, Chris Marrs, Peter Salomon). Also Tom Monteleone, F. Paul Wilson, and David Morrell for the lessons they taught me, and Mort Castle for a boost of confidence when it was sorely needed.

An extra-special thank you goes to Richard Christy, a heavy metal demon in his own right, for giving me permission to use lyrics from his Charred Walls of the Damned albums. It was an honor to include them, because I love those CDs; the songs kick ass! It's great having you as part of the horror community.

If you take away anything from this book, I hope it's the lesson to treat everyone the way you'd like to be treated, instead of judging books by their covers.

Please note: No actual bikers were harmed or defamed in the making of this book. In the real world, the motorcycle club members I've known have always been friendly and eager to help in the community.

PERMISSIONS

FLAME TREE PRESS
FICTION WITHOUT FRONTIERS
Award-Winning Authors & Original Voices

Flame Tree Press is the trade fiction imprint of Flame Tree Publishing, focusing on excellent writing in horror and the supernatural, crime and mystery, science fiction and fantasy. Our aim is to explore beyond the boundaries of the everyday, with tales from both award-winning authors and original voices.

•

Other horror titles available include:
Thirteen Days by Sunset Beach by Ramsey Campbell
Think Yourself Lucky by Ramsey Campbell
The Hungry Moon by Ramsey Campbell
The Haunting of Henderson Close by Catherine Cavendish
The House by the Cemetery by John Everson
The Devil's Equinox by John Everson
The Toy Thief by D.W. Gillespie
Black Wings by Megan Hart
Stoker's Wilde by Steven Hopstaken & Melissa Prusi
The Playing Card Killer by Russell James
The Siren and the Specter by Jonathan Janz
Wolf Land by Jonathan Janz
The Sorrows by Jonathan Janz
Savage Species by Jonathan Janz
The Nightmare Girl by Jonathan Janz
The Dark Game by Jonathan Janz
House of Skin by Jonathan Janz
Dust Devils by Jonathan Janz
Castle of Sorrows by Jonathan Janz
The Darkest Lullaby by Jonathan Janz
Will Haunt You by Brian Kirk
Creature by Hunter Shea
Ghost Mine by Hunter Shea
The Mouth of the Dark by Tim Waggonner
They Kill by Tim Waggonner

•

Join our mailing list for free short stories, new release details, news about our authors and special promotions:

flametreepress.com